## "You take care of the house, and in exchange, I'll provide the food and I'll pay what I can."

Her eyes brightened with unshed tears. "You don't need a housekeeper."

"It's a luxury," Guthrie admitted, and he didn't often indulge in luxuries.

"I—I really appreciate this. I'll do my best—" There were several ways Olivia could finish. *To earn my keep. To stay out of your way. To not be a problem. To not take your land away from you.* Instead, she simply shrugged.

"We'd better get back." He had chores to catch up on and a hell of a new situation to get used to. The chores he could handle in a few hours. The getting-used-to part, though...

Olivia called her girls. He watched Elly leap off the stool, then race out the door, watched Emma Rae step daintily to the floor, then prissily follow her sister, watched Olivia tuck a strand of hair behind her ear with purely feminine, graceful gestures, and he gave a regretful sigh.

The getting-used-to part was going to be so damned hard.

Or so damned easy.

Dear Reader,

Spring always seems like a good time to start something new, so this month it's Marilyn Pappano's wonderful new Western miniseries, HEARTBREAK CANYON. *Cattleman's Promise* is a terrific introduction to the men of Heartbreak, Oklahoma—not to mention the women who change their lives. So settle in for the story of this rugged loner and the single mom who teaches him the joys of family life.

Unfortunately, all good things must end someday, and this month we bid farewell to Justine Davis's TRINITY STREET WEST. But what a finale! Clay Yeager has been an unseen presence in all the books in this miniseries, and at last here he is in the flesh, hero of his own story in *Clay Yeager's Redemption*. And, as befits the conclusion to such a fabulous group of novels, you'll get one last look at the lives and loves of all your favorite characters before the book is through. And in more miniseries news, Doreen Roberts continues RODEO MEN with *A Forever Kind of Cowboy*, a runaway bride story you'll fall in love with. *The Tough Guy and the Toddler* is the newest from Diane Pershing, and it's our MEN IN BLUE title, with a great cop hero. Christine Scott makes the move to Intimate Moments with *Her Second Chance Family*, an emotional and memorable FAMILIES ARE FOREVER title. Finally, welcome new writer Claire King, whose *Knight in a White Stetson* is both our WAY OUT WEST title and a fun and unforgettable debut.

As always, we hope you enjoy all our books—and that you'll come back next month, when Silhouette Intimate Moments brings you six more examples of the most exciting romance reading around.

Yours,

Leslie J. Wainger
Executive Senior Editor

Please address questions and book requests to:
Silhouette Reader Service
U.S.: 3010 Walden Ave., P.O. Box 1325, Buffalo, NY 14269
Canadian: P.O. Box 609, Fort Erie, Ont. L2A 5X3

# MARILYN PAPPANO

## CATTLEMAN'S PROMISE

Published by Silhouette Books

**America's Publisher of Contemporary Romance**

SILHOUETTE BOOKS

ISBN 0-373-07925-7

CATTLEMAN'S PROMISE

Copyright © 1999 by Marilyn Pappano

Look us up on-line at: http://www.romance.net

Printed in U.S.A.

**Books by Marilyn Pappano**

## MARILYN PAPPANO

After following her career navy husband around the country for sixteen years, Marilyn Pappano now makes her home high on a hill overlooking her hometown. With acreage, an orchard and the best view in the state, she's not planning on pulling out the moving boxes ever again. When not writing, she makes apple butter from their own apples (when the thieves don't get to them first), putts around the pond in the boat and tends a yard that she thinks would look better as a wildflower field, if the darn things would just grow there. You can write to Marilyn via snail mail at P.O. Box 643, Sapulpa, OK 74067-0643.

For Meg Reid, Apple R Ranch, Arpelar, Oklahoma,
and Juno Thompson & Jeff Yount, Big V Ranch,
McAlester, Oklahoma.

Thanks for the tours, your time and your patience in
answering this greenhorn's questions. I couldn't have
written this book without you.

# Chapter 1

One muggy May morning, to the sound of rain rushing through the gutters and *Sesame Street* on TV, Olivia Miles's life fell apart.

Though two weeks and a lot of miles had passed, she could still remember the moment with the crystal clarity reserved for impending doom. The dishwasher had been running, the air conditioner humming, and the low-battery light on the cordless phone had been flashing. It had provided her a moment's distraction, reminding her of all the calls that had come after David's death, all the people who'd filled the house after his funeral, all the obligations and regrets and sorrows that had filled her mind. Then the dishwasher had begun to leak *again*, and she'd been annoyed because David had said he would call someone but, of course, he hadn't. And then she'd felt guilty because in eight years of saying he would do things he never did, he finally had a good excuse.

He was dead.

And in the still moment created by her anger and guilt, the lawyer's words had finally sunk in.

Debt. Foreclosure. Repossession. Lapsed life insurance policy. Investments liquidated. College fund wiped out.

Her husband—her estranged, soon-to-be *ex*-husband—and the father of her daughters had left them with nothing. No house. No car. No money. No future.

That was when the pieces that had once been Olivia Rae Miles went crashing to the floor. Two weeks later she still didn't have a clue whether she'd be able to put them back together again.

Not that she had a choice. She had the girls to think of. God knows, David hadn't thought of them when he'd swiped every penny set aside for their future. He probably hadn't thought of them at all when he'd quit making payments on the house where they lived, the car they depended on or the life insurance they needed to survive.

Damn his soul, if he weren't already dead, she'd kill him herself.

A gnat buzzed her ear and she idly brushed it away as she leaned over the road map spread across the hood of the car. According to the index, their destination was located in section 7B, which was crisscrossed with a lot of blue highways, the red lines that signified unimproved roads and plenty of tiny dots standing in for tiny towns. According to her calculations, she was right smack in the middle of section 7B, and she was *not* impressed. Trees, pastures, not a city in sight and a dry, dusty heat that made her long for Atlanta and home.

Except, thanks to David, home was no longer Atlanta. It was here, on the only piece of property he hadn't managed to lose. A ranch.

In Heartbreak, Oklahoma.

The name brought the thin smile that was all she could manage these days. How appropriate that, after losing her entire life except for the girls, she should end up in a town called Heartbreak. Her heart was certainly breaking.

Her best guess put them about twenty miles from the town. Barring any disasters, they should be there by two, which would give her plenty of time before dinner to locate the ranch and introduce herself as the new boss. She hoped these cowboys wouldn't have a problem working for a woman, because she could sum up what she knew about ranching in one word. Nothing.

No, she did know one thing. If she, Emma and Elly were going to survive, they *needed* this ranch.

"Let's go, kids," she called as she tried to return the map to its former folded and creased glory. She wound up using her fist to flatten it to a manageable size, then opened the back door of the battered station wagon that had replaced her repossessed Mercedes. Air-conditioning, leather seats and precision engineering aside, there wasn't much difference between the two vehicles, she'd kept telling herself. They were both transportation. The wagon had gotten them from Atlanta to Oklahoma as well as the Mercedes would have—if she didn't count being windblown, sunburned, slightly deaf and gritty eyed.

"Elly, Emmy, come on!"

As she watched, the five-year-olds rose as one from the ground and started toward her. This morning she'd dressed them in lavender knit skirts and matching striped tops, with socks of pristine white and expensive sandals Velcroed to their feet. Their fine brown hair had been neatly combed and tied with lavender bows, and they had looked adorable.

Younger-by-eighteen-minutes Emma still looked adorable. Elly's hair was tangled, her bow drooped, her skirt was twisted, her top looked as if it were on backward, her socks were filthy and there was a smudge of dirt across her nose.

But she looked pretty darn adorable, too, when she wrapped her arms around Olivia's waist and used her as an anchor while she swung from side to side. "Are we almost there yet?"

"Almost."

"I found a lizard. Can he go to our new house with us and be my pet?"

"Don't you think the lizards here would miss him?" Olivia

smoothed her daughter's hair and repositioned the bow. "Besides, I bet we have lizards at the new house, too."

Emma leaned forward from the back seat, where she was already belted in with a book open on her lap. "I told you she'd say no, so you'd better take him out of your pocket. You prob'ly already suffercated him dead."

"Did not. See?" Elly pulled free of Olivia and drew the wriggling creature from her skirt pocket.

As soon as she held it up to Olivia's face for inspection, the lizard leaped. So did Olivia. "Get in the car and get your seat belt on," she instructed, hearing the tremble in her voice. She *hated* creepy, crawly, reptilian creatures. Something told her she'd be dealing with a lot of them here in Oklahoma. "We'll be home before you know it."

As she closed the door behind Elly, she caught Emma's plaintive murmur. "Home is back in Georgia. We'll prob'ly never go there again."

"Be quiet or I'll pinch you!" Elly snarled.

Tightening her grip on the map as well as on her emotions, Olivia circled behind the car. Emma had wanted to leave Atlanta even less than *she* had. She hadn't understood why they couldn't just stay in their house, seeing the same familiar people and going to the same familiar places. Frankly, at times, Olivia hadn't understood, either. David had been the one with the gambling problem, the one to lose all the money. Why did *they* have to pay for *his* sins?

Tossing the map through the open window, she took a moment to compose herself, then slid behind the wheel. The old engine cranked to life, its rough idle sending vibrations through the entire car. Then, as she eased back onto the two-lane road, she calmly said, "We'll go back to Atlanta someday, Emmy—just as soon as we can. I promise."

From the back seat, she heard a faint noise that sounded like flesh against flesh, followed by a gasp that was definitely Emma reacting to Elly. Feeling like a bad mother as well as a coward, she pretended not to have heard a thing.

Exactly half an hour had passed when they drove past a

faded, crooked sign welcoming them to Heartbreak. Olivia automatically moved her foot off the gas pedal and swiveled her head from side to side. At first, it was hard to tell that this was a town. There were a few scattered houses on either side of the road, along with a gas station where three men huddled together under the open hood of a brand-new truck.

Within a thousand yards, though, the road curved around a bend and the town appeared before them. There were a few side streets leading north and south under the branches of tall oaks, and a few businesses, with houses dropped between them. On the far side of a vacant lot was an imposing three-story brick building, with a squat concrete-and-glass addition, trailers in neat rows and playground equipment inside its chain-link fence. The school, she presumed, where she was expected to send her girls to learn 'ritin' and 'rithmetic. Oh, joy.

It took only a minute to drive through the few blocks that made up downtown, circle the block and come back to park in the gravel lot that fronted the post office. The engine died as soon as the car came to a stop—an annoying habit it'd developed somewhere in Arkansas—but she paid it no mind.

There was one thing she could say about Heartbreak.

It lived up to its name.

"Is this it, Mommy?" The question came from Elly, and her use of Mommy made Olivia cringe. Elly was her oldest, her boldest and found adventure in *everything*. She was easy to please and loved change and called her mother Mom, Mama and even on occasion Olivia dear, but she never called her Mommy unless she was afraid or unsure.

*Very* afraid or unsure.

"I guess it is." Olivia forced her fingers to release their grip on the steering wheel, turned off and removed the keys, then climbed out of the car. "Let's go inside and see if we can get directions to the ranch."

"Couldn't we maybe wait here?" Emma asked in her smallest voice. "We'll roll up the windows and lock the doors and won't let nobody come around."

The Elly Olivia desperately needed reappeared with a disdainful snort. "And then *we'd* suffercate dead. 'Sides, the doors don't lock, and the front window don't roll up. Get outta the car, you big baby."

It was a measure of Emma's own uncertainty that she didn't respond to the insult, that she did respond to the order. She climbed out, sidled close to Olivia, then tucked her hand in hers for extra comfort.

The post office was nothing more than a small aluminum-sided trailer with steps at one end and wood ramps that sloped first this way, then that. Elly raced up the ramps, her small feet echoing with cowboy-size clumps, and reached the door seconds before Olivia and Emma. "I won!" she shouted, dancing around, hands in the air, before waltzing inside.

The woman behind the counter offered Elly a smile. "Well, hello there, young lady. What can I do ya for?"

Elly marched up to the counter, discovered she couldn't see over it and backed away a few feet. "You talk funny."

"Elly!" With her free hand, Olivia caught her daughter's shoulder and gave her a warning squeeze. "Don't be rude!"

"But, Mama, you say always tell the truth, and it's true. She does talk funny."

"Hush. Not one more word." She gave the girl her sternest look, before turning to the clerk. "I apologize."

The woman's smile beamed again. "Oh, no offense taken. I reckon I do sound pretty funny to her, 'cause you all sound different to me. What can I help you with?"

"We're looking for the Harris Ranch. Can you give me directions?"

"Sure thing, hon. You just go out here, turn left, go down to Cody Street, take a right and follow it out past Oakley and—" She must have seen the glazed look slide over Olivia's eyes, because she broke off and reached for paper and pen. "I'll draw you a map. It's not too difficult."

When she slid the paper across the counter a moment later, she gave them a speculative look. "You visiting someone out there at the Harrises'?"

"Yes." No doubt Heartbreak was like every other small town in the world. Within a few hours of their settling in at the ranch, the whole town would know that the ranch's new owner had arrived, but Olivia would rather not start the gossip right away.

She studied the map for a moment. It involved a fair number of turns, but, as the clerk had said, it didn't seem difficult. With that same thin smile, she thanked the woman and herded the girls back out to the car. Once they were settled in the back seat, she took a moment to study the street.

There was an entire block of abandoned buildings to her left. The grocery store across the street wasn't much bigger than the convenience store near their house back home. The busiest place appeared to be the feed store/lumberyard a half block to her right. The other businesses on the street—a lawyer, an insurance agency, a hair salon, a clothing store, a junk store—seemed to be having a slow afternoon.

If appearances indicated prosperity, *all* their afternoons were slow.

Olivia gave a huge sigh and was dismayed to feel the tremble that accompanied it. She'd known before she left Atlanta that Heartbreak wasn't likely to be much of a town, but she'd expected better than this. Damn it, she *deserved* better than this. So did her girls.

But this was what she had, she acknowledged as she squared her shoulders, and she would damn well make the best of it. Sooner or later she would scrape together enough money to buy them a new life back home. Maybe she'd sell the ranch. Maybe she'd find the same sort of sucker Ethan James, the former owner, had found in David—a city slicker with more money than sense, who thought it perfectly reasonable to buy an Oklahoma ranch sight unseen, who'd grown up watching *Rawhide* and *Bonanza* and believed in the romance of the cowboy.

In the meantime, it was time to see that unseen ranch.

The postal clerk's directions were clear and guided Olivia out of town and from one narrow street through a series of gravel roads. Watch for an arched gate topped with an *H*, the woman had written, and she instructed the girls to do just that, while in her mind she envisioned the entrance to their new home. Miles of whitewashed fence, pretty brick pillars supporting a wrought-iron gate, fancy curlicues dancing in and around the letter. The gate would open onto a broad graveled lane, planted alongside with flowers, and the lane would meander through pastoral fields and over a bubbling brook before climbing to the top of the highest hill and the house Mr. James had described to them in detail. Three stories, huge windows, a view to take your breath away, swimming pool out—

Both girls cried out at once. "There it is, Mama! There's the *H!*"

Jerked out of her daydream, Olivia hit the brakes, then backed up even with the drive.

She stared.

Whitewashed fence, brick pillars, elaborate wrought iron? Try barbed wire, rusted pipe and a crooked *H* fashioned from more pipe. There was a cattle guard across the drive, which was one dusty lane that ran straight and true to the house a hundred yards off the road. Visible behind it was a barn, corrals, weathered wood and dirt and lots more barbed wire and rusted pipe.

She felt queasy. Was it possible that there were two ranches in the area known as the Harris Ranch? Ranching ran in families, didn't it? Sons followed in their father's footsteps. It was conceivable that some junior Harris had struck out on his own, and both his and the senior Harris's places were known by the same name.

But if that were the case, wouldn't the clerk have asked which Harris she was looking for?

Maybe this was the right place, just not the right house. Maybe this was the foreman's house, and back behind it, out of her sight, the road wound off over the land to the distant owner's house. After all, the owner wouldn't want his view to include barns and corrals and cattle. He'd want the loveliest setting on the spread for his three-story house and swimming pool.

"Maybe it's a sideways *I*," Emma suggested. "Maybe a twister came and blewed it over so's it looks like an *H*."

"Maybe a twister'll come and blow *you* over so's you look like—" Elly clapped both palms to her cheeks in feigned shock. "You'd look like a crybaby no matter how a twister blewed you."

"They don't have twisters here, do they, Mama?" Emma asked, sounding worried, as she so often did, and Elly pounced on it, as *she* so often did.

"Uh-huh, they do. I seen the movie, an' it took place in Oklahoma—right *here* in this part of Oklahoma. *This* is where the cow went flyin', and he could've been one of our very own cows—"

"Hush," Olivia said, and something in her tone left them both silent.

Swallowing hard to ease the dryness in her mouth, she backed up a few more yards, then turned into the driveway. The station wagon bumped mercilessly—no shocks—over the cattle guard, then the tires kicked up a cloud of dust that rolled through the open windows, coating everything inside.

The driveway ended beside the house, with a pickup truck parked there. The truck was neither new nor old, and it looked to be in pretty good shape, considering that it was used for work. She wondered if it belonged to the foreman or if it was property of the ranch—wondered if the ranch might have a vehicle she could use instead of this old junk heap. Something with air-conditioning and a radio that worked and shock absorbers.

She could really use some shock absorbers about now.

"Is this our house?" Elly asked, unfastening her seat belt and climbing onto the seat to stick her head out the window.

God, she hoped not! Olivia thought, then was immediately ashamed of herself. There wasn't anything wrong with the house. It was two stories, white clapboard needing a coat of paint, with a broad porch that stretched all the way across the front. It was a perfectly fine house. It just didn't hold a candle to *her* house—Mediterranean in style, red tile roof, imported tile floors, four thousand square feet of space and simple elegance and...

And now belonging to the mortgage company.

"You guys wait here while I see if anyone's home." She turned off the engine that had already died, took the keys as a precaution and left the car.

Wood steps of pale, scuffed-up gray led to the porch. She walked past two rockers painted black to match the shutters and coated with dust, stopped at the old-fashioned screen door and looked blankly for the doorbell. Finding none, she opened the door and rapped sharply. While waiting, she prayed for some nice, motherly person to open the door, welcome her warmly and send her down the road to the three-storied, swimming-pooled haven Mr. James had described.

There was no answer, not even after a second loud knock. She let the screen door close and was wondering what to do next when sound split the quiet country air—the rhythmic, hollow raps of a hammer on wood. They were coming from around back. After once again reminding the girls to wait in the car, she headed that way.

Lord, it was hot. And dry. And quiet, except for the hammering. She'd lived all her life in Atlanta and had never imagined herself in a place without traffic, people, planes circling overhead, construction all around. She *liked* the city, with its noise and chaos and millions of people. She would give anything if she were back there right now instead of braving the heat and dust in search of some elusive handyman and—

As she drew closer to the barn, she became aware of music—country music, she thought distastefully—coming from inside the shadowy space. She couldn't make out anyone inside, though, and the hammering seemed to come from around back. Following the racket around the back corner of the barn, she came to an abrupt stop. The handyman had just stopped being elusive. He stood not ten feet away, his back to her, as he positioned a fence board to replace the one broken in two on the ground. He wore snug jeans, no shirt and a cowboy hat of straw that allowed just a glimpse of sweat-dampened brown hair.

Everybody loves a cowboy, or so she'd heard, and here was a prime example why. She hadn't gotten even a glimpse of his face, but with a body like that—narrow hips, broad shoulders, hard muscles—what woman could possibly care about his face?

She must have made some sound, or perhaps he just had some second sense that warned him when he was being ogled, because abruptly he glanced over his shoulder. He slowly lowered the board to the ground and turned to face her. "Can I help you?"

Brown seemed such an unremarkable color, a synonym for drab, dull. But there was nothing drab or dull about this man with brown hair, brown eyes, brown skin—lots and lots of warm brown skin. In fact, he was pretty damn remarkable.

And he was waiting for her to stop staring as if she'd never seen *remarkable* before.

Giving herself a mental shake, she shoved her hands into her pockets. "I'm looking for Ethan James. Can you tell me where to find him?"

A subtle change came over the cowboy—a slight narrowing of his eyes, a faint hardening of his jaw. Picking up the board again, he went back to work. "Nope. Don't have a clue."

She waited until he'd hammered one end into place and was gathering nails to secure the other, then asked, "Will he be back soon?"

"Not likely."

"Will he be back this evening?"

It seemed the blows he struck the nails were unnecessarily hard. When he finished, he faced her again, using the flat head of the hammer to tilt the hat back a bit on his head. "With Ethan, anything's possible. He might sprout wings and come flying over the barn in the very next minute. Hell, he might even be hard at work and living a responsible life. But coming here this evening or any other… I don't think it's gonna happen."

Olivia swallowed hard. She had a sick feeling in the pit of her stomach that chased away the sun's warmth, that made her skin feel damp and cold. Struggling to keep her voice even, she asked, "Then can I speak to whoever's in charge?"

"That would be me." He laid the hammer aside, picked up the shirt that hung on a fence post and shrugged into it. When he'd finished fastening the buttons, he offered his hand. "I'm Guthrie Harris. Ethan's my brother."

Harris. As in Harris Ranch. Another hard swallow did little to slow the sick feeling in its upward rise. She weakly shook his hand, vaguely noticing warm skin, tough calluses, controlled strength, then completed the introductions. "I'm Olivia Miles."

The cowboy's face was blank.

"From Atlanta."

Still no hint of recognition.

"D-David Miles was my—my husband." When his expression remained unchanged, she gave a great sigh and blurted out, "I'm the new owner of Harris Ranch."

Guthrie stared at Olivia Miles of Atlanta. Maybe she was suffering sunstroke and talking out of her head—though it got pretty damn hot in Atlanta. She should be used to the heat. But then, she didn't look like the type who would spend much time out in it. Her skin was pale, and she had a pampered look about her, as if her only time outside was spent lounging under a big umbrella, wearing a floppy hat and sipping mint juleps at a poolside tea party.

Maybe the heat had nothing to do with it and she was just flat-out crazy.

Or maybe… He didn't want to acknowledge the possibility, but a lifetime's experience with Ethan forced him to. Maybe she was the victim of another of his half brother's scams.

Tamping down his rising temper, he steeled his voice and

asked, "What do you mean—the new owner of Harris Ranch?"

"My—my husband bought out Mr. James nearly a year ago. I don't know all the details, but Mr. James agreed to run the place. It was an investment for David." Her smile was thin and strained. "He got bored with the stock market."

"Where is your husband now?"

Tiny lines appeared at the corners of her mouth. "He—he's dead. He died three weeks ago. In a car crash."

"I'm sorry." The anger surged higher, but Guthrie kept it under control. Getting angry did no good when Ethan was nowhere around to unload on. Hell, it did no good when his brother stood right there in front of him. The words went in one ear and out the other, and Ethan went on his merry way as if they'd never been said.

He forced his attention back to Olivia Miles of Atlanta. "And your husband left his investment to you."

Her nod set her pale brown hair swinging. She wore it in a ponytail, but strands had worked free around her face and the tail was tangled. Her outfit—red checked shorts and a white blouse with red checked trim—was obviously expensive and just as obviously rumpled. Her skin was flushed and damp, and her eyes were marked with fine red lines. From crying over her dead husband?

All in all, she looked like she'd had a tough few weeks—like she'd been rode hard and put away wet, his granddaddy would have said.

Guthrie put a stop to the smile that automatically started to form and instead scowled harder. In this instance, his granddaddy's saying was unkind and damn inappropriate. Olivia Miles was a brand-new widow—and, apparently, another of Ethan's suckers. She deserved sympathy—if he could find any underneath all the anger.

"And you came here to do what? Look the place over? Maybe consider unloading it?"

He expected another emphatic nod. What he got was a

nervous-edged, wary but dead-on-steady look. "No, Mr. Harris. I came here to live."

He stared at her for another long, silent minute—stared so hard that she shifted uneasily from one foot to the other. "Live," he repeated at last, his voice low, sounding cold and deadly in the afternoon heat. "On my ranch."

"N-no, Mr. Harris. On—on *my* ranch."

"There's a little problem with that, Mrs. Miles. You see, your ranch *is* my ranch. Ethan couldn't sell it to you because it's not his to sell."

For a moment, her expression was utterly blank, as if he'd suddenly started speaking a foreign language. Then, abruptly, pure panic crossed her face, swept through her body. "No, there must be a mistake. He said the property was his, free and clear. He signed a contract, a deed, a check! I've got them in the car! David *bought* this ranch!"

He shook his head. "Ethan might have conned your husband out of some money. He might have signed a contract and drawn up a deed, but they're bogus. He can't sell something he doesn't own, and he's never owned—"

Now it was Guthrie's turn to suddenly go blank. Dread rushed through him, stopping his words in mid-denial, turning him cold from the inside out as a long-forgotten memory blew into his mind. Ten years ago, the summer after their mother died. Nadine Harris James had been the one calming influence in Ethan's life. Without her, he'd been lost, drifting, unable to find any stability. Afraid of losing the only family he had left, Guthrie had taken the drastic action of signing over half of the ranch that had been in his family for four generations to his half brother. He'd thought it would give Ethan roots, that the responsibility would make him settle down and grow up.

It hadn't.

Oh, he'd stayed a few months, worked hard and made plans, and then one morning Guthrie had gotten up to find a note on the table and Ethan gone. The roots weren't holding. The responsibility was more than he wanted. Just as he'd always done when he got in a tight spot—just as his father had always done—he'd run away, leaving Guthrie and the ranch behind. With time—and hard work—Guthrie had forgotten his mistake.

Apparently, Ethan hadn't.

Sweet damnation.

"There must be some misunderstanding!" she insisted, her voice trembling, increasing in both pitch and loudness. "The deed can't be bogus! David bought this ranch from Mr. James! He paid him a fortune, and it was the only thing he didn't lose before he died—the only thing he didn't sell or quit making payments on, the only thing he *left* us! We *need* this—"

"Mommy? Mommy, where are you?"

The interruption made the woman freeze. She sucked in a breath and the rest of her protest with it, and her face turned even paler as her gaze darted anxiously to the corner of the barn. "It's okay, Elly, Emmy. I'm right back here."

Guthrie's gaze shifted, too, in time to see two matching little girls come flying around the building. One of them launched herself at her mother and hugged her tight. The other one skidded to a stop and looked him up and down.

"Hey," she said in greeting. "Are you a real cowboy?"

He looked from her to her mother and replayed her desperate, pleading words in his mind. *...it was the only thing he didn't lose before he died—the only thing...he left us! We need this*— Furious, he silently muttered every curse he'd ever known. What the hell had Ethan pulled this time, and why in hell had he involved Guthrie in it?

The little girl came a step closer. "I get it," she said with a knowing grin. "You're the strong, silent type."

Crouching to her level, he offered his hand. "I'm Guthrie Harris."

She gave his hand a firm squeeze. "I'm Elly Miles. Olivia's my mother. The scaredy-cat over there is my baby sister Emma Rae. She doesn't like cowboys. Or strangers. Or Oklahoma. Or twisters or lizards or spiders or snakes or horses or dogs, 'cept little bitty ones. She doesn't like nothin'. Are you *our* cowboy?''

He looked at her mother again. Now two spots of color had appeared in the stark whiteness of her cheeks. "Elly, I told you girls to wait in the car."

"We got tired of waiting, and Emmy got 'fraid, so I told her I'd find you, but she was too big a baby to wait in the car by herself so she came, too. Where're the cows?"

"Out in the pasture." Guthrie got slowly to his feet. He needed to talk to Olivia Miles—and to his lawyer—and get this mess straightened out. And then he was going to hunt Ethan down, kill him and be done with him once and for all. "Why don't we go in the house, Mrs. Miles, and see if we can figure out where we stand?"

She looked as if she wanted to refuse. In fact, she looked as if she simply wanted to crawl into some dark corner, hide her head and not come out until her world was right again.

Thanks to his worthless brother, that could be a while.

She nodded resolutely, then peeled the girl's arms from around her waist. Holding Emma Rae's hand, she grabbed Elly's on the way past and started toward the barn. Guthrie took a moment to tilt his head to the sky and whisper a heart-felt curse before he followed.

At the back of the house, she stopped with the girls, waiting for him to catch up. "Can we talk on the front porch? I can watch the girls while they play."

And then they wouldn't have to overhear what might be a less-than-pleasant conversation—less pleasant for him, he feared, than for her.

Taking his shrug for agreement, she headed for the front of the house. On the way she made a stop at her car, older and junkier than anything he'd ever owned, and took a large manila envelope from the front seat.

Elly was happy to skip off and explore. Emma Rae required an order, and even then, rather than join her sister, she climbed into the back seat of the station wagon, fastened her seat belt and did her best to look cranky, whiny and scared.

Her best was pretty damn good.

Guthrie followed the mother up the steps, then leaned against the porch rail, arms folded across his chest, while she seated herself on the edge of one dusty rocker. ''Why don't you start from the beginning?'' he suggested, all his anger and apprehension coming out in his voice. It made her stiffen, made her look just a little more panicked, and that made him feel more than a little guilty, but he ignored it.

She hugged the envelope tightly and, keeping her gaze locked on her daughter, began. ''It—it was about a year ago. Mr. James came to Atlanta to find a buyer for his ranch. David met him at the—the country club. He was looking for something different to invest in, and Mr. James was offering it. I tried to talk him out of it. It was a lot of money, and he knew nothing about ranches or cattle or Oklahoma, but once he made up his mind...''

The man sounded like Ethan's favorite kind of victim—too much money, not enough brains, gullible as hell. Why else would he buy a ranch a thousand miles away without seeing it first? Without having the paperwork looked over by an attorney? Without doing a title search? If he'd had even the slightest bit of sense, he would've known the deal was too good to be true—and Guthrie wouldn't have his widow to deal with now.

''Before I knew it, it was a done deal. The papers had been signed. The money had been paid.''

''And Ethan had left town.''

She nodded.

''Is that the deed he gave you?'' When she nodded again, he held out one hand. ''Can I see it?''

Her blue eyes turned wary, and for an instant, her grip on the envelope tightened.

''I'm not going to run off with it, Mrs. Miles,'' he said impatiently. ''I just want to see how much trouble we're in.''

Clearly reluctant—but aware she had little choice—she handed over the envelope. Guthrie fished out the papers, then settled against a rounded post to read them.

The contract was remarkably detailed, illustrating just how much thought Ethan had put into this scam. The price, though, was laughable. A lot of money, yes, but not half what the place was worth. If David Miles had bothered to learn anything about his investment, the price alone would have told him something was wrong with the deal. Had Ethan priced it low as part of the come-on? Had he thought that the fact he was taking only what his share was rightfully worth made the deal less of a scam?

More likely he'd discovered that that was all Miles was willing to pay.

The deed looked good, but was as worthless as the contract. Unfortunately for Mrs. Miles, the only paper in the envelope that was a hundred percent legitimate was the check her husband had written Ethan, the check Ethan had cashed before disappearing from their lives.

"Didn't it strike either of you as a little odd that a man would travel from Oklahoma to *Atlanta* to sell his ranch?"

"I tried to tell David… There aren't that many prospective ranchers in Atlanta. He pointed out that there was a lot of money in Atlanta, that that was why Mr. James had come there."

"And it never occurred to him to have an attorney look at the contract or the deed."

"Mr. James was on a tight schedule. He needed an answer immediately. He told David he had other interested buyers and if he wanted it—" She closed her eyes, pinched the bridge of her nose, exhaled heavily. "It was all a big lie, wasn't it?"

Her words, as soft as a whisper, made him uncomfortable. She looked defeated. Troubled. Worried as hell.

For just an instant, he was tempted to say, yes, it was, and send her and her kids on their way. But if he did that, he'd be no better than his brother—and he'd *always* been better than his brother. Guthrie Harris didn't lie, cheat or steal. Those activities were reserved for the James side of the family.

He blew his breath out hard enough to rattle the papers in his hands. "Not exactly."

Her gaze jerked up to meet his, lit by a sudden flare of hope.

"Years ago, in a moment of incredible stupidity, I gave Ethan..." His desire to avoid saying the awful words out loud made his jaw tighten and his scowl turn harsher. "I gave him part of the ranch. Not the entire thing, like he claims here, but..." The papers rattled again, and he realized how tightly he was holding them. He offered them to her, then had to force his fingers to let go on the third tug.

"How much did you give him?"

He swallowed hard, forced out the answer. "Half." Not the best half. Not the half that would be worth anything to anyone besides *him,* but half just the same.

"So I own his half?"

"I don't know. The papers say 290 acres, all livestock, buildings, houses and equipment. The fact that he owned only 145 acres and none of the rest might invalidate the whole deal." Which would work great for him. It would put that 145 acres back in the family and give him time to hunt down Ethan, force him to sign it back over to him legally and then kill him.

And where would that put Mrs. Miles and her little girls? *...it was the only thing he didn't lose before he died—the only thing...he left us! We need this—*

Out in the cold. No money, no land, no place to live.

He glanced at his watch. If he left now, he could get into town before his lawyer closed up—except, he remembered, it was Thursday, and Jerry wasn't in his Heartbreak office on Thursdays. There wasn't enough business around here to keep him going, so he had other offices in a three-county area. He spent more of his work hours traveling than lawyering.

"If you'll give me the number where you're staying..."

She met his gaze. Hers was level, flat, empty of everything, including pride. "If you'll show me one of the acres that might be mine, that's where we'll be."

"There's a motel—"

"We can't afford a motel."

He'd known she was going to say that. Knowing what he was going to say, too, he postponed it by looking away. His gaze settled on Emma Rae, sweltering in the station wagon but asleep all the same, her head tilted to one side, her mouth open, her hair frizzing around her face where the sweat dampened it. Just the sight of her guaranteed what he was about to say. "Then I guess you'll have to stay here."

She looked at the front door, at him, then her daughters, and shook her head. "We can't—"

"Not in this house. There's a cabin. You can use it." He gestured off to the west, where the cabin was visible at the tree line. "It's been empty a long time, but it's usable. You're welcome to it until we get this mess straightened out."

The desire for a refusal—hers to give one, his to accept it—was strong. When she spoke, though, *no* wasn't a part of the conversation. "I appreciate your generosity, Mr. Harris."

Not feeling particularly generous—just trapped—he pushed away from the post. "Go back down the driveway. Just this side of the gate, there's an old road that leads to the cabin. I'll get the keys and meet you over there."

For a moment, she sat motionless, then, with a sudden burst of energy, she got to her feet and offered her hand. "Thank you, Mr. Harris."

He looked at her hand—so much smaller than his, so soft, pale, smooth—then finally took it. Amazing how different soft and smooth—and feminine—were from the textures he was accustomed to.

Amazing—and one more reason to straighten out Ethan's mess as quickly as possible.

After a quick handshake, he pulled away and unlocked the front door. Her sandals made little noise on the wood floor as she crossed to the steps, called to Elly and circled the car. The little girl raced off, chattering about lizards and trees and wouldn't this be a great place to finally have a dog, and Guthrie stepped inside, closing the door before he heard more.

His boots echoed in the empty house as he went down the hall to his office, where the keys to the cabin were kept in the desk drawer. As he picked them up, his gaze settled on a photograph on top of the old rolltop desk—him and his mom, Ethan and his dad, looking like one happy family.

Appearances were deceiving, though. Nadine Harris and Gordon James had married for several reasons—she thought Guthrie needed a father after his own died, and Gordon had thought he might like being a rancher. But he'd been no substitute for Vernon Harris, not in the rancher department and sure as hell not in the father department. It wasn't long after Ethan's birth that Gordon had begun spending more time away from home than there, and by the time Ethan turned ten, Gordon was out of their lives completely. Instead of finding a father for her older son, Nadine had wound up with two sons to support on her own.

Ethan was about six in the photo—blond-haired, blue-eyed, grinning what their mother had described as Gordon's scoundrel grin. He'd had eighteen years of Nadine's strict upbringing, with minimal contact with Gordon, and yet it was his father whose influence had counted, his father whose footsteps he had followed. He was as worthless as Gordon had proven to be, only he'd gone one step further in selling the ranch.

And he'd succeeded at that only because Guthrie had been stupid enough to think that the bonds of family counted for something. Now he knew they didn't.

Picking up the photograph, he tossed it into the bottom drawer, then nudged it shut with his boot before leaving the office.

As far as he was concerned, he had no brother. It was just him and his ranch.

And Olivia, Elly and Emma Rae Miles.

God help him.

# Chapter 2

Olivia followed the cowboy's directions, finding a faint trail that followed along the fence line before turning into the trees where the cabin sat. She stopped underneath the spreading branches of a tall oak, listened to the engine die and clutched the steering wheel more tightly as she looked.

The cabin sat two dozen feet away, surrounded on three sides by scrub oaks and one tall Austrian pine. It stood two stories high, fronted by a narrow porch with steps and a door at the nearest end and six empty windows looking out. Nestled on the banks of some lake or river, it would make a great little getaway—a rustic cabin in the woods.

Oh, God, what was she doing here?

What had David gotten her into?

In the back seat, Emma woke up and looked around, and her lower lip began to tremble. "Mommy, I want to go home," she whimpered. "Please... I don't like it here. Please let's go home!"

Olivia clenched her jaw to keep from snapping, We have no home! Her big, beautiful, red-tiled house was gone. So was the three-storied ranch house marvel. As of fifteen minutes ago, they had joined the ranks of the homeless and were damn lucky to have the temporary use of this place.

How temporary? What if it turned out that her claim to the property wasn't valid? What if she lost this last hope and had absolutely nothing to show for it? What in the world would she do then?

She fought down the hysteria with a line borrowed from her home state's most famous Southern belle. *I'll think about it tomorrow.* Tomorrow would be a better day.

It couldn't possibly be any worse.

*"Mommy!"* Emma's voice began to rise into a wail that Olivia tried to quell with a sharp look.

"We're staying here, Emma, for a while, at least. Grab your things and help me take them inside." She unfolded her fingers from the steering wheel and climbed out as Guthrie Harris, with Elly skipping along beside him, reached the overgrown lane. He waited at the back of the car while she lowered the tailgate, then took the heaviest suitcases without a word. If he recognized the pricey label sewn into the leather, he didn't show it. His handsome face was set in lines too grim to show anything.

She took two more bags and followed him up the steps. Emma remained in the car, while Elly was already on the porch, peering in the window. She turned, shaking her head, as Guthrie opened the screen door, then unlocked the wood door. "It's nothing like our old house, Mom," she warned.

Olivia gave her half a smile. "Toto, we're not in Kansas anymore," she murmured.

"Of course we're not in Kansas, Mom. It's Oklahoma, and our very own ranch with our very own cows and cowboys and a real live cabin." As soon as the door was open, she darted between Guthrie and the jamb and raced inside. "I'm gonna find our bedroom!"

Olivia stepped over the threshold to the accompaniment of small feet pounding up the stairs. The door opened directly into the living room with no space wasted for the luxury of a foyer. The room was about ten by twelve feet, with dust-covered humps of furniture—a sofa there, one chair near the front window, another at the side. There was one door leading to the kitchen in back, another going into a bedroom next door. Just outside the bedroom door, stairs with a no-frill rail led straight to the second floor.

As Elly had warned, it was nothing like home. Maybe that would help in their favor. Maybe she could persuade the girls they were on sort of a vacation—an adventure. How many of their friends back in Atlanta had ever gotten to live in a cabin in the woods on a ranch in Oklahoma? How jealous would they be that Elly and Emma had gotten the opportunity?

Guthrie set the suitcases down in the center of the room and looked around. "She's right. It's not much."

"That's not what she said," Olivia gently corrected him. "She said it's not like our house in Atlanta. That doesn't automatically make one better than the other."

"Where do you want these bags?"

"Right there will be fine. I'll have to sort out everything."

"The kitchen's through here."

He led, and once again she followed. The kitchen and dining room were one long, narrow space that stretched across the back of the house. The back door opened onto a tiny stoop and an up-close-and-personal view of the woods. The door at the far end led into a small bathroom, which had a second door that went into the front bedroom. No foyer, no hallways. Just the efficient use of space.

It took little time to unload the rest of their belongings. In the middle of the living room, the five suitcases and twelve boxes made a pitifully small pile for everything she owned in life. Limited wardrobes, the kids' favorite toys and games, a small supply of dishes and linens, and the photographs and mementoes she couldn't bear to discard. Like their house, their car, their secure lives, everything else was gone.

Guthrie straightened after depositing his last load of boxes. "I'll get the pump running and turn the power on, then bring the vacuum over. It'll help get rid of some of this dust. Do you need sheets and pillows?''

''No, thanks. We've got them.''

''Why don't you bring the kids over around seven for supper?''

''I don't—'' She thought about cleaning up, driving back into town and spending part of her precious stash on dinner, swallowed her pride and said instead, ''I will. Thanks.''

After one more look around, he went outside, catching the screen door so it closed quietly, then gestured toward the car. ''Is she going to stay there?''

Emma sat staring straight ahead, her brows knit into a frown, her jaw set. Olivia indulged a moment's wish that she were more adaptable, like Elly, then immediately felt guilty. She loved her girls dearly and most of the time wouldn't change either of them for anything. ''She'll come out eventually, when her curiosity gets the better of her. This has just been so hard…''

He gave her a look that she couldn't quite read through the dusty screen, then nodded once. ''I'll be back.''

She watched him walk away, thought about coaxing Emma inside, then decided to work instead. She walked through the cabin, opening every window upstairs and down so the occasional breeze could exchange fresh air for musty. In the kitchen, she located a broom and dustpan and started sweeping the wood floors. She carried throw rugs out back to hang over a wire line strung between two trees. Elly wanted to help and did a fair job of sweeping the room she'd claimed as her own, while Emma stayed where she was.

Olivia was watching her through the side window when Elly, dirty and flushed and looking happier than she had in weeks, joined her. ''Want me to go get her?''

''Do you mind?''

''Nope.'' She dashed out, screen door slamming behind her, and poked her head in the car window, leaning so far forward that her feet dangled off the ground. When her earnest conversation was greeted with stubborn refusals, she wiggled the rest of the way into the car and settled her arm around Emma's shoulders.

Olivia's eyes filled with tears. She should have been better prepared to take care of her children. From the moment David had moved out, when she'd known that divorce was inevitable, she should have been taking steps to one day provide for the girls. But David had paid the bills—or so she'd thought—and he'd talked about continuing to do so while she got on her feet. He'd wanted her to be available to the girls until they started first grade, and so he had promised her generous alimony, as well as child support, and he'd had the income to cover both. Or so she'd thought.

She'd gone complacently on with her routine, making a home for the girls and being a full-time mother, convincing herself that *later* was soon enough to prepare for the future. And then *later* had hit her right square between the eyes.

When had things gone wrong? When had he begun losing money hand over fist? And why hadn't he told her? They could have sold the house, could have moved someplace smaller and more affordable. She could have traded down from the Mercedes to an economy car, gotten a job and learned to budget.

Pride, stubbornness and independence. David had hated being wrong, hated making bad decisions. He'd wanted no one else's opinion, not even hers. He'd wanted to be able to look at everything around him and say, "*I* did this."

Olivia watched her older daughter comfort her younger and thought bitterly, Yes, David, *you* did this.

After a time, Elly reversed her wiggling and exited the car the same way she'd gone in, then opened the door. Clutching her pillow, her favorite storybook and her most cherished doll, Emma slid out, then took halting steps across the ground, up the steps and into the house.

"Come on, I'll show you our rooms," Elly was saying importantly. "They're upstairs." She galloped up the stairs. Emma followed at a listless pace.

Olivia found a box filled with the girls' treasures and carried it upstairs. The hallway there was short—less than four feet—with a door at each end opening into a bedroom and one straight ahead leading into a tiny bathroom. The twins were in the room on the right, where Elly was showing off her twin bed, her dresser, her closet, her window.

"I don't want my own room," Emma whispered as Olivia walked in.

"Oh, don't be a baby about it," Elly said briskly. "Bethany and Caitlan and Amber Lynn and Tiffany and everyone else at home has their own room. We're not babies anymore. We're almost in the first grade. 'Sides, I'll be right here."

"Mama, I don't *want* a room all by myself," Emma pleaded.

Olivia gave Elly a beseeching look, which her daughter pretended to not see, then hugged Emma. "Let's give it a try, darlin', and see how it works out, okay?"

Her lower lip trembling, Emma nodded, and Olivia made her escape. Through the next two hours, while she worked, she kept telling herself that everything would be all right. Emma would adapt. At least a portion of the sale would be valid so she wasn't completely broke. A buyer for her share of the ranch would show up, offering cash and return tickets to Atlanta. Ethan James would magically appear, saying, I made a mistake; here's your money back.

His brother didn't think there was the remotest chance in hell of that last happening.

Maybe everything *wouldn't* be all right, she thought glumly as she called it quits at six-thirty. Maybe the best she could hope for was that it wouldn't get any worse.

She hustled the kids into the shower that filled half the space in their bathroom, then ran tepid water into the claw-foot tub that dominated the downstairs bathroom. The bath felt good and worked a few cramps out of long-unused muscles, but it didn't do much to relieve the stress that knotted her neck muscles.

By ten minutes till seven, they were all clean and neatly dressed. Rather than dig out the hair dryer, she braided the girls' hair and her own into matching French braids, then hurried them out the door.

"I don't want to eat dinner with that man," Emma whined as they set off across the—field? pasture? out-of-control lawn? Olivia wasn't sure what to call it. "He's big and scary."

Guthrie Harris *was* big, no denying that. Probably six foot two, broad shoulders, hard muscles. But scary? Only to a woman susceptible to generous, decent and handsome as sin, or to a brother who'd betrayed him, or to a hapless, helpless family of three who had to rely on this stranger's kindness for a roof over their heads.

Under the circumstances, he would have been perfectly within his rights to escort them from his property and leave them to their own problems. After all, hadn't David, who owed them far more than any other man in the world, done just that? Of course, in all fairness to David, he hadn't intended to die in that accident, and no doubt he'd been convinced that he could win back everything he'd lost without ever having to admit a thing.

At exactly seven o'clock, Elly knocked at Guthrie's front door. Feeling miserably like a charity case, Olivia fixed the best smile she could manage as the door swung open.

He was recently showered, with his damp hair slicked back from his forehead, and had changed dirty jeans and chambray shirt for clean. He was barefoot—an intimate little detail to notice, she thought foolishly—and making no effort at all to smile. Why should he? This morning all was right with his world, and this afternoon he'd found out that half of his ranch might no longer be his and had gotten saddled with *them* at the same time.

"Dinner's almost ready. Have a seat." He gestured toward the living room that opened on the left.

Elly burst inside and headed straight for the recliner. Olivia had to drag Emma through the door.

"Hey, can we watch TV?" Elly called, then abruptly remembered her manners. "Mr. Guthrie, may we watch television, please?"

"Sure. And it's not 'Mr.' Just Guthrie."

She detoured to get the remote control from atop the television, then plopped into the recliner. "We're not allowed to call grown-ups by their first names. It's not r'spectful. C'mon, Emmy. Let's see what's on."

Olivia got Emma settled with her sister, then walked down the broad hall to the kitchen. It was easily twice the size of the cabin's kitchen and contained all the modern conveniences, but it didn't look as if they were used often. Apparently, there was no Mrs. Harris—the place was lacking a feminine touch—and Mr. Harris didn't have much time to invest in cooking. Right now he was bent in front of the oven, removing from the oven a baking sheet that held a foil casserole pan.

She waited until he laid the pan on the stove, then asked, "Can I help?"

He gave her only the slightest of glances over one shoulder. "Everything's ready except the drinks. What will they want?"

"They'll drink anything—milk, soda, juice."

"You can get that out of the refrigerator." Using two thick pads, he transferred the pan—lasagna, she could see and smell—to the square table near the back door. "Will they eat lasagna?"

Olivia resisted the urge to gently point out that *they* had names and generally responded quite obediently to them. Instead, she took a two-liter bottle of soda from the refrigerator and began filling the glasses already on the table. "It's one of their favorites. It smells homemade."

"It is."

"So you find time to cook, too?"

"No. Mary Stephens—my nearest neighbor—fills my freezer with these every couple months. She started when she thought we were going to be family and never stopped."

At that moment Olivia wouldn't have minded possession

of one bit of Elly's breezy unawareness—or was it uncaring?—of what was proper and what wasn't so she could pursue his last statement. Going to be family in what way? Had he had a relationship with Mary or with a daughter/niece/sister? And what had happened to end it? Had it been his decision? Not likely, or else Mary was a most forgiving woman.

But she'd been too properly brought up to exhibit even the slightest nosiness about a stranger, and so she said nothing.

He set a basket of steaming garlic toast on the table, then finally looked at her. "I guess that's it."

Wishing she was anywhere in the world but here, she managed another strained smile. "I'll get Elly and Emma."

Somewhere in his thirty-four years, he must have had a more awkward meal, Guthrie thought when it was over, but he couldn't remember when. He'd done the right thing. He'd fed these people and given them a place to stay. Now he wished they would go there.

Immediately he felt bad for the unkind thought. They were still here because Olivia was cleaning the kitchen. He would have preferred to do it himself, just so he could have some privacy, but she'd insisted, and something in her eyes—some little bit of shredded dignity—had persuaded him to let her. She wasn't used to charity—the obviously expensive clothes, pampered hands and high-dollar luggage, of which she had a full set, attested to that—and she was in the position of having to accept it now in part because of his brother. The least he could do was make it a little easier for her.

Thoughts of Ethan made his jaw tighten. Tomorrow he would see his lawyer—he'd already called and left a message on Jerry's machine—and after that, he intended to suggest that Olivia Miles make a visit to the district attorney's office. Land fraud was a serious crime, especially around here where everyone's livelihood, in one way or another, was tied to the land. Maybe having to face the legal consequences of his actions for once would be the push Ethan needed to straighten up and fly right.

She started the dishwasher, gave the counters one last swipe, then returned a dusty silk flower arrangement to the middle of the breakfast table. He didn't care much about flowers, but his mother had bought that the week before she died, and so he'd kept it.

It would break her heart to know what her younger son was up to these days. She'd done her best with both her sons, and in both cases, they'd taken more after the fathers they'd barely known. Fortunately, *his* father had been worth taking after. Ethan's wasn't.

But there came a point where a man had to take responsibility for himself—for who he was and what he did, good or bad. Guthrie had reached that point sixteen years ago, when he'd taken over the running of the ranch. Ethan wasn't likely to ever reach it.

And that was none of Guthrie's concern. Once this matter of Olivia's bogus deed had been straightened out, nothing Ethan ever did would matter to him. He could cease to exist, and Guthrie wouldn't care.

"Pretty flowers. You know, they make this spray that cleans silk flowers and makes them look like new."

He stared at the flowers for a moment, blinked, then refocused his gaze on Olivia. What was he supposed to reply to a comment like that? Like dusting fake flowers had any place at all on his long list of priorities?

She slid into the chair across from him and folded her hands together on the tabletop. "This—this land you gave your brother... If it's mine, can I—can I sell it?"

"If it's yours, you can do whatever you damn well please with it."

The sharpness of his answer made her blink and brought color to both her face and his. "I meant...would I be able to find a buyer for it?"

He thought of someone else, some stranger, owning half his land and felt sick inside, but forced himself to answer.

"Maybe. I doubt your husband was the last fool in this country." The instant he heard his words aloud, the heat increased and shame cranked the tension in his muscles a notch higher. "I'm sorry. I shouldn't have said that."

"David *was* a fool," she said in a quiet voice. For a moment she studied her hands, and so did he—small, long-fingered, knuckles and fingertips white from squeezing so tightly. They didn't look capable of much work, not the kind of hard work that was part of living on a ranch. When she looked up again, he did, too. "Would you— Would you be interested in buying it?"

Guthrie's laugh was sharp with bitterness. "Buy back my own land? That would teach me not to trust my worthless brother again, wouldn't it? Not that I need the lesson." Then, turning grim, he gave her a real answer. "I can't afford the debt. People generally don't get rich in ranching. Most of us are lucky to keep our heads above water."

She looked so disappointed that he ventured a question he would normally never ask a stranger. "Just how bad off are you?"

"If the sale was invalid and I have no legal claim to Mr. James's share of the ranch…" She smiled a faint, bleak smile. "I have nothing."

For an instant he wondered if she was exaggerating, but the hopeless look in her blue eyes assured him she wasn't. Clothes, toys, dishes, pots and pans and an old car that was about to give up the ghost—that was the total of her belongings.

That, and two little girls who'd lost their father, their home and everything else.

"Didn't your husband have life insurance?"

"I thought he did. He quit making payments on it about the same time he quit paying for the house and the cars. I thought the girls and I were well provided for until a week after his funeral. That's when the lawyer told me that everything was gone. Everything except the ranch. I'd forgotten all about it. I guess David had, too, or he would have tried to get some money out of it, too.''

"Or he'd already found out that Ethan had conned him."

The thought obviously hadn't occurred to her before. He wished he hadn't mentioned it now because with those few words, he'd destroyed whatever bit of faint hope she'd been clinging to. Her shoulders rounded and her voice turned dull. "Of course. He sold or lost everything else. He must have tried to sell this place and found out—" Her words choked off, and she pressed one hand to her mouth as if trying to hold in the despair.

He shifted his gaze to the window. He could see her reflection, but the glass distorted it—softened her fear, put a haze over her panic. "Did your husband have any contact with Ethan after they made the deal?"

"I don't know." Her smile was painfully sad. "We're old-fashioned Southerners, Mr. Harris. David took care of business, and my job was the house and the girls. I was remarkably ignorant of what was going on. I do know that Mr. James gave him a phone number, but he said it would change when he moved from the main—the main house to the foreman's house. He said he would give him the new number once he got it. David and I never discussed the ranch again, so I never knew..."

*The main house.* Guthrie restrained his disgusted snort. Ethan had probably filled Miles's head with images of ranch life as seen on *Dallas* or some other TV show. He'd always been good at spinning tales, but no one around here had ever been foolish enough to fall for them. He'd had to go all the way to Atlanta for that.

The chair scraped the floor as Olivia slid it back. She stood up, pushed her hands into the pockets of her long, summery dress and faced him. "I really do appreciate everything. We—we'll try not to be any more trouble than we already are."

He knew he should say they were no trouble. The cabin was just sitting over there empty, and he would've heated that lasagna for dinner whether they were here or not. But he didn't say anything. He just nodded once, then got to his feet as she left the kitchen.

She got the kids from the living room, prompted them to thank him for dinner as he walked down the hall toward them. Elly did. Emma Rae stuck out her bottom lip, hung her head and refused.

And then they were gone.

*Finally.*

He turned off the television, switched off the kitchen lights, then stood in the dark, staring out the window. He hadn't had more than a minute to brood when the phone rang, disturbing the quiet. He considered ignoring it, but he didn't ignore calls, letters or knocks at the door. Unlike Ethan, he'd never had any reason to.

His curt hello was greeted with a laugh. "I'd ask how your day has been, but I'd say that about answers it."

"Sorry, Mary. I've got something on my mind."

"Could it be a lovely young Southern belle with adorable—I repeat, absolutely *adorable*—twin girls?"

He closed his eyes and rubbed the ache centered in his forehead. He should have known news of his visitors would be all over town by now. Olivia must have asked for directions in town, and in a place like Heartbreak, that was all it took. The only surprise was that his neighbor had waited this long to call for details.

"What have you been keeping from us, Guthrie?" she teased.

"You know I don't keep secrets."

"So who is she?"

He was silent a long time, uncomfortable with any answer he might give. He wasn't ready to tell the whole truth, not before he'd talked to his lawyer, but he also didn't want to refuse to answer and fuel speculation about his connection to Olivia and her daughters. Finally he settled on a half truth. "She came here looking for Ethan."

Though she hadn't made a sound, he knew Mary's lighthearted mood had disappeared. He knew her well—so much better than her daughter whom he'd almost married.

When she broke her silence, her voice was grim. "Tell me Ethan's not the father of those little girls."

He managed a bitter smile in the dark. That possibility had never occurred to him. Taking all the proper precautions when it came to sex was about the only responsible thing Ethan had ever done. No kids for him, he'd always sworn. Not now, not ever.

Lucky kids.

"No. Their father—her husband—is dead."

"So what does she want?"

"I really can't talk about this right now, Mary."

"Corliss over at the post office said she's awful pretty. Is she?"

If a man's tastes ran to fragile, insubstantial, pampered, then, yeah, she was pretty. Her eyes were a nice shade of blue, and her mouth had a nice shape to it. Her hair looked silky, and so did her skin, and her hands seemed so small and delicate.

But what she mostly was, he thought, remembering the moment when she'd pressed her hand to her mouth to hold back the fear, was tragic. Her whole world had fallen apart, and there wasn't much she could do to put it back together.

"You're taking a long time to answer, Guthrie," Mary chided. "It's a simple question. Yes, she's pretty, or no, she's not."

"She's a widow," he said impatiently. "Her husband's only been dead three weeks."

There was a moment's silence, followed by a curious, "Oh."

He knew Mary's *ohs* well enough to know that that one meant a whole lot more than just *oh*. "What?" he asked flatly.

"I was merely asking for your first impression. Obviously, you've moved on to second and third ones."

"Why do you say that?"

"You've gone past thinking yes, she's pretty, in an uninvolved, person-to-person sort of way to thinking yes-she's-pretty-but-her-husband-just-died-so-I-shouldn't-be-thinking-that sort of way. Hmm."

Her logic annoyed Guthrie no end. His only interest in Olivia Miles was finding a solution to this mess Ethan had gotten them into that both of them could live with. He wasn't looking to get involved, wasn't looking for anything but the peace and solitude she'd stolen from him today. "Listen, Mary, I can't talk now. I'll be in touch with you later."

Before she could protest, he hung up. He felt bad for cutting her off—she'd been a good friend to him since his mother died—but he had too many troublesome females in his life right now. He couldn't deal with one more.

Too restless to settle inside, he went out onto the front porch, taking up a position in the shadows at the west end. With the sun set, the temperature had dropped ten degrees and a slight breeze cooled the air a bit more. Across the field lights were on in all three bedrooms in the cabin, as well as the living room.

Nothing like their old house, Elly had announced with a grim shake of her head. He didn't need to ask to know that their old house had been a mansion compared to either of his places. Olivia had that look of privilege and an easy life. She no more belonged on a ranch than he would in her old mansion.

But her life wasn't easy anymore, and though it wasn't his fault, though he was even less to blame for this situation than she was, the fact was he felt responsible. If he and his mother hadn't somehow failed Ethan, if he hadn't given Ethan the land, if he'd put restrictions on the gift...

Ethan still would have done what he'd done. He'd had no qualms about selling the half of the ranch that didn't belong to him. He wouldn't have had any reluctance if none of it had belonged to him. He was immoral. Unethical. A thief and con artist.

Upstairs in the cabin, the lights went off in one room, then the other. A moment later the downstairs bedroom went dark, too. After their long trip from Georgia and all the shocks of the day, they were calling it an early night, he thought, but at that moment, Olivia passed in front of the living room window, then came out the screen door to the porch. She still wore that flowery sundress she'd worn to dinner, but her hair was down now, loose past her shoulders. For a long time, she stood motionless, hands braced on the porch rail, lit by the soft light coming through the window.

Was she pretty? Mary had asked, and he had danced around the answer. He should have been straightforward and honest. *Yes. Hell, yes.* She was soft, lovely, womanly, and in need of his help, and he was a sucker for all of the above. Toss in one bold, brash kid and another nursing a broken heart over the upheaval in her life, and he could be in serious trouble.

He was about to go back inside when abruptly she moved, sinking to the porch floor in a heap. He'd moved an instinctive step in that direction before he realized that she hadn't collapsed. She wasn't in pain—at least, not physical pain. She was crying—huddled there against the rail, sobbing as if her heart had broken.

For the husband who had died and left her in such dire straits? For the easy, privileged life she'd lost? Or for the future that seemed so hopeless and bleak?

He didn't want to know.

He retreated into the house, shutting the door, shutting out the breeze that carried the sounds of her tears, but the image remained in his mind. The sobs still echoed in his ears. Damn Ethan and David Miles, he thought grimly, for putting them in this mess.

And damn himself for feeling the need to get them out of it.

Olivia awoke to a headache, a stuffy nose and puffy, red-rimmed eyes. Crying had seemed the only solution last night, but she'd found no release in it, and she felt worse for it this morning. She washed down aspirin with a mouthful of rusty-tasting well water, patted her eyes with a washcloth soaked in cool water, then got dressed. She was so sore from two days' travel, the heavy-duty cleaning the cabin had required and tossing and turning in a strange bed that she couldn't tell where the aches in her body ended and the ones in her heart began.

She dressed in another sundress and sandals, pulled her hair back and clipped it, then went upstairs to wake the girls. She'd expected a middle-of-the-night visit from a frightened Emma, who'd hated the idea of sleeping in her own room. It hadn't come, though, and she found out why when she walked through the door—Elly had given up her own bed down the hall to share her sister's rumpled bed.

She opened the curtains, then woke both girls. Elly literally sprang from the bed and hopped from one foot to the other. "Can we see the cows today? Can I ride a horse? Can we get a dog? Can we help the cowboys round up the cows?" Her eyes widened. "D'ya think they might be brandin' 'em today? If they are, can we watch?"

When she paused for breath, Emma, looking forlorn on the side of the bed, asked her own plaintive question. "Can we go home?"

Olivia ignored all the questions. "First thing we're going to do today is go into town and buy some groceries."

Elly laughed as if she were silly. "Oh, Mom, the *first* thing we're gonna do is go pee and brush our teeth and put on some clothes. *Then* we'll go to town. D'ya think they sell dogs in town?"

"No dog yet, sweetie," Olivia said. Right now she could barely afford to feed the three of them—and not for long. There was no way she could take on the expense of dog food, too. "Emmy, how did you sleep?"

"Not like in my own bed. I don't like it here, Mommy. There's noises."

Olivia opened her arms, and her younger daughter slipped into her embrace. There was no denying the noises. Through the open windows last night, she'd heard whippoorwills, bobwhites, owls and, for a few minutes, a chorus of yips and howls that had made her shiver. Dogs, she'd told herself. Coyotes or worse, she'd feared.

"Nothing's going to get you, baby," she assured Emma. "Not with Elly and me here."

Elly bounced onto the bed beside them. "And not with Mr. Guthrie right next door. You said he was big and scary, 'member? Nobody's gonna mess with a big and scary cowboy. He'll keep you safe."

He looked capable of keeping them all safe, Olivia thought. After the last few weeks, safe sounded pretty darn good.

But they weren't his responsibility. He wasn't their savior. He was just a decent guy trying to do the right thing for the moment. But the moment was going to pass, and doing the right thing was going to fall on *her*. She prayed she could handle it, but she was afraid she couldn't. Right now, in fact, she didn't have a clue what the right thing even was. She was too defeated to even think about it.

She sent the girls off to brush their teeth while she made their beds, then went downstairs to wait. She was studying a family portrait on the end table when a knock sounded at the door.

She opened the door but left the screen door closed between them. It was their neighbor and benefactor, wearing jeans, a white shirt and that straw cowboy hat. In the bright morning light, he looked bigger, stronger, more capable, than he had last night.

He looked perfectly able to keep them safe forever.

"Good morning," she greeted him.

He tilted his hat back an inch or two. "I'm going into town this morning to meet with my lawyer. I thought you might like to come along."

She considered his invitation a moment before hesitantly suggesting, "Maybe I should have a lawyer of my own."

"Why?"

"Because we both have problems, Mr. Harris, and the best

solution for you isn't likely to be the best solution for the girls and me.''

His gaze narrowed subtly, as if he'd taken offense at her words. She'd meant none. She was just trying to be realistic.

"Jerry Danvers is the only lawyer in Heartbreak. Before you go spending money you don't have on someone else, you should talk to him first. Depending on the validity of your claim, you may not need a lawyer at all.''

He was right. She didn't have money to spend on legal fees and maybe—please, God—she wouldn't have to. Maybe she could take ownership of Ethan James's property free and clear.

And then what? Sell it out from under his brother? Pitch a tent and live on it? Try to work some partnership deal with Guthrie? Oh, yes, and wouldn't he be happy with that? First she'd asked him to buy back his own land. Now she was considering offering him the use of it in return for a share of his profits. It wasn't right. Of course, he'd voluntarily given the land to his brother—she couldn't bear any blame for that—but he'd done it with the apparent understanding that it would remain in the family and under his control. It wasn't fair that Ethan and David—and, yes, Olivia, too—had put him in this situation.

"All right," she agreed quietly. "The girls are getting dressed now. I'll get my papers and we'll meet you—or would you prefer that I take my car?''

He gave the junk heap a flat look, then said, "You can ride with me.''

She nodded. "Can we stop at the grocery store afterward?''

"Sure. No problem.''

Her smile came a fraction more easily than usual. "Kind words, Mr. Harris, but I know we've been nothing *but* problems.''

Her acknowledgment seemed to loosen just a bit of the tension that held him so stiff. "My name is Guthrie.''

"I'm Olivia.''

For a moment, they simply stood there, looking at each

other, then she smiled again. "We'll be over in a few minutes."

He nodded, then walked away. She was watching him go—some long-dormant part of her appreciating the view—when footsteps pounded down the stairs.

"We're ready to go," Elly announced in a voice that could be heard next door as she skipped the last steps to land with a jarring thud.

Olivia turned from the door and stifled the laughter that tried to escape. There was a reason why she rarely left the girls to dress themselves. Emma had chosen her favorite ensemble—a long, full dress with poufy sleeves and a matching sun hat. And Elly had chosen her own favorite—blue-and-white striped shorts a shade too small; a T-shirt colored in blocks of red, green, yellow and purple; an Atlanta Braves baseball cap, turned backward; and a pair of scuffed Doc Martens, unlaced, of course.

"Honey," Olivia began, directing the single endearment to both of them, and their expressions simultaneously turned mutinous. As quickly as her protest had begun, it ended. Their choice of clothing wasn't worth a battle that she simply didn't have the energy to fight. No matter how they looked, they were going to get plenty of attention when they showed up in town with Guthrie, so why not give the folks of Heartbreak something to look at?

"Let's go, girls," she said, picking up her purse and the keys from the coffee table, then collecting the manila envelope with the ranch papers from the end table drawer. "Mr. Guthrie's going to take us into town."

"I'd really rather take our car," Emma announced as she walked out the door.

"I know you would."

"Can I ride in the back, please, Mom?" Elly asked as she followed her sister. "I've never ridden in the back of a truck before. Please, please, I won't fall out or nothin'."

"'Fraid not, darlin'." Olivia locked up, breathed deeply of the fresh warm air, then started across the field with the girls.

Guthrie was waiting beside the truck, staring off at the buildings out back. She wondered what work he was missing because of them, wondered just how big an inconvenience they really were to him. But wondering was all she would do. When he turned at the sound of their approach, he didn't look the least bit inclined to talk.

"Hey, Mr. Guthrie," Elly greeted him. "Where're the cows?"

"Still in the pasture."

"Do you have horses?"

"Yup. They're in a different pasture."

She stopped close enough that she had to tilt her head back to see his face. "Can I ride?"

"I don't know," he answered gravely. "Can you?"

Her giggle sounded so relaxed and normal and gave Olivia the faintest hope that everything would eventually be all right. "I mean, can I ride one of your—one of *our* horses?"

A muscle clenched in his jaw as he gave the same answer. "I don't know." To Olivia he said, "We'd better get going."

The pickup had a cramped back seat, Olivia discovered when she opened the door, and she lifted Emma into it. Elly climbed up behind her, fastened her lap belt, then tattled. "Mama, Emma Rae doesn't have her seat belt on."

"I don't have a seat belt," her sister announced defensively.

Guthrie pushed the driver's seat forward while Olivia fastened her own belt. "There's one back here," he said, leaning in. "It must have fallen—"

Emma fixed her steeliest gaze on him. "If you touch me, I'm gonna scream and tell the police," she warned.

"Emma Rae!" Shocked, Olivia twisted around. "Don't you dare speak to him like that! You apologize right now."

The mutinous look was back. "I won't. He's a stranger, and strangers aren't s'posed to touch little girls. My daddy told me so."

Before Olivia could say anything else, Guthrie retreated and scowled at her across the cab. "*You* fix her seat belt," he said, irritation making his voice sharp. "And make it quick. I don't want to be late for this appointment."

"I'll get it, Mama," Elly said quickly, eager to smooth things over. "Look, I already founded one." She located the other half of the belt, snapped the ends together, then tugged one end to fit it more snugly. Judging from Emma's squeal, she pulled it a tad tighter than necessary.

Please behave, Olivia silently entreated her daughters. *Please don't antagonize this man who's the only thing standing between us and disaster. Please don't give him reason to be sorry he helped us.*

And before her prayers were finished, she got an answer. Unfortunately, Elly's gasp and Emma's resulting wail weren't the answer she was hoping for. She twisted in her seat to scold them both, then stole a look at Guthrie as she settled in again. His gaze was directed straight ahead, his fingers were curled tightly around the steering wheel, and his jaw was set so hard that she suspected his teeth must ache. She considered making excuses—they're tired, they're scared, they're five years old—then thought better of it. As long as he could pretend they weren't there, creating chaos in his life, she could let him.

## Chapter 3

When he pulled into a parking space in front of Jerry Danvers's office, it was all Guthrie could do to keep from heaving a great sigh of relief. For nine solid miles, the kids had done nothing but fuss and their mother's frequent admonitions had done nothing to calm them. Elly was a devil, and Emma Rae really was a crybaby, as her twin insisted, and his headache from last night was back full force.

He climbed out of the truck and closed the door, leaving prissy Emma Rae to slide across the seat and exit the passenger door. She clung to her mother's hand while Elly skipped onto the sidewalk and looked first one way, then the other. "Where're we goin?"

He gestured to the storefront that housed Jerry's offices and Elly muscled open the door and marched inside right up to Ann Screechowl's desk. He followed Olivia and Emma Rae inside in time to hear Elly announce, "And I'm gonna ride and have a rope and hat and boots just like a real cowboy, and I'm gonna practice lassoing Emmy 'cause she's so whiny."

Ann looked the way Guthrie felt—overwhelmed. When she saw him, she smiled, then her expression quickly shifted to Olivia. She had about a million questions—everyone in town would—but she didn't ask one. ''Jerry's in his office, Guthrie. You can go on back.''

''Thanks, Ann. Can you watch the kids?'' When Olivia started to protest, he cut her off. ''Would you rather have them sit in on this meeting?''

She wavered—and why not? He was asking her to leave her kids with a complete stranger who appeared to be no more accustomed to rambunctious kids than he was. But apparently she agreed that the lawyer's office wasn't the best place for them, because she sternly warned both girls, then followed him down the hall to Jerry's office.

After the introductions, Jerry leaned back in his chair and asked, ''What can I do for you, Guthrie?''

He gestured to Olivia to hand over the envelope. Jerry scanned the documents inside, looked from her to Guthrie as if he suspected it might be a joke, then muttered, ''Well, hell.''

Guthrie's sentiments exactly. ''So what do we do?''

''Well, obviously Ethan can't sell your ranch, so the deed and contract are pretty much worthless.''

Olivia, who'd been sitting upright on the edge of her seat, sank back, and that panicked look that was becoming too damn familiar crossed her face. ''So I don't have the money,'' she said thickly, ''and I don't own the land.''

Jerry looked over the contract again, then shrugged. ''Honestly, I don't know. Guthrie could probably make a pretty good case in court that the whole deal is invalid because it includes property that didn't belong to Ethan to sell.'' He shifted his attention to Guthrie. ''Is that your intent?''

There was no question it was what he *wanted* to do, though the admission shamed him. If the sale was declared invalid, life would go back to the way it was—just him and his ranch—while he tracked down Ethan and coerced him into deeding the place back to him.

But if the sale was declared invalid, Olivia and her daughters would be homeless and hopeless. No matter how foolish David Miles was, he'd made the deal with Ethan in good faith. He'd paid a hefty chunk of cash and believed he was getting a piece of land in exchange. At the very least, that was what his widow deserved.

But this was his business, his *life*. Not fighting Ethan's deal would hurt him financially. It would cost more than he could afford to lose, and it could conceivably put him out of business.

But the one thing he couldn't afford *most* to lose was his honor. Going to court, asking a judge to undo Ethan's wrongs, trying to keep his property intact and the ranch on stable footing and, in the process, putting a woman and her little girls out on the street... Those things would cost him his honor.

The longer he delayed answering, the more fearful Olivia's expression grew. She looked as if she was about to crumple into tears again when finally he spoke. "No. That's not my intent." He didn't look straight at her, but still he saw the relief sweep over her. "Ethan sold her husband his land. Now her husband's dead. *She* owns the land."

His answer didn't satisfy Jerry. "Guthrie, maybe we should discuss this in private."

The lawyer couldn't come up with any arguments he hadn't already tried on himself. "There's nothing to discuss."

"What about your operation? You use every square foot of that acreage. You can't run your herd on what you've got left. What are you going to do? Lease your own land back?"

"It's not my land anymore." Guthrie felt sick deep inside as the reality of that fact sank in. That land had been in the Harris family for nearly a hundred years. He was the first in all those years who'd ever lost so much as one acre. "I guess that's something I'll have to work out with..." He hesitated, then forced himself to say the words that left a bitter taste in his mouth. "With my new partner. What does she have to do to get a clear title?"

"She'll have to—" At a gesture from Guthrie, Jerry broke off, flushed and directed his gaze to Olivia. "You'll have to hire an attorney and go to court over in Buffalo Plains, the county seat, and file a quiet title suit. Then— Do you have any idea where Ethan is?"

Both Olivia and Guthrie shook their heads.

"Well, then you have to run a notice in the county legal news and in the legal notices column in the newspaper where you think he might be. You can run it consecutively or every second or third day, whatever, for thirty days. You also have to make some effort to locate him—do a credit check, hire an investigator, run him on the Internet, whatever. After thirty days, if he hasn't been located, then you ask the judge to enter a default judgment granting you a deed and ownership of the property."

"And how much does all this cost?" she asked in a small voice.

Jerry shrugged. "Depends on the lawyer and the cost of the legal notices and the costs of the search. A couple thousand dollars, maybe more, maybe less."

She swallowed hard as she looked at Guthrie. "I can't afford it."

Neither could he. But... "You can't afford not to. Next time Ethan needs money, he may try selling the place again. You need a clear title to protect your interests." The ache in his head intensified its pounding. "We'll see what we can do." He stood up and shook the lawyer's hand. "Jerry, thanks for your time."

Looking shell-shocked, Olivia led the way from the office, collected the girls and went outside. For a moment she simply stood on the sidewalk, her eyes closed against the bright morning sun. She looked so lost that even the twins noticed.

"What's wrong, Mommy?" Elly asked, sounding exactly like the more timid Emma Rae for the first time since Guthrie had met them.

Olivia drew a deep breath, summoned a poor smile and

looked down at her daughters. "Nothing's wrong, sweetie. Were you two good for Miss Ann?"

"*I* was,"? Emma Rae announced smugly. "I sat in a chair and readed a book the whole time."

Elly sidled closer to Guthrie and said in a stage whisper, "She only pretended. She can't really read, 'cept little baby books."

"Neither can you," Emma Rae said.

"So? Least I don't pretend." The window art next door caught Elly's attention and made her forget teasing her sister. "Mama, look. That place has ice-cream cones. Can we have one? Please?"

"I don't—"

Though he knew it was wrong, Guthrie interrupted. "Let 'em have one. My treat." Food in their mouths, he'd learned last night at dinner, would slow down the teasing, arguing and incessant talking at least a little. Since it was a sure bet he wouldn't get much peace on the drive home, he could use a few minutes of it now.

When Olivia reluctantly agreed, they went inside the diner. Except for two old farmers down at one end and the teenage girl—Doc Hanson's niece, he thought—behind the counter, the place was empty, a fact for which he was grateful. He wasn't much in the mood to be making introductions or offering explanations.

The girls climbed onto stools at the counter and ordered ice-cream cones. Guthrie ordered pop, Olivia iced tea, and they sat at the nearest table. She looked frazzled as she stirred sweetener into her tea.

"They must seem like the worst behaved children in the world to you," she said apologetically. "I used to be so much better at things. I was organized and capable, and I could make them behave with no more than a glance. Now I've lost control of my life and my kids—" She broke off, but not in time to disguise the quaver in her voice. Very carefully laying the spoon on the table, she took a sip of tea, then met his gaze. "Thank you."

He didn't ask for what. He didn't want to be reminded that for the first time in history, part of Harris Ranch belonged to an outsider and it was all his fault. He could blame Ethan all he wanted, but the simple fact remained that if *he* hadn't been stupid enough to give that half to his brother, Ethan still might have sold it, but Olivia's claim wouldn't be valid.

"What are your plans?" he asked, watching as Elly and Emma Rae spun their stools in opposite circles, their outstretched legs tangling once every whirl.

"First, I've got to find a job."

In Heartbreak? he thought cynically. *Good luck.* "What are you good at?"

"Nothing." She smiled thinly. "I've never held a paying job. I was in college when David and I got married. Afterward, I was his wife and the girls' mother." She said the two words as if they were all-inclusive, self-explanatory titles that should be written with capital letters—Wife, Mother—as if that were *all* she was. Maybe in the way she'd been taught to view life, that was true. *We're old-fashioned Southerners,* she'd said last night. *David took care of business, and my job was the house and the girls.*

"I can keep house," she went on. "I can cook. I can plan fabulous parties, I can volunteer with the best of them, and I can keep other people's lives on schedule. That's about the extent of my usefulness."

"Unfortunately, there's not a big demand for wives and mothers or fabulous parties in Heartbreak."

"Of course there's not." She gave that same little smile again and made him wonder how a real smile looked on her. He bet the difference would be like night and day. He bet it would make her gorgeous.

And the last thing he needed was *gorgeous* living a hundred yards away.

"What about the ranch?" he asked grimly. "I assume you plan to put it up for sale."

The look that settled over her features was pure regret. "I don't see any other choice. The girls want to go back to Atlanta. *I* want to go back to Atlanta. It's our home. It's where we belong.'' Her voice turned hopeful. ''Maybe we can work something out. Maybe you could lease it or buy it back without going through the bank.''

He didn't know how. She needed an income to support her kids. He couldn't squeeze more than a couple hundred bucks a month out of his budget, if even that.

She took his silence as rejection of her suggestion. ''It's not important right now. I can't sell it until I have a legal title, and I can't get that until I come up with the money for the lawsuit, and I can't do that until I get a job, and... Oh, God.'' Hiding her face in her hands, she whispered, ''If David weren't dead, I'd kill him.''

Guthrie silently echoed the words. And as long as he was feeling murderous, he wouldn't mind wrapping his hands around Ethan's throat, too—which might bring him some satisfaction, but it wouldn't solve any of their problems. They were going to have to work together to do that.

''Look, I need that pasture, and you need a place to live. For now, I'll trade you the use of the cabin for the use of the land. Okay?''

Letting her hands slide away from her face, she slowly nodded.

''As for a job, you're not going to find anything in Heartbreak that can support all three of you, and that car of yours isn't up to commuting to Buffalo Plains or anywhere else, and you'd wind up spending most of what you earn on a baby-sitter. So—'' He broke off, gave himself a chance to talk himself out of the deal he was about to offer, then offered it anyway. ''You take care of the house, do the cooking and the laundry and help me if I need it, and in exchange, I'll provide the food and I'll pay what I can.''

Her eyes brightened with unshed tears and her voice dropped to a fragile whisper. ''I've been inside your house. You don't need a housekeeper. You just need to dust once in a while.''

''It's a luxury,'' he admitted, and he didn't often indulge

in luxuries. All he did, all he'd done since he'd awakened ten years ago and found Ethan gone, was work. Well, housework was one chore he would gladly relinquish, and if it made her feel less like a charity case…

"All right." She hated saying the words. It showed in her too-expressive eyes. "I—I really appreciate this. I'll do my best…" There were several ways she could finish. *To earn my keep. To stay out of your way. To not be a problem. To not take your land away from you.* Instead, she simply shrugged.

"We'd better get groceries, then get back." He had chores to catch up and a hell of a new situation to get used to. The chores could be handled in a few hours. The getting-used-to part, though…

Olivia called the girls, told them they were going. He watched Elly leap off the stool, then race out the door with suitable sound effects, watched Emma Rae step daintily to the floor, smooth her dress and adjust her hat, then prissily follow Elly, watched Olivia smooth her own dress and tuck a strand of hair behind her ear with purely feminine, graceful gestures, and he gave a regretful sigh.

The getting-used-to part was going to be so damn hard.

Or so damn easy.

And so damn much trouble either way.

It was after six o'clock Friday evening when Olivia gave herself permission to sit down and relax. Her feet felt as if she'd walked all the way to Oklahoma from Georgia and her shoulders ached as if she'd carried the girls every step of the way. But Guthrie's house—the first floor, at least—was spotless, a week's worth of groceries were put away in their proper cabinets, his laundry was done and waiting in a basket at the top of the stairs, and dinner—supper, he'd called it— was right on schedule for a six-thirty serving.

For the first time since she'd arranged David's funeral, she felt as if she'd accomplished something, and the tasks were so common, so everyday normal that they made her feel the slightest bit normal. After more than two weeks of fear, shock and panic, she desperately needed to feel normal.

She scooted her chair back from the kitchen table, propped her feet on another chair and gazed out the window at their new, temporary home. Back in Atlanta, when she'd made the decision to come here—when she'd accepted that she had no other choice, she bitterly corrected—she'd tried to imagine what it would be like, but all she could see had been the three-storied house and pool. Barns, corrals, fence, dirt and cattle—none of those things had entered into her daydreams. Lord, she'd been foolish.

And, Lord, she wanted to go home!

She missed her house and her housekeeper, missed her beautiful lawn with its rich velvety green grass and manicured flower beds and her lawn service that kept them looking perfect. She missed her neighbors and friends, the private school they'd chosen for the girls when they were barely out of diapers, the lunches at the club. She missed the familiar lushness of Georgia's hot, humid summers, the giant live oaks draped in Spanish moss, the kudzu covering every stationary object in its path.

Everything dear and familiar was back home. All she had here was a barn. Corrals. Cattle, weeds and dirt.

And a stranger who cared more about a woman in trouble than her own husband had.

If anyone had told her six months ago that men like Guthrie Harris still existed, she would have laughed. Honor, decency, compassion—those qualities were in short supply among the people she knew. Not one of their friends back home who'd heard about the situation David had left her in had offered their help—some of them, not even their sympathy. It was too bad, but, hey, it wasn't *their* problem.

Well, it wasn't Guthrie's problem, either, but that hadn't stopped him from doing what he could. She was amazed. Grateful. Determined to prove herself worthy. And if there was *any* way possible, when she left here to return home, she would leave ownership of his property with him.

*If* there was any way.

Movement out back caught her attention, and she watched him come out of the barn. He took his hat off, dragged his fingers through his hair, then wiped his face with his shirt-sleeve. He looked hot and tired.

And handsome.

Shying away from that last thought, she left the table and filled a glass with ice and soda. He entered the house through the back door, which led into the utility room, where he left his hat and took off his boots. When he came into the kitchen, the soda was on the table. Olivia was beside the stove.

He stopped short, as if he'd forgotten that she was there. His shirt was damp with sweat, and a fine layer of dust coated him from head to toe. He was big, as Emma had pointed out, and looked tough. He also looked endearingly ill at ease.

"The soda's for you," she said when he continued to simply stand there.

"Soda?"

Her smile felt more like a grimace. "I suppose I should learn to call it pop while we're here."

He looked at the glass, looked back at her, then muttered thanks. He didn't reach for it, though.

"Dinner will be ready in about fifteen minutes."

"I have to shower."

"Okay. It can wait."

After another long moment, he started toward the hall. At the doorway, though, he detoured back, picked up the soda— the pop—and took it with him.

His bedroom, she'd discovered when she gathered the laundry, was directly above the kitchen. It was the biggest of the three bedrooms, with an old double bed, a dresser and chest of drawers, an easy chair and a rocker. It was a room in which he spent little time, she'd guessed, judging from the unmade bed, the dust that covered everything, the piles of clothes on the chairs.

She'd spent little time there herself—had simply gathered the clothes, then retreated. She'd gone back only to hang the jeans and shirts she'd taken from the dryer—if he wanted them ironed, she would figure that out later. The rest of his laundry—the socks, the T-shirts, the underwear—she'd neatly folded and left in the basket in the hallway. Going through his drawers to find out what went where was just a little too personal for her first day on the job.

Now she listened to the sound of running water overhead—thought of him stripped down naked up there and showering, and heat flushed her face. Maybe it would be a good idea in the future if she scheduled the girls' baths about this time each evening, then returned with them, fresh and clean, for dinner.

The water stopped. The floorboards creaked. One door snapped shut, then another. Less than five minutes later, he was walking down the hall to the kitchen, dressed in what she knew now made up the bulk of his wardrobe—jeans and a cotton shirt. Like last night, he was barefoot.

Like last night, she found something intimate about that.

She'd made roasted chicken and mashed potatoes, had heated home-canned green beans from the pantry and dinner rolls from a box. She set everything on the table while he filled three more glasses with ice, then soda. It felt strange, working with a man in the kitchen. David had had so little interest in woman's work that he hadn't even known in which cabinet to find a glass. When he was single like Guthrie, he'd simply taken all his meals elsewhere.

Leaving him with his task, she went down the hall to the living room and switched off the television. "Dinner's ready, girls—and please behave. No fussing, no arguing, no teasing, no whining."

"I don't whine," Elly said matter-of-factly.

"No, you make your sister whine."

"'Cause she's a crybaby."

"I am not!" Emma started, but Olivia clamped her hand over her mouth and gave Elly a sharp look.

"*Behave.*" If they didn't, she decided, they would have to

take their meals separately, because, after all his generosity, the least Guthrie deserved was to eat his supper in peace.

The girls walked sedately down the hall to the kitchen, slid into the same chairs where they'd eaten last night's supper and today's lunch and politely—quietly—waited to be served.

Halfway through the meal, Guthrie finally broke the silence. "Did you find everything you need?"

Olivia used the side of her fork to cut a piece of chicken, then stabbed it. "Yes."

"The house looks nice." The last word sounded foreign, as if *nice* wasn't something he often said.

"Thank you." It did look nice. It was spick-and-span spotless, as good as her housekeeper back home would have done, and it smelled faintly of the potpourri scent of the furniture polish with which she polished every bit of wood she could reach. "I'll get to the upstairs tomorrow."

"Tomorrow's Saturday."

"Don't you work on Saturday?"

He nodded.

"Then I can, too. What else do I have to do?"

"You could explore your new property. Just stay away from the cattle, be careful climbing fences, watch out for snakes and scorpions and—"

She and both girls stared at him, wide-eyed. "All we have to worry about at home is the occasional yellow jacket."

"We've got those, too, and wasps and bees and centipedes and fiddlebacks and tarantulas."

"Maybe I'll just stay inside and keep the girls there, too."

His thin smile was closer to natural than any she'd yet seen. "Unfortunately, we've got 'em inside, too. Be sure you shake out your clothes and empty your shoes before you put them on, and keep your bedcovers off the floor. If you go outside at night, watch for the spiders that spin webs from the trees down to the ground and for the snakes that curl up on the rocks. Don't reach into a bush and stay away from the brush, and if you—" he gestured to include the girls "—do get bit, don't do something stupid like trying to suck out the poison or putting on a tourniquet. Just get to Doc Hanson's office, next to the post office, right away.''

Emma scooted her chair an inch closer to Olivia's. "Mommy, I don't like it here,'' she wailed. "I don't like snakes and spiders! I want to go home!''

But across the table, Elly was grinning. "This is cool! Snakes and spiders and scorpions! Back home at our other house, we didn't have nothin' 'cept mosquitoes.''

"We've got those, too.'' Guthrie's gaze shifted to Emma. "I'm not trying to scare you. You just have to be a little more careful in the country.''

Her lower lip began to tremble. "I hate the country, and I hate Oklahoma, and I hate snakes and spiders and scorpions, and I hate—''

Well aware of how Emma's litany of dislikes usually ended—*and I hate you!*—Olivia gave her hand a warning squeeze. Emma grasped her fingers, slid from her chair and wormed in as close as she could get, burying her face in Olivia's shoulder, then giving a huge quavering sigh that trembled through her entire body.

"She's a little…sensitive, isn't she?'' Guthrie asked, his voice perfectly even, perfectly blank of emotion.

What had he been about to say before that hesitation—before he thought better of it? Olivia wondered. Spoiled? Whiny? Bratty? Her protective maternal temper flared, then just as quickly faded. Even under the best of circumstances, Emma was sensitive, as he'd tactfully put it—and the last few weeks, particularly the last few days, had been far from the best of circumstances.

She didn't respond to his comment. Instead, she smoothed Emma's hair back from her face and smiled down at her. "We're not afraid of any ol' spiders or snakes, are we?''

"*Yes.*''

"We-ell… Sometimes being afraid is good. It makes you careful and keeps you from getting hurt. We'll do everything Mr. Guthrie said, and maybe we won't even see any spiders or snakes before we go home.''

Emma raised her head and fixed her sweet, worried gaze on Olivia. "Can we go home tomorrow?"

"No, honey, not that soon."

"Next week?"

"I'm afraid not, babe."

"Then when? You promised, Mama. You *promised!*"

"I know, and I'll keep my promise. Don't I always?"

Reluctantly Emma nodded.

"We'll go home just as soon as we can, but it's going to be a while. Don't you think you can learn to like Oklahoma a little? Just while we're here?"

Emma drew back, hung her head and shook it. "I like Georgia. And Atlanta. And our house. And our bedroom. And my bed. I don't like *anything*—" she emphasized her words with a scowl at their host "—in Oklahoma." Still pouting, she gave a listless sigh, then asked, "May I be excused?"

"Sure, honey."

As she left the kitchen for the living room, silence settled. Finally Guthrie spoke. "I didn't mean to get her stirred up."

Elly chewed the last bite of her dinner, swallowed with a gulp, then replied, "Emma's *always* stirred up. Daddy said she was 'citable and needed backbone. Our daddy's dead, you know."

"I know," Guthrie replied. "I'm sorry."

"Me, too. May I be excused, too?"

When Olivia nodded, Elly slid to her feet, then circled behind to grasp the back of her chair. "Dinner was good, Olivia dear," she said in her most grown-up voice. She spoiled the effect, though, with a loud, smacking kiss on Olivia's cheek before racing off to join Emma in front of the television.

After a moment, Olivia pushed her plate aside and traced a scratch in the tabletop with her fingertip. "Emma *is* excitable," she agreed softly. "She wasn't exactly the child David was hoping for. Actually, neither of them were. He wanted sons. When he got daughters..." They'd found out in the course of all the tests her doctor had done once they'd realized she was carrying twins, and it'd taken the entire rest of her pregnancy for David to deal with the disappointment. And dealing with it was all he'd done. He'd never completely gotten over it.

"I shouldn't have said anything in front of them."

"She would have reacted the same way if I'd told her privately. She's very timid." Olivia smiled at her understatement. "You don't have any children?"

"I've never been married," he said as if that made a difference. She supposed, to a man like him, it did.

"What about family? Besides your brother?" To excuse her nosiness, she explained, "I was just wondering if there were many people who would object to my being here." It wasn't entirely a lie—she did wonder if there were Harris relatives who might resent her ownership of family property—but not the entire truth, either. Truth was, she was curious about him, plain and simple.

"My father died when I was six. My mother died ten years ago. He was the last of his family. Her family lives over around Tahlequah—cousins mostly, plus two brothers and their wives."

"What about Ethan's father?"

The muscles in his jaw tightened. "He took off years ago. He wasn't cut out for family life. Or responsibility. Or work, or anything but having a good time. Like Ethan."

And, to some extent, like David, she thought. Oh, he'd done his best, but it was hard to be a good husband and father to a wife you didn't love and kids you'd never wanted. He'd reached a point where he'd regretted their marriage, regretted the girls. She was convinced that was why he'd been so generous once they'd split up. He'd simply been trying to ease his guilty conscience.

"How long has it been since you saw Ethan?"

"I don't know. Four, maybe five years ago."

"So you weren't close."

"Actually, we were, considering he's six years younger. But after what he's done now, I don't care if I never see him again."

"You don't mean that," she said automatically, but his harsh expression suggested otherwise. "He's your *brother*."

"No. Not anymore."

He said it as if saying could make it so, but it wasn't that simple, she thought as she began gathering dishes. You couldn't just wave a wand and do away with unwanted family ties. He might never forgive Ethan for selling the family ranch, but he could never undo the fact that they shared the same blood, that they'd come from the same mother.

She stacked the dishes on the counter, wrapped the leftover chicken for the refrigerator and began loading the dishwasher. Guthrie didn't offer his help, but neither did he make any move to leave the table.

"What about your family?" he asked as she sprinkled soap powder into the dispenser, then secured the door.

"I come from a long line of only children. My grandparents died years ago, so when my parents died, that was it. No cousins, no aunts, no uncles."

"What about your husband?"

"He was estranged from his parents in Florida and his sister in London. They weren't invited to our wedding, and they refused to come to David's funeral." Their disinterest had astounded her. She'd loved her parents and mourned them deeply, and she absolutely couldn't imagine not being an everyday part of her daughters' lives. But David had cared no more about his family than they had about him.

Sometimes she thought that was why he'd never truly loved his own children. Maybe he simply hadn't been capable of it.

After wiping the counters with a damp cloth, she did the same at the dining table before slipping into her seat once more. "What time do you want breakfast?"

"I can fix it myself."

"It's no problem."

"I get up at five."

She swallowed hard. She hadn't seen daylight at five a.m. in her life unless one of the girls was sick. But she could handle it. She could handle anything.

Apparently reading her reaction, he grinned—the first real, sincere, honest-to-goodness expression of amusement she'd seen. It took twenty years off the age in his dark eyes and gave him a certain appeal that could prove lethal if a woman was susceptible.

After all those years with David, she feared she was susceptible.

"I can get my own breakfast," he said. "I usually just have coffee and leftovers from the night before. There's no reason for you to drag the kids out that early. They probably wouldn't appreciate it."

And if *they* didn't appreciate it, no one else would, either, she acknowledged.

With a sigh, she pushed to her feet again and tried to ignore her muscles' protest. She hung the washcloth over the side of the dish drainer, gave the kitchen one last look to be sure everything was in place, then faced him. "I guess we'll go now."

"Hang on." He disappeared down the hall, then returned with a set of keys. One was for the house, two for the truck parked outside. He offered, and she accepted them with some reluctance.

"You're awfully trusting," she commented. "How do you know I won't steal you blind and take off?"

"What kind of thief cleans a place up before cleaning it out? Besides, there's not much worth taking."

"You're wrong about that. Maybe it takes losing everything to fully appreciate it. Back home we had a big house filled with stuff that I didn't care about at all—until we lost it. Then…" She trailed off with a shrug.

"How did he lose it?"

Folding her fingers around the keys, she slid both hands into her pockets. "A few years ago he discovered the thrills of gambling. He started innocently enough—the office football pool, occasional lottery tickets—but every win, no matter how small, drew him in a little deeper. I had no idea how bad it had gotten until the lawyer broke the news after the funeral. Everything was gone. *Everything.*" She gave him a level look. "You're not a gambler, are you?"

"Of course I am. I'm a rancher. I bet my future every day on good weather, good market prices and good luck."

She smiled a little, and so did he. "I'd better go," she murmured, circling around him and starting down the hall. Halfway to the living room, though, she looked back. "Thank you. For everything."

"You're welcome."

It was the oddest thing, but she swore she could feel it. In spite of all the problems, all the tension and troubles, at that very moment, she *felt* welcome.

Good thing she was going back home to Atlanta before too long. With everything else that had gone wrong lately, the last thing in the world she needed was to risk heartbreak in Heartbreak.

# Chapter 4

Guthrie had finished brushing his horse Saturday morning and was swinging the blanket over the animal's back when the small figure standing motionless at the corner of the corral caught his attention. Covertly keeping an eye on her, he hefted the saddle into place, tightened the girths, then fastened the tie-down to a ring on the cinch. Then, finally, he looked straight at her.

Realizing that she'd been spotted, Elly gave up trying to hide and came forward. Her hair stood on end, she wore heavy, untied boots, and her thin cotton outfit looked suspiciously more like a nightgown than a dress. But she was grinning as confidently as if she hadn't sneaked out of the house half-dressed when she was supposed to be tucked snug in her bed.

"Morning."

Her grin widened a notch. "Mornin'. Is 'at your horse?"

"Yep. This is Buck."

"Why'd you call him that?"

"'Cause that's what he used to do."

"Can I pet him?"

"Sure." He held out his hand, and she skipped right over. Keeping one reassuring hand on the gelding's neck, he showed her where to rub and where to scratch for maximum effect. After a moment, she stepped back and flashed him a smile brighter than any morning sun.

"All my life I wanted a pony—not even one all my own. I'd've shared him with Emma, too. But Mama always said no, we couldn't, 'cause we lived in town. I don't know why that mattered, though. We had a great big yard. But now…" Her expression turned sly. "Now we got a ranch with hunnerds of acres, and we *got* to have horses. Now she can't say no no more, can she?"

"Mothers can always say no," he said, lifting her to sit on the top rail of the wooden fence. "It's what they do."

"Then maybe if *you* ask…"

Uh-uh. The middle of a mother-daughter standoff was no place for a man. "If I ask, your mom might think you don't want it bad enough to ask for yourself."

"Oh, no, she knows I want it more'n anything in the whole world. A pony and a dog—and maybe a four-wheeler," she added thoughtfully. "And cowboy boots and a cowboy hat… Can I wear your hat?"

"Nope. You never mess with a man's Stetson. Listen, Elly Mae—"

She giggled. "My name's not Elly Mae."

"Are you sure? It rhymes with Emma Rae."

"'Course I'm sure." She drew her shoulders back and regally lifted her head. "My name's Eleanor Marie Miles, and when I'm in trouble, Mama calls me all three names."

"You? Get in trouble?" he teased, but she answered in all seriousness.

"I'm okay on my own, but Emma Rae gets me in trouble *all* the time. She's just so easy to be mean to 'cause it makes her whine, and I tell Mama that if she didn't make it so fun, then I wouldn't do it so much, but Mama still gets onto me like it's all my fault." Shaking her head with an aggrieved expression, she launched into one of those sudden subject changes. "Can I ride your horse?"

His first impulse was to say no. His second was to relent. "I'll give you a ride back to the cabin on my way out. Later, if you guys stay long enough, I'll teach you to ride by yourself."

He swung into the saddle, then settled her on the saddle in front of him. As Buck turned away from the fence, she wrapped both hands around the horn and held on tightly for someone bold and fearless. Within a minute, though, she relaxed and gave a great sigh. "You know what? I don't want to go back to Atlanta," she said in a quiet, just-between-us tone. "Daddy's gone, and our house is gone, and our car is gone, and we can't live in our old neighborhood, and we can't go to school with our old friends, and nothing would ever be the same again. I'd just as soon stay right here forever."

Guthrie didn't have anything to say to that. He didn't want a partner for forever—just long enough, maybe, to give him a chance to buy back his land. Besides, while Olivia was willing to make the best of a bad situation, she'd made it clear that her main goal was to return home as quickly as possible. That was his goal, too—to regain the even keel of his life as quickly as he could.

They circled behind the house and cut across the field to the cabin. If Elly had harbored any hopes of returning to the house unnoticed, they were dashed the instant she and Guthrie spotted her mother sitting on the porch with a cup of coffee.

Olivia looked at Elly, then at the open door, then slowly rose to her feet. "Eleanor Marie Miles, get inside this house *right now*."

Guthrie reined in the horse beside the steps and gave Elly a hand down. She tugged her nightgown down and rolled her eyes at him. "I told you. All three names. Thanks for the ride." Whirling, she dashed inside, leaving the screen door to bang behind her, leaving him to face her mother.

Her mother, who looked drowsy and soft, as if she hadn't been long out of bed. Whose hair tumbled down over her shoulders, as tousled as Elly's but with a much different effect. Whose nightgown was sleeveless and white and fitted long and narrow over full breasts, slim waist, rounded hips, all the way to midcalf. Who looked, aw, hell, exactly the way he didn't need somebody looking.

"She just came—" He had to clear his throat, had to shift in the saddle to ease the tightening in his body. "To—to watch me saddle Buck. She hasn't been gone more than a few minutes."

"She should know better than to sneak off—and in her nightgown, no…less…" Abruptly, she realized that was exactly what *she* was wearing and color flooded her face. Balancing her coffee mug on the porch railing, she folded her arms across her chest, which only served to pull the thin cotton taut in interesting places and to create a hint of swelling above the rounded neckline where a moment ago there'd been none. "I, uh…uh… Would you excuse me a moment, please?"

Without waiting for a response from him, she disappeared inside. He saw a flash of white pass in front of the living room window, then another flash returning. She'd pulled on a robe in white terry cloth heavy enough to disguise every detail about the body underneath it. The hem brushed the floor, the sleeves fell inches past the tips of her fingers, and the neck gapped just enough to reveal the utterly plain, remarkably feminine gown underneath.

He was glad she'd covered up—and, perversely, glad he'd seen enough to know *what* she'd covered up. He wished she would shed the robe and let him look again—and hoped he never saw more than he already had. There was no future in learning to want this woman. She was his partner. A brand-new widow. Single mother to two overwhelming children. Victim of Ethan's schemes.

She was a great many things, but *not* someone for him to get involved with. Not someone for a casual affair, someone cut out for ranch life, someone who might be happy living the next fifty years in Heartbreak, Oklahoma.

And he was someone who couldn't live anywhere else.

She picked up the coffee with hands that were less than steady and avoided meeting his gaze. "I'm sorry she bothered you. I'll make sure it doesn't happen again."

"How? By hog-tying her to the bed at night?" Her gaze darted to his—to make sure he was teasing?—then away as he went on. "She didn't bother me. She just kept me company while I saddled the horse. I figured it was safer to deliver her home than sending her back on her own."

"Definitely safer." She relaxed enough to lean one shoulder against the post. "Is it proper to say a horse is pretty?"

"I don't think Buck would mind."

"He *is* pretty. Elly's always wanted a horse."

"So she said. She asked me to intercede on her behalf."

Shaking her head, Olivia smiled ruefully. "I made the mistake of telling her once that the reason she couldn't have any animals was because we lived in the city. I never *dreamed* we might move to the country, even temporarily. I may have to pay now for not telling her the truth then."

"What was the truth?" he asked, pretty sure he already knew.

"David was allergic to cats, he didn't like dogs, hamsters looked too much like mice, goldfish tend to have a life span of mere days..." She finished with a shrug.

What kind of man denied his kid the pet she wanted more than anything in the world simply because *he* didn't want one? he wondered, then answered his own question. The same kind of man who left that kid—and her mother and sister—homeless and penniless so he could indulge his penchant for gambling. The kind of man that he absolutely could not imagine Olivia with. She seemed so responsible, so caring, so devoted to the kids.

Had she been equally caring and devoted to their father?

He didn't know and didn't care. Honest.

He latched onto the conversation to distract himself. "There are cats in the barn, if they like cats, and you're welcome to get them a dog if you want."

She looked both interested and not. A dog would be no problem here, but what about when they left? She would have to move him back to Atlanta with them, then find a place where pets were allowed and come up with the money for food and vet bills, or leave him behind and break the kids' hearts. She was a sucker for her kids. She wouldn't break their hearts. "Where do you buy a dog around here?"

"You don't. You go by old Miz Wilson's in town. She's Heartbreak's unofficial animal shelter. Every stray in the county finds its way there. So does everyone looking for a pet."

"I'll keep that in mind." As Buck impatiently pawed the ground, she took a step back from the railing. "I'll persuade Elly that it's not in her best interests to slip off again. I'm sorry she—we've—kept you from your work."

"It's no big deal." He wheeled the horse around, then hesitated. "What are you doing up so early?" He'd gotten the impression last night that what he called morning, she considered the tail end of night. Was she so determined to earn her keep that she was willing to rearrange her schedule?

Her shrug that aimed for careless but scored on awkward suggested he was right. "I just thought that, being in a new place, with a new life, I should find a new routine to go with it."

Meaning that once she'd become accustomed to the early-morning hours, he could expect a real breakfast on the table—with her sitting across from him. He thought of the sight that had greeted him *this* morning—drowsy, soft, womanly—and swallowed hard.

What a hell of a way to start the day.

What a hell of a way to *end* it.

He murmured something about being back for lunch, then rode away. Once the cabin was out of sight behind him, he gave a deep, jarring sigh that made Buck's ears twitch and said aloud, "You've got enough trouble, son. Don't go borrowing more."

This thing with Olivia Miles was strictly business. The

sooner he convinced himself of that, the better off they would all be—and the *safer* he would be.

He did more of his work behind the wheel of an old beat-up truck than on horseback, but there were times when the horse offered maneuverability the truck couldn't match. For this morning's job—checking fence—he needed to cross creek beds and get into timber where the truck couldn't go. Sometimes he just needed to feel like an old-time cowboy— like his father and grandfather before him. There were places off away from the road where he could forget about modern conveniences and modern pressures, where all he could see in any direction was pasture, cattle and timber, where there were no power lines, no roads, no houses with TV antennas. Sometimes he'd spend the whole day out here, just him and Buck, packing a lunch and water and reminding himself why he did what he did.

He took his time this morning and kept his thoughts centered on the job. Buck was tall, nearly sixteen hands, and the branches of the blackjacks that dominated this area weren't forgiving of distracted riders. Over the years one Harris or another had used axes, chain saws and bulldozers to fell entire scrub oak forests and clear the land for pasture, but uncounted acres of the scraggly trees remained. Every time he had to round up a cow that took to the brush for cover, he swore he'd get rid of them all, but there were always more pressing needs. Now, though, this technically wasn't his land. These trees were Olivia's problem.

And Olivia's problems were *his* problems, he acknowledged with a scowl, at least for a few months—maybe, realistically, a few years. There was no way she could return to Georgia without selling the land, no way she could sell the land without getting a clear title first, no way she could earn enough working for him to file the quiet title suit. Until he came up with the money for the lawsuit, or the money to buy back his land, she was stuck here.

And he was stuck with her.

The sound of fabric ripping jerked him from his contemplation of that last thought with about as much force as the branch that had caught his sleeve. With an annoyed frown, he fingered the tear, scowled harder and narrowed his attention once more to the job he was doing and nothing else.

At least until the grumble of his stomach reminded him that it was lunchtime.

By one o'clock, he was back at the barn. Freed of his saddle, Buck had found a cool, shaded place to graze, and Guthrie was crossing the yard on his way to his own cool place when a truck turning off the road caught his attention. He recognized the blue-and-white Chevy immediately and realized he'd been preparing for this visit. Mary knew he broke for lunch about this time every day. She also knew he'd have a harder time avoiding her questions in person than over the phone.

He changed direction, bypassing the back door for the front porch. By the time he reached the steps, his neighbor was climbing out of the truck, wearing a floppy hat and a big grin and carrying an armload of frozen casseroles. "Afternoon, Guthrie."

"Mary."

"I brought you some food. I understand you've still got guests—'' her attention shifted to the old clunker parked by the cabin "—and thought you might be running low."

"Aw, Mary, admit it. You came to pry, and you feel more comfortable about doing it when you can trade food for information."

"You know me too well," she said with a laugh. "So…where is she? Who is she? What is she?"

He took the casseroles, cushioned in a box with newspaper, and set it on a rocker. "She has a name."

"So I've been told—though certainly not by you. Olivia, is it?"

"You've been talking to Jerry, haven't you? Whatever happened to attorney/client privilege?"

"He just told me her name. He didn't breathe a hint of what your business is with her, not even on threat of never tasting my pecan blondies again. By the way, that top foil packet is blondies. I figured the kids might like them." She tucked a strand of steel gray hair behind her ear. "So...who is Olivia, and why is she staying at your stepgranny's cabin?"

Before Guthrie had decided what to answer—or even *if* to answer—the screen door flew open and two pairs of feet pounded out. "You just wait and see," Elly was saying belligerently. "Mr. Guthrie, I did, too, ride your horse today, didn't I, while ol' lazy Emma was still in bed— Oh." Seeing Mary, Elly came to such an abrupt stop that Emma skidded into her from behind. "Sorry. We didn't know you got company."

"Elly, Emma Rae, this is Mary Stephens. She lives just down the road at the Rocking S. Mary, the Miles sisters."

"Sounds like an old-time musical group," she remarked as she watched the girls approach.

Elly stuck out her hand first. "Hey. I'm Elly."

"And I'm really just Emma, but..." Her sister gave Guthrie a fearful look, then leaned forward and whispered, "He keeps calling me Emma Rae."

"Elly calls you Emma Rae, too," Guthrie protested.

"Only when she's being a baby," Elly said with a shake of her head. "Which is just about all the time. And Mama calls her Emma Rae when she's mad, like this morning when she said, 'Eleanor Marie Miles, get inside this house right now!'"

Mary's eyes were bright with amusement when she admonished him. "Heavens, Guthrie, the least you could do is find out what a lady wants to be called."

"And what do *you* want to be called?" Elly asked.

"Mary is fine with me."

Emma Rae—no, really just Emma—parroted the same response her sister had given him Thursday evening. "We don't call grown-ups by their first names. It's not r'spectful. We can call you Miss Mary, if that's all right."

"That's perfectly all right." Mary shifted her steady gaze to him. "Corliss was right. They're dolls. *Whose* dolls?"

Again, before he could answer, the screen door swung open and Olivia took one step out. "Kids, I asked you to tell Mr. Guthrie— Oh, I'm sorry. I didn't mean to interrupt."

"Oh, honey, you're not interrupting a thing," Mary said, her voice friendlier and warmer than usual. "Come on out here and let's get acquainted."

Hesitantly, Olivia obeyed, catching the screen door so it wouldn't bang behind her. She was wearing a sleeveless dress of emerald green that fitted snugly from shoulder to hip before sweeping practically to her ankles. Her hair was pulled back in some fancy braid with a bow the same color of green, and she looked fresh and young and surprisingly *pretty*.

She also looked nervous as hell as she took a few steps toward them. She expected people to resent her presence here, he remembered from their conversation last night, and no doubt, some might. But not Mary. She would feel bad for Guthrie, losing half his land, but she knew Ethan. She knew where to lay the blame.

"I've already met Miss Elly and Miss Emma," Mary said, taking Olivia's hand in both of hers. "They are absolutely adorable—which I see they get from their mama. I'm Mary Stephens, the only other woman on this five-mile stretch of road. Guthrie's mama, Nadine, was my best friend, and he's been like a son to me since she died. And you are…?"

"Olivia Miles." She gave her hand a slight tug, but Mary didn't let go.

"And you came here from…?"

"Georgia. Atlanta."

"Really? And what brings you all this way?"

Olivia gave Guthrie a helpless look. He didn't blame her for feeling uncomfortable. He'd known Mary and everyone else in town all his life, and he wasn't looking forward to breaking the news that he had a new partner. After the first ten or twelve times, it might get easier, but these first few times…

He claimed Mary's arm, leaving her no choice but to re-

lease Olivia. "Come inside and have lunch with us, Mary—
and if you behave, we'll answer all your questions."

"*All*? Don't forget, son, you were once engaged to my
daughter. You'd better put a limit on exactly which subjects
you're agreeing to be forthright about." She reclaimed the
box of food, then let him escort her past the girls and Olivia
to the front door.

After she was inside, he held the door for the others. Olivia,
all but wringing her hands, hesitated. "I can take the girls
back to the cabin for lunch," she offered in a low voice.

"And disappoint Mary like that? You're the whole reason
she's here." He watched as the twins ducked under his arm
and raced inside, then looked at their mother again. "We're
going to have to start telling people sooner or later—and
knowing the good folks of Heartbreak, they're not going to
settle for later. We may as well practice on Mary."

"We don't really have to tell anyone at all, do we? I mean,
the situation *is* just temporary. As soon as everything's settled
here, the girls and I are going back to Atlanta. In the meantime—"

"Everyone will think we're having an affair." His blunt
statement made her blush. It increased his own temperature a
steamy degree or two, but he ignored it and pushed on.
"What would you expect, with you suddenly showing up and
moving in here with no explanation?"

Her blush deepened, and she laced her fingers tightly together.

"Heartbreak is a small town, and until everything's settled,
you've got to live here. Do you want people knowing that
you bought out Ethan and—much to my surprise—we're partners? Or would you rather have them thinking that we're engaged in an illicit relationship?"

She managed a faint smile. "Considering that I've never
done anything even remotely illicit in my life, having people
think I have doesn't sound so bad."

"Telling the truth doesn't sound so bad, either."

"I just thought you might feel more comfortable keeping it between us and your lawyer."

She thought he might like to avoid the sympathy the news was sure to bring him. Everybody in town knew how important the ranch was to him, how hard he'd worked to keep it. They also knew that it was only through his own foolish sentimentality that he'd wound up in this mess. Ethan never could have sold him out if he hadn't given him the land in the first place.

"I've been on the receiving end of their pity before," he said grimly. "I can deal with it again."

She looked as if she wanted to ask for details. It was just as well that she didn't, because being left for another man—hell, for his best man—a few days before the wedding wasn't the sort of conversation he indulged in with virtual strangers, especially not with Shay's mother just down the hall.

"We'd better go in," he said stiffly. "Lunch is getting cold."

With a single nod, she went inside. He followed.

Lunch was already cold—and meant to be that way. Before going outside to see what was delaying them, she'd laid out the makings for roast chicken sandwiches, along with potato salad and deviled eggs. There were also thick tomato slices sprinkled with oil and vinegar and a few shreds of cheese, an open jar of Mary's homemade pickles and a plate piled high with pecan blondies.

Mary kept the conversation flowing through the meal, right up to the moment the girls excused themselves to play on the front porch and the screen door slammed behind them. She stopped in midlighthearted sentence, looked from Olivia to Guthrie, then said, "Either the girls are confused, or there've been some big changes at Harris Ranch in the last few days. Which is it?"

Olivia's smile was weak. "The girls are often confused," she said, then gave a small sigh. She looked at him, too.

He tried for a casual tone, but even to his own ears, his

voice sounded strained. "Remember after Mom died, I gave part of the ranch to Ethan?"

"Yes. And I told you then it was a *bad* idea. The boy was too irresponsible, too young."

"I was that young when I took it over."

"Yes, but you were never irresponsible."

Sometimes he wished he was, Guthrie thought. If he weren't so damn responsible, he wouldn't have tried to make Ethan feel wanted, wouldn't have given him what he thought was a reason to stay. He wouldn't feel an obligation to Olivia and her kids, wouldn't feel the need to make right the wrongs Ethan and her husband had done them.

"Not a day in my life," he agreed grimly. "I gave Ethan the land, he left, and I forgot about it. Until Olivia arrived Thursday with a contract and a deed transferring ownership of the whole operation to her late husband, whose estate now belongs to her."

Mary stared at him. "Ethan *sold* it? He sold your land?" When he nodded, she leaned forward. "But he can't do that! It's not legal! You're going to fight this, right?"

"He couldn't sell my share, but he owned the rest. He had the right…" The surge of pain was surprising in its swiftness and intensity. Ethan had no rights. He hadn't earned any. Even as a teenager, his efforts on the ranch had been half-hearted at best. He'd disliked the hard work, the long hours, the dirt and the animals and the pay. All he'd ever wanted was a way out—and he'd found it in David Miles.

"Giving him the land was foolish, but your heart was in the right place. But not fighting this—Guthrie, that goes beyond foolishness! This ranch can't survive split in half like that! All your years of hard work, all your sacrifices, all your dreams…" Mary gave Olivia an apologetic look. "It's nothing personal, Olivia, but I've watched him work and struggle year after year, and now—"

Guthrie pushed his chair back. "I'm not going to court over it, Mary," he said stiffly. "Whatever happens, I'll deal with it, and I'll survive. Now if you'll excuse me, I've got work to do.''

Olivia watched him leave, his hat clamped on his head, his spine rigid. When he disappeared into the deep shadows of the barn, she glanced at Mary Stephens. ''His heart is still in the right place,'' she said softly. ''If he got a judge to declare the sale invalid, the girls and I would be out on the streets. This questionable share in Guthrie's ranch is the only thing my husband left us. We have nothing else.''

''I'm sorry,'' Mary said, and Olivia believed she meant it. ''But this is *his* property. Even if he did sign it over to Ethan, even if Ethan did sign it over to you, it's still his. He never intended for it to pass outside the family. He and Ethan had an agreement that if Ethan wanted to sell it, he had to offer it to Guthrie first.''

Olivia sighed, feeling both a little more lost and a lot more amazed. That was the first she'd heard of any agreement, but it made sense. Valuing the land the way he did, Guthrie would have wanted some assurance that it would remain in the family. And being determined to honor his brother's deal with David, he would have neglected to mention that small detail, which would surely sway any judge his way.

''So what are your intentions for the property?''

As she began putting away the leftovers, Olivia explained the deal she and Guthrie had made. She also told the woman that she planned, if she could find a way, to return the land to him when she left.

''How?'' Mary asked flatly. ''He can't afford to buy it. You can't afford to start over again without selling it. To do that, you may have to stay here a *long* time.''

Now there was a depressing thought. Olivia wanted to go home. She'd promised the girls they would go home. Though Elly didn't seem to care, Emma did—deeply. How could she tell her younger daughter that they were staying here indefinitely? How could she face it herself?

But after the help Guthrie had given them, how could she

turn around and sell his land to someone else? When he'd behaved honorably in a bad situation, how could she do less?

But why couldn't she be honorable back in Georgia, where she belonged? she wondered in a moment of homesick panic. Why couldn't she do the right thing for him *and* the right thing for the girls and herself?

She was rinsing dishes to load in the dishwasher when Mary came over to help. "I'm not being very neighborly, am I?" she asked with a wry smile. "We're generally a lot friendlier around here. It's just that Guthrie's awfully well-liked in the community. He'd do anything for anyone—as you've seen for yourself—and he's had some pretty tough times, what with his father dying, and his mother, and his stepfather being so worthless, and Ethan and Shay and Easy... Most of us feel a bit protective of him. Lord, I hate to see Ethan do this to him."

Olivia handed her the last plate, then wrung out a cloth to wipe the table. "Who are Shay and Easy?"

Mary was silent for so long, staring into the half-full dishwasher, that Olivia thought her question would go unanswered. Finally, the woman closed the door, turned to lean against the counter and gave her a tight smile. "The Rafferty place is down the road another half mile. Easy—short for Ezekiel—and Guthrie were best friends since they were in diapers. They grew up together, worked together, played together, double-dated together...until Shay came between them." Her smile grew thinner. "Shay's my daughter."

Her movements slow and distracted, Olivia dried the table with a dishcloth. Mary had started filling his freezer, Guthrie had said Thursday evening, when she thought they were going to be family. And just a short while ago, he commented that he'd been on the receiving end of the town's pity before. Because Mary's daughter had left him for his best friend?

Either Easy Rafferty must be one hell of a catch, or Shay Stephens had rocks in her head. Knowing that men like Guthrie were sadly few and far between, Olivia would have to vote for the rocks.

"I know this is a bad situation and it's not fair and I'm sorry to be a part of it," she said at last. "But I'll do my best to make it work out."

"I'm trusting you will." This time Mary's smile was more relaxed. "Why don't we grab us a glass of pop and go sit out on the porch and get acquainted?"

Olivia considered the suggestion only a moment before nodding. She'd spent the morning making the upstairs shine, and she already had a head start on the roast she was fixing for tonight's supper. She could afford a little time to visit with the woman who claimed Guthrie as almost a son.

Emma was seated in one of the rockers, her favorite doll cradled in her arms. At Olivia's suggestion, she politely moved to the glider at the end of the porch and left the two rocking chairs to the women. In her sundress and sandals, with her hair held back by a bow, she looked solemn and pretty and almost too good to be true.

"Little girls are so precious," Mary said, watching her for a moment. Then she chuckled as Elly raced by, shoelaces undone, dirt on her face and arms and a lizard cupped in her hands. "So are little tomboys. Doesn't she look the picture of happiness?"

"Elly's adaptable. She can make a place for herself anywhere."

"But Emma misses home." Mary glanced at her. "So do you."

"I lived all my life in Atlanta. I thought I would die there." But David *had* died there, and his doing so had forced her and the girls nearly a thousand miles away.

"You got family back there?"

Olivia shook her head.

"Lots of good friends, I imagine."

She started to nod in agreement, but caught herself after the first bob of her head. Good friends? She'd thought so— but none good enough to be there for her when she needed them. None who'd offered a shoulder to cry on when David died. None who'd showed any concern about where they would go or what they would do. None who'd said, Keep in touch, or, I'll miss you.

And when they went back to Atlanta, it wouldn't be to friends. Their friends, because of David's job, because of where they lived, were all in a certain economic bracket. They all lived in the same exclusive parts of town, shopped in the same expensive shops, sent their children to the same private schools. When they went home, they would live in an apartment or, if they were lucky, a small rental house. They would shop at Kroger and Wal-Mart, and the girls would go to the public schools that weren't good enough for their friends.

When they went home, they would be living a life almost as foreign as the life they'd found here.

But they'd be living at *home*. That would count for a lot.

"Have you always lived here?" she asked, not wanting to think anymore about home lest she get as whiny and teary-eyed as Emma was prone to do.

"Heavens, no. I'm from California. San Diego. I met my husband when the Navy stationed him out there. Oklahoma sounded so exotic, and being a rancher's wife seemed romantic to someone who'd grown up on Westerns. It didn't take me long to discover there wasn't any romance, but I fell in love with it anyway. I can't imagine doing anything else." She gave Olivia a sly look. "Give yourself enough time, and you might fall in love, too."

Olivia would have liked to pretend that those last words referred to the ranch or the town, but she wouldn't be fooling anyone, least of all Mary. And, truthfully, the words sent a little quiver of longing through her too strong to be denied. She would like to fall in love, would like to love a man who felt the same for her. Wasn't that one of the reasons she'd finally asked David for a divorce? Because she wanted to be important to someone, wanted passion, devotion, undying commitment.

Guthrie could provide devotion and undying commitment, and she had no doubt that the passion he felt for his land extended to other parts of his life. But his roots were sunk as deep in this Oklahoma soil as hers were in Georgia's red clay. He wasn't looking for passion, but for a way out of this unwanted partnership, and all she wanted was a way back home.

"Are you Heartbreak's unofficial matchmaker?" she asked dryly.

"Matchmaker? Me? Mother of Shay, who waited until the church was being decorated for the wedding to take off with Easy Rafferty? If I could make matches, hon, I would've done a whole lot better for my empty-headed, fool-minded daughter than that good-for-nothing rodeo cowboy who wouldn't even marry her after stealing her away. Fourteen years it's been, and people are still paying for it." Shaking her gray head, she sighed. "If I could make matches, hon, I would've made her stick with the one nature intended."

Olivia set her chair in motion with one foot, making the floorboards creak on every forward rock. "If nature intended it, then maybe someday they'll get back together."

"No." Mary said it flatly, with no elaboration and no room for argument. "So if you're interested in Guthrie, you've got a clear field."

*Interested in Guthrie.* She was alive, wasn't she? But she wasn't in the market for more than a few fantasies, not until she was back on her feet, back home and settled into their new life. *Then* she could go looking with the intent of finding and keeping.

Right now *all* she could do was look.

With a sigh, Mary pushed to her feet. "I'd better get home. A ranch wife's work is never done. Drop in to see me sometime, Olivia. We're at the first mailbox on the way back into town. I'll see you next time, Miss Emma."

Emma looked up from her doll. "It was a pleasure meeting you, Miss Mary," she said, her voice soft, small, so Southern.

"It was a pleasure meeting you, too—all of you." Mary's smile included Olivia as she passed on her way to the truck. Once she settled behind the wheel, she waved, then tapped the horn twice on the way down the driveway to catch Elly's attention for another wave.

Emma came to sit in the rocker Mary had vacated. "She's a nice lady."

"Yes, she is."

"She bringed us brownies, only not."

"They're called blondies."

"Yeah. At home we have brownies." Emma fussed with the doll's dress, then smoothed her hair. "I like brownies."

Olivia stifled a sigh. "Honey, do you understand that when we go home, things aren't going to be the same as before? We can't live in our old house. You can't go to school with your old friends. Daddy won't be there."

Emma ignored her first two points—the ones she didn't want to deal with—and focused on the last. "Of course he won't, Mama. He's in heaven."

For a moment Olivia considered the unlikelihood of that statement. David's idea of heaven would include plenty of booze, lovely women and games of chance, along with no responsibility, no obligations and no family or job to hold him back. Plunk him down with angels, saints and good, righteous people, and he would think he'd died and gone to hell.

"What if you come to like Oklahoma while we're here?" It would be a blessing, since it looked as if they would be here a long time.

"I won't."

"Elly's having a good time." Her older daughter was perched on the lowest branch of a small tree growing in the field out front, swinging her legs and talking—to her captive lizard, to herself, maybe to the sky. With Elly, one was never sure.

"I'm not having a good time. I don't like it here."

"Couldn't you pretend it's an adventure?" Olivia heard the slightest pleading seep into her voice and gave herself a mental shake. Emma was five years old. Maybe she wasn't as flexible as Elly, but she *would* adjust. If she wanted to pout and be difficult in the meantime, well, she would just have to pout.

"I don't *want* a 'venture. I want to go home." Abruptly

she stopped fussing with the doll and fixed a mutinous stare on Olivia. "You promised we could go home soon. I don't like that house. I don't like this place. I don't like *him*, and I'm never gonna like any of it. I want to go *home*. You *promised*. You said you always keep your promises!"

She *had* promised, Olivia thought grimly. It wasn't the first mistake she'd made. It surely wouldn't be the last. "I do, Emmy, but this one's going to take some time. It may be a *long* time, and things would be so much easier for you—" for them all "—if you would just try to find something to like about the place. Why don't you go play with Elly? Do some exploring?"

"I don't wanna 'splore!" she snapped, tears welling in her big blue eyes. "There's spiders and snakes and scorpions and dirt, and I don't wanna go, I don't wanna play, I don't wanna do nothin' but go home!" The words ended in a wail as she jumped from the chair and drew back the arm that clutched the doll. She faced Olivia, thought better of it and turned toward the steps, flinging the doll with all her might. It sailed through the air, head over feet, and hit Guthrie square in the face as he came around the corner of the house.

For a moment Emma was stunned into utter stillness; then, ignoring Olivia's outstretched hand, she raced off the porch and tore across the field toward the cabin.

Feeling helpless, embarrassed and pretty damn tearful herself, Olivia rose from the rocker. "I—I'm sorry," she murmured, her face hot, her gaze settling somewhere around Guthrie's knees. "She—she's—"

Elly swung to the ground and sauntered toward them. "She's got a pretty good arm, don't she, Mr. Guthrie?"

He picked up the doll, straightened the skirt that had turned up over her head and brushed the dust off. "That she does."

"I'll go talk to her, Mom. I can handle this." Without waiting for a response, Elly started across the field. "Hey, Em, wait up!"

Guthrie came slowly up the steps. "I saw Mary leave and thought it was safe to come back. Apparently, I was wrong."

He offered her the doll, then leaned against the rail. "Do you need to see to her?"

She sank back into the rocker. "No. When she's upset, she always prefers Elly. They've got quite a bond." She set the doll on her lap and, for a moment, envied its perpetually cheerful face. No matter what misfortunes befell it, it would always be able to smile.

Sometimes she thought neither she nor Emma would ever smile again.

With a sigh, she hugged the doll to her chest. "So that work you had to get back to after lunch was just an excuse."

"It was really you she wanted to see and talk to." He removed his hat, ran his hand through his hair, then fingered the brim. "What'd you talk about?"

She suspected what he wanted to know. He'd made a few comments himself about his near-miss with marriage, and she knew her curiosity had shown before lunch. Still, she wasn't sure she should tell him that Mary had discussed what he hadn't. There was an issue of privacy here, after all. "We talked about Heartbreak, the ranch, the girls, my plans. She was full of compliments—and concern—for you."

A faint flush colored his cheeks as a faint discomfort crept into his eyes.

Taking a deep breath, Olivia went on. "She wasn't quite so generous with Shay and Easy."

The flush deepened. So did the discomfort. He slid down until the spindles were at his back and stiffly, sharply asked, "What did she tell you?"

Embarrassed herself and wishing she'd left him to wonder, Olivia tried to be tactful. "That Shay waited until the last minute to—to call off the wedding."

The sound he made could have been a snort of disgust or a scornful chuckle. "That doesn't sound like Mary. Usually there's a line in there about her fool-minded daughter and that good-for-nothing cowboy." He gave a shake of his head. "She was about as fond of Easy before this happened as she was of me. Did she give you all the details?"

"No, and I didn't ask."

"Good, because it's none of your business." He got easily to his feet and walked away, clamping his hat on his head as he stepped off the porch into the bright afternoon sunshine.

Alone with nothing but the sting of his last words for company, she resumed rocking. Fourteen years had passed since the wedding that wasn't, and he was still sensitive about it. Had he loved Shay so deeply, or was it wounded ego because she'd chosen another man over him?

She hoped it was ego, though he didn't strike her as a particularly egotistical man. It just seemed a more comfortable answer than the alternative.

With a sigh, she locked up the house, then started toward the cabin, where Emma and Elly were snuggled together on the porch. She had plenty of other things to worry over—like her kids, her homesickness, their precarious future. Her new partner's love life didn't make the list. It couldn't.

She wouldn't let it.

# Chapter 5

It was after seven when Guthrie awakened. Sunday was the one morning of the week that he didn't set his alarm, but slept as late as he was able. It was his day for catching up on the books, cleaning the house and doing the laundry and the grocery shopping, but today everything was already done except the books. He wondered as he rolled onto his back if Olivia might be willing to do that, too. He never had cared much for paperwork.

But her presence here was temporary. He couldn't come to count on her too much, because as soon as he did, she would be gone, and he'd be in sorrier shape than before she'd come.

After stuffing the extra pillow underneath his head, he gave the room a long look. She'd spent a lot of time up here yesterday—had wiped away three months' accumulation of dust from the furniture and polished it to a high gleam, had made the bed with clean sheets that smelled of flowers, had vacuumed in all the corners and under the bed and put everything away where it belonged. The two empty rooms appeared ready for company, and both bathrooms gleamed as if prepared for inspection. It was a hell of a change from the dust and disorder he'd become accustomed to.

And it made him somewhat... Uneasy, he decided, was as good a word as any. It wasn't that he didn't appreciate the heavy-duty cleaning. He did. It just felt odd knowing that *she* had done it. That she'd handled his things. That she'd come into places exclusively his, places where no woman had been in more years than he could count. Hell, her scent had lingered long after she had gone.

It had reminded him of how long he'd been alone. Of how tired he was of being alone. Of the satisfaction a woman could bring into his life.

The *right* woman, he reminded himself, which Olivia Miles most certainly was not.

But maybe it was time to start looking for whoever was.

Downstairs the front door opened, visitors shuffled in, then the door quietly closed again. Hushed voices made their way to the kitchen, and a few short minutes later the smell of coffee brewing drifted up the stairs.

He wondered if she knew he was still in bed or if she thought he'd left the house long ago. Last night at supper, she hadn't asked him for his Sunday morning schedule. In fact, after he'd told her on the porch that what had happened between him, Shay and Easy was none of her business, she'd taken his statement to heart. She'd hardly spoken to him at supper and hadn't asked any questions. He hadn't found anything to say, either, and as soon as he'd finished eating, he'd retreated into his office. As soon as she'd finished cleaning, she'd taken the girls and gone home.

All in all, it hadn't been one of his better evenings.

The smell of bacon frying drew him from the bed. He got dressed, went into the hall, then returned to haphazardly make the bed. The fewer reasons he could give her for coming into his bedroom, he reasoned, the safer he would be.

He was halfway down the stairs before he noticed the twin sitting on the lower landing, her shoulder and head leaned against the wall. Even without seeing her face, he knew it was Emma Rae—no, just Emma. He didn't imagine Elly could be that still even if she were sound asleep.

The last stair before the landing creaked, and she turned, then tilted her head way back to see him. With a disinterested look, she turned back to lean against the wall. He slid past her and went on to the bottom, then looked back. "Why are you sitting on the stairs?"

"I'm being punished."

"Why?"

"'Cause Mama's mean."

"Oh." He started to go on, but came back. "So why does she make you sit on the stairs?"

The look she gave him fairly shouted, How dumb can you be? while she explained with exaggerated patience. "Because there's nothin' to do here. No TV to watch, no books to read, no games to play, *no one to talk to*." She gave him a meaningful scowl before resting her head against the paneling once more.

"Once you're through being punished, would you like to see the horses?"

With her head tilted at an absurd angle, she watched him. "Are they big?"

"Pretty big."

"Do they bite?"

"They could, but they never have."

"Can Mommy come, too?"

"Sure." He had no intention of going even as far as the barn with two five-year-olds, one who needed a tight rein and one who, according to the tantrum he'd overheard on his way to the porch, didn't like him and wasn't ever gonna like him.

She heaved a great sigh that seemed to come from her toes all the way up. "All right. I guess I can go."

"Oh, gee, thanks for the excitement," he said dryly as he started toward the kitchen.

"Hey, Mr. Guthrie," Elly greeted him as he walked through the door. Standing on a chair pulled up to the counter in front of the electric griddle, she wore a dish towel as an apron and brandished a pancake turner in her left fist. "We're makin' bacon and pancakes. D'ya like pancakes?"

"Doesn't everybody?"

She looked at Olivia, busy at the stove, then lowered her voice a decibel or two. "Not Emma. Cereal and toast. That's all she wants for breakfast, every day of her whole entire life. Just cereal and toast." She beamed a brilliant smile. "*She's in trouble.*"

Guthrie took a mug from the cabinet and filled it with coffee. "And that pleases you?"

"Oh, yes. It's usually me, you know."

He tasted his coffee and found it potent, exactly the way he liked it. Finally he shifted his attention to the woman who'd made it. "Good morning."

She darted a cautious glance his way and answered in an equally cautious voice. "Good morning."

"Breakfast smells good."

"Thank you."

"I haven't had pancakes and bacon in longer than I can remember."

It was Elly who responded as she expertly flipped a pancake. "We have 'em ever' Sunday—just Mom and me. And Emma has cereal and toast and Daddy..." Her small face puckered into a frown, then relaxed. "I don't 'member what Daddy ate for breakfast. It was a long time ago."

David Miles had been dead only a few weeks, Guthrie thought. Granted, children's sense of time was different from adults', but a few weeks wasn't long enough for a bright kid to forget one part of a multipart routine, was it?

"Your father didn't usually eat breakfast," Olivia reminded her in a voice that sounded strained. "Remember, Elly? Daddy slept late on Sundays."

"Oh, yeah, that's right. 'Cause he was always out late on Saturdays."

Color seeped into Olivia's cheeks, and he didn't think the stove's heat was responsible. However, she pretended not to hear her daughter's comment and went about removing strips of bacon from the pan. After a moment of uncomfortable silence, she glanced at him again. "You don't work on Sundays?"

"If there's something that has to be done, I do it, but usually it's reserved for things around the house."

"Oh. Well, after breakfast, I'll take the girls back to the cabin so you can—"

"I told Emma I'd take her out to see the horses."

"And she agreed?"

Beside him, Elly removed the last pancake to a plate, then jumped to the floor with a clatter. "*Woo-hoo!* I *love* horses!"

Guthrie couldn't help but smile as he watched her little dance—or when he looked back at Olivia, who looked so surprised...and soft...and lovely. He had to swallow hard before he could answer her. "She agreed—provided you come, too."

The caution returned to her gaze, but this time for a different reason. "I don't know. Animals and I don't normally get along."

"You've never had any pets. When have you gotten close enough to figure that out?"

"When we took the girls to Charleston last summer, one of the miniature horses at the plantation we toured bit me, and the seagull I fed tried to eat my hand. When we went into a pet store once just to look, a cockatoo attacked me, and one of the goats at the farm the girls' day school visited butted me into the mud."

Elly burst into giggles. "It was the funniest thing we ever seen. She was just standin' there, talkin' to Mrs. O'Keefe, who's the teacher, and all of a sudden, *splat!* She's facedown in the mud."

Olivia gave her daughter a restrained smile. "I'm glad my misfortune still amuses you."

Elly wrapped her arms around her mother's waist. "Oh, Mama, please come see the horses. We got a ranch now, and we got to have horses. Maybe they'll be different. Maybe they'll *like* you."

"Thanks for the vote of confidence." Olivia untangled Elly's arms and turned her toward the hall. "Go tell your sister breakfast is ready."

"*Em—*"

Olivia clamped her hand over her mouth, then gave her a little push. "Don't bellow. Go."

As soon as Elly stepped through the door, an uneasy stillness fell over the kitchen. He'd run out of things to say, and there was no food cooking to distract her. They uneasily avoided looking at each other, until finally he remembered one thing he did have to say. "What I said yesterday... I shouldn't have."

She took plates from one cabinet, glasses from another and silverware from a drawer and began setting the table. "About your life being none of my business? It's true—and you're right. It should have gone without saying." Her voice sounded brittle, but it was impossible to see if her expression matched because she kept her back to him. "But I wasn't gossiping. I didn't ask questions. I just thought, when you asked, that you wanted to know."

And he *had*, he admitted grimly. Hell, he'd known Mary would talk about Heartbreak, the ranch, the girls and Olivia's plans. He'd known she would have nothing but good to say about him, along with maybe a few protective warnings. What he hadn't known—had wanted to know—was if she'd discussed what surely ranked as one of the three worst times of his life.

Finding out that she had, he'd been... Not angry. Plain and simple, he'd been embarrassed. He didn't want his personal life talked about behind his back, and he sure as hell didn't want it talked about with Olivia. Whatever she needed to know about him and Shay and Easy should come from him, even if it was common knowledge, even if everyone in the whole damn county knew the details—the hurt—as well as he did. It was *his* broken heart, *his* pride. He wanted the right to discuss it or not.

"Do you want to ask questions?"

She looked at him then, her startled expression quickly giving way to impassivity. "No. No, thank you."

He knew she was curious, but that was natural enough. Hell, he was about the least curious person he knew when it came to other folks' business—which wasn't always a good thing. Maybe if he'd paid more attention, he would have noticed that his fiancée was falling in love with his best friend. But there were a few questions he'd ask of Olivia, given the chance. Such as why her husband had always stayed out late on Saturday nights—and with whom, doing what—while his wife was home with the kids. Exactly how devoted to him she had been. Whether she was a *grieving* widow or merely a widow.

That last could make a difference.

If he let it.

She wasn't inviting questions, though, and even if she were, the girls' arrival at the table would have put an end to it. Elly was cheerful, as usual. Emma was pouting. As usual. They provided the only conversation through breakfast, talking about the horses, about giving them treats, going for rides, having one for a pet. "Mr. Guthrie said if we stay 'round long enough, he'll teach us to ride," Elly announced as she drew the tines of her fork through the syrup that was all that remained of her breakfast.

"Uh-uh," Emma murmured around the spoon caught between her teeth.

"Yes, he did. Didn't you, Mr. Guthrie?"

"Yes, I did." He caught the look on Olivia's face and quickly added, "If it's all right with your mother."

"It's all right," Elly said confidently. "After all, we're ranchers now. We gotta learn to rope and brand and shoot and ride, else all the other ranchers'll laugh at us and call us city slickers."

Leaning forward, Olivia claimed both girls' silverware at the same time. "If the shoe fits…"

"What shoe?" Elly ducked her head under the table. "I'm wearin' my boots, and Emma's got on sandals, and Mr. Guthrie—'' When she popped up again, her hair was mussed and her grin was wide. ''Mr. Guthrie don't got no shoes on at all, and, Mama—'' her whisper somehow managed to be even louder than her normal voice ''—he's got *big* feet.''

Olivia flushed and started to scold, but with a chuckle, Guthrie brushed it off. ''Why don't you girls help your mother with the dishes while I get my big boots on my big feet, and then we'll go see the horses.''

Elly jumped to obey. Emma gave him a long, distrustful look before sliding from her chair and carrying her bowl and spoon to the counter. She returned for her napkin and glass, then made a third trip, stopping behind her empty chair, wrapping her small fingers around the spindles while fixing her gaze on him.

''I think she wants your dishes,'' Olivia said.

Guthrie glanced at her, then back at Emma. He set his empty coffee mug on the plate, placed his silverware on either side and offered the entire stack to her. When she didn't take it, he was tempted to call Elly over. Instead, he set the dishes on the table, slid them closer to Emma, then drew back. Still watching him warily, she snatched them up and headed for the counter.

Olivia saw the look he gave her daughter and felt equal measures exasperation, defensiveness and frustration. She hated for Emma's sake that Elly was so much more outgoing, so much funnier and friendlier and more adventurous. She hated that Emma was fearful and timid, stubborn and slow to trust. She hated that people took them at face value and liked Elly more, showed her more tolerance, more affection. David had done it—had made no effort to hide the fact that, while he'd be happiest of all with no children at all, he considered Elly less of a burden than Emma. Now, apparently, Guthrie was going to feel that way, too.

Leaving the table, she joined the girls in the kitchen and got the dishwasher loaded, the pans scrubbed and the counters wiped down in record time. By the time she finished, Guthrie had put on his boots, collected his Stetson and was waiting.

The horses were in the pasture a hundred yards behind the house, next to the barn and a maze of pens and alleys that he identified as the cow lot. Olivia braced her arms on the warm pipe that formed the top rail of the fence and watched as they responded to his whistle, tossing their heads, trotting to the fence. The big one he'd been riding yesterday, Buck, stayed some distance away, disdainful of the others' eagerness for attention, but the other three trotted right up.

Elly all but squealed with delight. "Mr. Guthrie, pick me up so's I can see better."

He lifted her easily onto one hip, and Olivia waited for him to turn back, ignoring Emma where she clutched the folds of her mother's dress. He didn't, though. "Emma, want to come up here?"

Burrowing deeper against Olivia, Emma hesitantly nodded. When he bent toward her, she was reluctant to leave safety, but finally she shuffled forward and let him swing her up. She didn't cling to him, the way Elly did, but she didn't try to escape him, either.

"This one's a paint. His name is Maverick," he said, gesturing to the horse nearest Olivia, a beautiful brown-and-white animal with huge brown eyes and a tad more friendliness than she wanted in an animal so much bigger than she. He stretched out his neck for attention, then shouldered in closer for more.

"So you're a *Top Gun* fan," she said, talking to cover the fact that she was uneasily retreating out of the horse's reach.

Guthrie gave her a long look. "*Maverick.* The TV series. With James Garner."

Olivia's flush added a few degrees to the day's heat. "Oh."

"Oh, Mama, isn't he beautiful?" Elly sighed. "Can we ride him, Mr. Guthrie?"

"We won't saddle him up right now, but sometime soon."

The nervous mother in her forced Olivia back up to the fence. "Is that safe? He's awfully big, and Elly's so small."

"Me, too, Mama," Emma whispered. "I'm small, too, and I wanna ride, too."

"Maverick's only about fourteen hands," Guthrie pointed out. "When you're talking horses, that's on the small side. And he's kid-broke. That means he's used to having kids on his back. He may take you or me for a pretty wild ride, but never a kid. He's as gentle with them as any horse you'll ever find." Then he gave her another of those flat looks over the girls' heads. "I'd never do anything to get your kids hurt."

She knew that, and she felt guilty for implying otherwise. He just didn't understand maternal instincts, thousand-pound animals and fifty-pound girls.

He introduced them to the other horses—Dusty, with the same great expressive eyes and a rather homely coat of mottled gray, and Mustang, a muscular, high-spirited creature. "Let me guess," she said, admiring the horse from a distance. "He's named in honor of the mustangs that once roamed the prairie."

"Nope. The guy I bought him from collected classic cars. Loved the early Mustangs." He gave her a sidelong look. "Come on over here and get a closer look."

"No, thank you. I can see quite well from here."

"Mama's 'fraid of horses," Elly sang, and Emma's baby-soft voice joined in. "Mama's 'fraid of horses."

She smiled fondly at both girls—and the man who held them—then took a long look around. "Does everything around here belong to you?"

"You and me."

"For how far?"

"The north border's the road. In the other directions, farther than you can see."

That wasn't saying a lot. With gently rolling hills rising in every direction, she couldn't see far.

"Want a tour?"

She glanced at him. His head was tilted so that all she could see was the lower part of his face, set in an expression that was neither friendly nor unfriendly, neither caring nor uncaring. If she said yes, fine. If she didn't, that was fine, too.

As the horses began wandering away, she glanced at them. "How?"

He bent his head toward the barn. "In the truck."

She'd been in the truck. It was comfortable, with plenty of room and a separate seat for the girls, and it wasn't likely to get ornery, toss her to the ground and run home without her. "All right. I'd like that."

"Why don't you pack a picnic lunch? After you see the place, we can take the kids swimming. They do swim, don't they?"

She smiled smugly. "Like fish."

He let both girls slide to the ground, and they returned to the house. There she fixed a batch of sandwiches and packed them, along with cold soda, potato salad and blondies, in the ice chest Guthrie brought in from out back. While he filled it with ice, she took the girls home to put on swimsuits underneath their shorts and T-shirts and to trade boots and sandals for sneakers. For a moment, she thought longingly of her own swimsuit downstairs in her dresser, then decided against it. She knew it was silly—women swam with men all the time, and no one thought anything of it—but she simply wasn't ready to be that exposed.

Not with this man.

A horn sounded out front, and she hustled the kids down the stairs and out the doors. It was Guthrie, but not in the comfortable, plenty-of-room pickup. This flatbed truck was old, rusted and looked as if it'd been driven a million miles, every one of them hard.

He leaned across the seat to open the passenger door, and Elly clambered inside. "As long as we're taking a tour, I thought I'd put out some feed. Save me from having to do it tomorrow."

Olivia gave Emma a boost, then climbed in after her. There were no seat belts to be found, but if the slow pace at which he set out was any indication, they wouldn't be going fast enough to need them.

He followed the overgrown lane back to the driveway, then

circled around behind the barn and through an open gate. The truck bounced over the cattle guard, then started up a gentle incline.

"How many cows do you have?"

"Head of cattle," he corrected her. "I can't have any partner of mine sounding like a city slicker."

"So sorry," she responded, feeling darn near lighthearted. "I didn't know terminology was so crucial. How many *head of cattle* do you have?"

"Five bulls and about 140 mama cows, plus calves."

"'Mama cows'?" she snorted. "That's proper terminology?"

Grinning, he tilted his hat back on his head. "It gets the idea across. Right now the herd is mostly Hereford, but we're getting away from that gradually and going to the blacks. All of our bulls are Angus or Brangus—a Brahman-Angus mix. Breed one of them to a Hereford, and you'll get a black baldy—a black cow with a white face. You'll see some out here in a bit. They're pretty little things."

"I thought you bred for beef, not beauty."

"Doesn't hurt when something's profitable *and* pretty." He guided the truck over a particularly deep rut, bouncing the girls off the seat and jarring Olivia's teeth.

"I suppose not," she murmured, turning to look out the side window. This portion of the road snaked through stands of scrub oaks, the way so narrow in places that she was forced to pull her arm inside to avoid low branches. For a city girl, it was an alien landscape—misshapen trees growing close enough to choke out the morning sun, the uneven ground littered with massive, moss-covered boulders that looked as if they'd been tumbled from the sky to land where they would, briars and brambles that tangled to make passage difficult, if not impossible. "Do the cows ever go back in there?"

"Just about every time I'm looking for them."

"How do you get them out?"

"With patience and a great deal of swearing."

"Swearing is naughty," Elly announced casually. "Mama washes our mouths out with soap when she catches us doin' it."

"Elly," she chided. "I've *never* washed your mouth out with soap."

"Well, you said you would."

"I did not."

"*Only* 'cause we don't swear," Elly said in a confidential tone to Guthrie. "If we did, she would."

"Stinker." Olivia mussed her hair, then returned to the subject. "So you have to go in after them?"

"Unless I want to wait for them to decide to wander out on their own. Some of the neighbors use dogs to bring them out. Me, I'd rather doze down every blackjack on the place. As trees go, they're pretty dam—darn worthless."

While she tried to envision the landscape without the scraggly trees, the truck eased over a rise, then onto the sort of country she imagined when she thought of ranches. Pasture stretched ahead and on both sides, the grass lush and as lovely in the distance as any manicured lawn. A large pond filled a hollow on the right, and farther ahead on the left was a smaller version. Near the edge of the tree line, black, red and white blobs morphed into individual creatures as they drew closer.

"Cows!" Elly exclaimed, rising onto her knees and leaning across both sister and mother to get a better look. "Look, Emma, our cows! Our first cows!"

Olivia caught hold of Elly's shirt to keep her from hanging out the window, then tugged her closer to make room for Emma, too. "Actually, El, these are Mr. Guthrie's cows."

"Where're ours? Will we see ours? Do they look like them?"

"We don't have any cows, babe. We have land."

The astonished look on her daughter's face would have been comical if it weren't so disappointed, too. "But how can we be cowboys if we don't have no cows?"

"We're not boys, either," Emma pointed out, earning a scowl from her twin.

"That *don't* matter. You can be a cowboy and not be a boy, but you can't be a cowboy without no cows."

"Sure, you can," Guthrie said. "A lot of cowboys take care of other people's cows. They don't have any of their own. You're helping take care of mine because some of them are living on your land, so that counts."

Satisfied for the moment, Elly turned back to the herd.

He stopped the truck a few yards off the road, blew the horn a couple of times, then climbed out. The girls watched in amazement—all right, Olivia admitted, so did *she*—as the cows began moving toward them. "They come when called," Emma murmured delightedly.

Olivia smiled indulgently at her younger daughter, grateful to see her looking anything but sad. "Better than you two do."

"Come on out," Guthrie invited as he tore open a feed sack, then began scattering the nuggets on the ground.

"No, thank you," Olivia replied, but Elly was already scooting out the driver's door. "Elly, come back here!"

Emma wriggled free. "I want to go, too."

There were too many cows gathered on her side of the truck, so Olivia slid across the seat, too. As she climbed out, Guthrie lifted first Emma, then Elly, onto the truck bed before turning to her. "Want a hand up?"

What she really wanted was to get back into the truck, close and lock the doors and roll up the windows. But her babies were up there, chattering excitedly. There was no way she could leave them so exposed while she cowered in safety.

Keeping a cautious eye on the animals milling about, she headed to the back of the truck. Guthrie climbed up, then half pulled, half lifted her onto the bed. His hand—big, warm, callused—remained clasped tightly around hers while she got her balance and was part of the reason, she suspected, it took her so long to regain it. When finally he released her, she had to stifle the wild urge to hold on just a little longer.

Totally unaffected, he joined the girls, crouching between them, pointing out features of various cows. Olivia remained where she was for a moment, working to steady her suddenly uneven breath, to ease the unaccustomed tightness in her chest.

It had been so long since she'd felt the slightest attraction to any man. Even the spark that had brought her and David together had died a long time ago. They had stayed together because of the girls, because it was familiar, because being together was easier than breaking apart, because the unsatisfying life they shared was less risky than the elusive possibility of something better alone.

But Guthrie wasn't the man to break her cold spell with. She was going back to Atlanta. *She was.* She was going home where she belonged, raising her kids where they belonged.

And he was never leaving Heartbreak.

Too bad she wasn't the type for pleasant diversions, for no-strings, no-promises affairs. Too bad she couldn't settle once more for physical attraction, for sexual satisfaction. But she'd made a promise to herself the day she'd told David she wanted a divorce—no casual affairs, no meaningless relationships. This time around, she wouldn't accept anything less than the grand prize—love, with all the bells and whistles. Passion, respect, friendship, trust, commitment, forever and ever.

And she wasn't falling in love with anyone who couldn't give her all those things and more.

That most especially included ranchers with Oklahoma soil flowing through their veins.

"Come on over here," that particular rancher said, rising easily to his feet. "I'll show you some of our stock."

Taking a deep, even breath, she picked her way around fifty-pound feed bags and stopped a fair distance from him.

"That big black one is a Brangus bull. The red-and-whites are Herefords. Over there's a black baldy, and this brindle here is a Braford—a Brahman-Hereford mix. They're excellent mamas."

She compared the red-and-white cows to the brindle—red streaked with black. "Maybe, but they're not nearly as pretty as the plain old Herefords. Why do you want to get rid of them?"

"They're a good breed, but they're prone to conjunctivitis and cancer of the eye. Plus, by breeding them with the blacks, we get a touch of ear. See how the blacks' ears are longer than the Herefords? That means we'll get more height, they'll grow faster and will be more marketable."

He moved a few steps closer as he talked. She couldn't move any farther away without climbing on top of the feed sacks—an option she considered. Keeping her gaze focused strictly on the animals, she asked, "What do you market them for?"

"Some I sell for breeding. An old cow who's lost her teeth goes to the slaughterhouse for hamburger. Even if she's still producing good calves, it's not cost-efficient to feed her. Yearlings go to the feedlots out around El Reno to be fattened up. That little guy there—" he pointed to a wide-eyed calf at his mother's side "—might show up on your table next year as T-bones."

Olivia's gaze swung around to connect with his. "Steaks come from *calves?* We're eating their babies?"

He contemplated her with the same degree of seriousness as the calf. "The tender meat always comes from the young."

She tried to swallow her distaste. "I may become a vegetarian."

His chuckle eased the lines of his face. "Watch out. No self-respecting rancher would ever make such a statement, not even in jest." Then, with a hint of understanding, he added, "It's easier to eat meat when you buy it in the supermarket and don't have to think about what it was before it became sirloin or pork chops, isn't it?"

She nodded solemnly as the girls approached.

"Mr. Guthrie?" Emma came close to get his attention, then took a step back and tilted her head all the way back, squint-

ing against the sun to see him. "You didn't give them very
much food. Aren't they still hungry?"

"Feed, Emma," he politely corrected her. "We eat food.
Animals eat feed. This isn't all they get. They eat grass and
hay and sometimes the leaves off the trees. We give them
this feed only because it's got an antibiotic—a medicine—in
it to keep them from getting sick."

Moving to the edge of the flatbed, he jumped to the ground,
lifted both twins down at the same time, then looked up at
Olivia, arms outstretched to give her the same assistance.
When she hesitated, he asked, "Are you coming?"

She considered the alternatives. With her luck, if she
jumped as he had, she would startle some poor cow and start
a stampede, break her ankle, or land in a smelly deposit left
behind by one of those big-eyed bovines—any of which
would be preferable to letting him lift her down. To having
his hands on her waist. To being that close. To admiring his
strength...his body...his face...his big dark eyes.

"I—I'll take the easy way down." She took a step back
and nearly tumbled over a feed sack. Catching herself with a
hot flush, she went to the back of the truck, where she had
to sit down, swing her feet down to the bumper, then jump
the remaining distance to the ground.

"The easy way, huh?" he murmured as he passed on his
way to the driver's side.

She took a deep breath and swore that, in addition to the
smells of rust and feed, of animals and muddy water and hot
air and summer days, she could detect some subtle scent that
was *him*. In light of that, yes, she'd taken the easy way. Because if she'd accepted his help, she very well might have
taken the first step on a fall that could break something far
more important than her ankle.

She could have started the process that could break her
heart.

They'd seen most of the ranch and traveled every back road
by the time they reached their final destination. The swim-

ming hole was little more than a large pond, spring-fed and—thanks to the fence that surrounded this three acres—unused by the livestock. They'd spread the old quilt his mother had kept for just this sort of outing, and Olivia had laid out the meal she'd fixed. Now the girls were splashing in shallow water while the adults were lounging...

Guthrie considered the word. Nah, that implied being relaxed, at ease, and Olivia didn't strike him as either. Truth be told, he wasn't feeling particularly at ease himself. Or maybe he was too much at ease. Maybe that was the problem.

He'd enjoyed the tour and the questions more than he'd thought possible when he'd suggested it this morning. The only time he'd felt at all tense was when they'd driven across the cattle guard that marked the beginning of Ethan's—Olivia's—property. As the engine had ground up a rocky slope, he'd announced that they were now on Miles land and she'd grown silent and stiff. So had he.

Other than that, though, he'd had a good time.

It had been a lifetime since he'd last said that.

A breeze stirred down the hill, rustling the leaves in the old oak above them. Its branches spread out and hung low, forming a giant canopy and lowering the temperature a few degrees. If he were alone, he could stretch out and take a nap. When the sun moved low enough to reach underneath the branches, he could strip off his clothes and go for a swim, the way he'd done countless times in the past. Usually with friends, often alone, sometimes—when he was older—with a girl.

Never with anyone like Olivia.

She had slathered the girls with sunscreen before sending them off to play. Now she was doing the same to herself, but it was too late for her right arm and her face. They'd already turned pink, courtesy of the sun coming through the open truck window.

She finished with the lotion, dried her hands on a napkin and sighed. "I am *so* pale."

Porcelain pale, he silently agreed. She looked as delicate as porcelain, too. As fragile. As costly.

She *wasn't* his type, he reminded himself, directing his gaze from her long legs stretched out in front of her to the twins. But the part of him that let his attention immediately drift back to her scoffed. What did he know about type? He'd only had one serious *type* in his entire life—Shay. Did that mean he could be attracted only to women who were beautiful, wild, deceitful and untrustworthy?

Maybe it was a family trait. After all, his stepfather had been a male version of Shay, and his mother had loved him.

Or maybe it was just a feeble attempt to keep himself from starting something that couldn't follow through to its natural conclusion. When he decided to find a woman in his life, he would look close to home.

And right now there was no one closer to home than Olivia.

He corrected that with a scowl. He would look for someone born and raised in Oklahoma. Someone who wasn't looking to leave it behind. Preferably someone raised on a ranch and as appreciative of the life as he was, who didn't mind hard work and little money and an uncertain future.

For years, he'd thought Shay was that someone. Along with Easy, they'd been best friends all their lives. At fifteen, they'd begun dating, by seventeen they'd become intimate, and by twenty they'd been in love and ready to marry.

Too bad that, while *he'd* been in love with her, *she'd* been in love with Easy.

Too sad he'd lived all these years alone.

"You look like you bit into something sour."

He looked at Olivia and realized that he was still scowling. Consciously he eased the muscles in his face, then, in an attempt at casual, he stretched out on one side, resting on one elbow so he could see both her and the girls in the water. "I was just thinking."

"Unpleasant thoughts in a lovely place like this?" She made a *tsking* sound. "I bet you spent a lot of hot summer days here when you were a kid."

He nodded.

"With Ethan?"

"Sometimes. Usually—" Avoiding her gaze, he traced a pattern in the quilt. "Usually with Easy and Shay."

For a moment a silence settled between them so still that the air fairly hummed with it. Then she quietly asked, "Do they live around here?"

"Shay has a place in town and runs the café on Main Street. Last I heard, Easy was still on the rodeo circuit. According to rumor, he's spent the last fourteen years drinking too much, partying too much, taking too many chances and raking in money hand over fist. I haven't seen him since he took off with Shay, so I don't know if any of it's true."

"Mary said he was your best friend."

"Yeah, well, he had her fooled, too."

"He sounds troubled."

Typical woman, ready to feel sympathy for a man she didn't even know. Well, Guthrie was fresh out of sympathy— had been for damn near half his life—and it showed in the unflinching hardness of his voice. "Whatever troubles he's got, he asked for."

A shriek at the pond commanded her attention, and she called to Elly to please quit splashing water in her sister's face before glancing back at him and changing the subject. "So…what's it like growing up in Heartbreak?"

"I finished growing up fourteen years ago, and I'm still here. That ought to tell you something."

"That you're in a rut?" she teased. "That you're not the adventurous sort?"

"Watch it," he warned with a scowl that was all surface and no threat. "You're not the adventurous sort, either, and you'd give anything in the world except your daughters to be stuck in your own rut back in Georgia."

"I know. Isn't it pitiful?"

"There's nothing wrong with having ties to the place you come from. But there's nothing wrong with creating ties to a new place, either." Hearing his last words made him frown.

Where had that come from? No one was creating any ties. They were merely making the best of a bad situation. As soon as circumstances improved, this arrangement would end. They would go back to Atlanta and he would stay here, and he would be glad they were gone and they would forget all about him.

End of story.

But it didn't look as if circumstances would improve for a long time—months, maybe even a year—and ties could create themselves, whether you wanted them or not. Hell, they were practically living together. Already he'd seen more of them in the past few days than he had of any of his neighbors in the last month. Already he'd started to become accustomed to their presence. Hell, he'd even gotten Emma to trust him to pick her up and set her down again unharmed.

Though he hadn't won the same trust from Olivia. Yet.

In months he could. In *months,* he could persuade her to let him set her down in his bed. He could convince her that she needed nothing as much as she needed him, could convince himself that he needed her. In months, lonely as he was, he could convince himself that he was in love—not just with her, but with pushy Elly and prissy Emma.

In months, he could be in far worse shape than when Shay and Easy had left him.

Leaning to one side, she plucked a bright, orange-red wildflower and examined it closely. "What are the schools like in town?"

"School. There's only one, kindergarten through twelfth grade." He took his hat off, laid it upside down on its crown. "You don't have to worry. They'll be learned readin', 'ritin' and that newfangled 'rithmetic. I heard tell they even got some brand-new itty-bitty addin' machines that ain't hardly been used at all and some real, honest-to-God books, bound and everything, so's they don't have to copy their lessons on their slates."

She gave him a wry smile. "Smart ass."

"Don't you know swearing is naughty? I'd hate to have to

wash your mouth out with soap. It wouldn't set a good example for the girls.''

Her smile deepened, softened her face, lightened her eyes. Friday morning in the diner, he'd wondered how a real smile would look on her, had speculated that it would make her gorgeous. He'd been partly wrong—she was pretty no matter what her expression—and partly right. The smile made her even prettier. It gave him a glimpse, he suspected, of the woman she'd been before her husband died and her safe, comfortable life fell apart. Of the woman she might once again become when she got it all put back together.

In Georgia.

"I wasn't being condescending," she informed him. "Merely curious."

"The school is comparable to any other small-town public school. They don't have enough money, but they do the best they can. A few teachers could try a little harder, but most of them are dedicated to the kids. They work hard for too little money—like most folks around here. We've got a good 4-H program, Scouts, a decent band, one of the best football teams in the state in our class, and our girls' basketball team won the state championship last year. We've never had any teachers assaulted by a student, any weapons confiscated on school grounds or any threats made against the students or the staff. About the worst that ever happens is a shoving match on the playground or a fistfight among the older kids.''

"It sounds good.''

"But nothing like the exclusive private school they would have gone to back in Atlanta.''

"What makes you think they would have gone to private school?''

The answer was so apparent that he couldn't help but laugh. "Look at you. It couldn't be more obvious that you're used to money if it was tattooed on your forehead. People with money—especially Southern people with money—do not mingle with the common crowd. They stick to their own kind, and they give their children the absolute best their old money can afford. That doesn't include public school.''

She tilted her head until she was looking down her perfectly shaped nose at him. ''Who's being condescending now? How do you know what you're mistaking for affluence isn't simply good breeding? How do you know I don't come from solid, middle-class working people?''

''Give me your hand.''

She transferred the flower to her right hand and extended the left. He turned it palm up and pretended to scrutinize it. He also pretended to not notice how soft it was, how slender and well-manicured and *womanly* it was. He definitely pretended not to think about how it would feel touching him— not like this, but intimately, in places he hadn't been touched for too damn long.

She was waiting for his next words, and he had to clear his throat to give them. ''Just as I thought. Not a callus, a scar or a mark of any kind. Did you even clean your own house back in Georgia?''

Her cheeks colored delicately, and she cleared her own throat before answering. ''Well, actually, no, I didn't. We had a housekeeper.''

''Did you cook? Did you shop? Did you do laundry? Did you scrub toilets or floors and carry out garbage? Or did you sip iced tea at garden parties, go to charity balls and make regular appearances at your husband's very expensive and very exclusive club?''

The color in her face flamed hot enough to give the wildflower a run for its money as she tugged her hand free. ''All right. The girls *were* enrolled in a private school soon after their first birthday. I *did* have a housekeeper and a very active social life, and we spent a great amount of time at the club. Satisfied?''

Not by a long shot, he thought as discomfort worked its way down his spine. Whatever description might fit his *type*, he knew beyond a doubt that it didn't include *accustomed to money.*

"None of that changes the fact that we are homeless and broke—a situation that doesn't appear likely to reverse itself anytime in the near or distant future," she said quietly.

They fell silent for a time. She watched the kids, and he watched anything but her. After a while, though, she offered a conciliatory gesture, laying the flower on the quilt between them. "If I transplanted these to the cabin, would they grow?"

He picked it up and twirled it by its stem. "Indian paintbrush grows damn near anywhere. I don't know about transplanting it. I've just always done my best to kill it. But if you want to give it a try, go ahead. That'll be a few less for me to spray."

"Why do you want to get rid of them?"

"Because they're *weeds,* darlin', and every weed I can get rid of means more grass for the cattle." He returned the flower to the quilt, then reluctantly sat up. "We need to head back. The kids have had enough sun, and I've still got the books to do."

She called Elly and Emma out of the water and wrapped them in towels while he secured the ice chest on the flatbed. He returned in time to help her shake out and fold the quilt, then they climbed into the truck.

Before they'd gone half a mile, Emma sank down, her head pillowed in her mother's lap. Soon after, Elly was sagging against him, sound asleep in spite of the rough ride.

"You want to push her this way?" Olivia asked.

"She's fine." He just had to reach over her to shift, and he couldn't rest his right arm at his side, but that was no problem.

"There was a time when they took naps every afternoon. As soon as they settled in, I'd wander through the house and just listen. There was such stillness that the house resonated with it. It felt *wonderful.*"

After that, she became so quiet, with her head turned away, that he wondered if she'd fallen asleep, too. But when he finally came to a stop in front of the cabin, she looked his way with a polite smile. "Thanks for the tour. We had a great time."

He shut off the engine. "I'll bring Elly if you can manage Emma."

She looked as if she wanted to protest. Was she reluctant to have him in her house? Eager to see the last of him for a while? Averse to imposing any further on his time? Whatever her reason, she set it aside and smiled again, this time with a little weariness, a little gratitude. "Thanks."

They carried the girls upstairs and laid them, hair and swimsuits still damp, on their beds. Elly murmured, rolled onto her side and fell immediately back into a deep sleep.

Olivia preceded him down the stairs and to the door. "Thanks," she said again.

Eager to see the last of him, he decided and his jaw tightened in response. But as he passed her on his way out the door, she touched him—nothing personal, just her hand on his forearm, a gentle squeeze. This time more than his jaw tightened.

"We'll see you at dinner."

He gave her a curt nod and headed for the truck. He could handle dinner. After a few hours of paperwork—and a cold shower—he could handle damn near anything.

# Chapter 6

By the end of the week, Olivia had settled into a routine of sorts. She was up by five-thirty—still not early enough to cook breakfast for Guthrie before he left the house, but she was making progress. She fixed breakfast for the girls and herself in the cabin's small kitchen, usually cereal and toast, then gave the cabin its daily cleaning. That done, she sent the girls to play while she went through the same chores at Guthrie's house. Picking up wasn't a problem—he spent little time in the house and was relatively neat—but dusting, thanks to the dirt road out front, was a daily job.

This Friday morning, she was finished by ten and, with the girls skipping ahead, was on her way to the barn. Elly raced to the fence and called the horses, laughing with delight when both Dusty and Maverick responded. Emma spied one of the barn cats and found a shady seat just inside the open doors to coax it onto her lap.

Olivia reminded them to be careful, then went deeper into the barn. Its shadows were a few degrees cooler than the heat outside, its smells a whole lot more pungent. Stalls lined the right side, five of them with doors that opened into the pasture for the horses. On the left was a small, windowless room that smelled of leather, horse and feed, and at the rear was a tall stack of hay bales. Elly would have fun with those once she discovered them, Olivia thought dryly.

She found what she was looking for in the end stall—a riding lawn mower, a matching trailer, a weed whacker and an assortment of garden tools. She'd done all she could for the inside of the house. Now it was time to do something about the outside and that field that passed as a yard.

The mower was dirty, with cobwebs stretching from the steering wheel to the nearest stud. She used a rake handle to brush them away, then gave the thing a perplexed look. The key was in the ignition and the gas gauge read three-quarters full—two problems solved. However, the biggest problem—that she'd never been this close to a lawn mower in her life—remained.

It couldn't be any more difficult than driving a car, she encouraged herself. Of course, she knew *how* to drive a car. She wasn't even sure how to start this. Just turn the key? Pull that knob? Move that lever? She could wait until lunch and ask Guthrie to show her, but after his comments Sunday, she would give a lot to master this small lesson with no help from him.

His words had stung more than she wanted to admit. Like those scrub oaks he wanted removed from his land, he obviously considered her damn near worthless. He thought she was some sort of pampered Southern belle who'd wasted her life in frivolous pursuits, who contributed nothing to society, who judged people by their money and their social standing rather than their character.

And it hurt because much of it was true. She *had* been pampered. About the only noteworthy thing she'd ever done was raising her daughters herself, instead of turning them over to a nanny as so many of their friends did. She'd done some charity fund-raising, along with her friends, but that had been the extent of her social conscience. She'd never done any hands-on work, had never even known much about the charities for which she'd helped raise money. She'd lived her easy, privileged life and done nothing that mattered.

Today, mowing the yard mattered.

It would be nice if the owner's manual was conveniently stored on the shelf up above, but all she found was a few rusted hand tools, a box of plant fertilizer so old that it was rock hard and a long-forgotten packet of morning glory seeds. "Face it, city girl," she murmured. "You're stumped."

At that very moment, an answer to her dilemma appeared outside. "Hello," Mary Stephens called. "Is anyone here?"

"Hey, Miss Mary," Elly responded excitedly. "Look at Maverick. He's lettin' me pet him."

"That he is, Elly. You keep scratching his ears like that, and you'll have a friend for life. What've you got there, Miss Emma?"

"A kitten." Emma's voice quavered with pleasure. "She rumbles when she sleeps, and she likes to lick me."

Olivia came out of the stall in time to see Mary bend to look at the cat, then gently correct Emma. "He, darlin'. That's a boy kitten."

"Good morning," Olivia greeted the older woman.

"Exploring this morning?"

"I found what I was looking for." She gestured inside the stall. "I just don't know what to do with it."

Mary looked at the mower, then back at Olivia. Her face grew warm. "No, I've never used a mower before," she said, forestalling her neighbor's response. "And please don't act incredulous. I was too busy going to tea parties to learn, so we always had a lawn service."

Mary's expression turned speculative, then she squared her shoulders and stepped inside the stall. "Come on over here and climb up in the seat. I can teach you everything you need to know in five minutes or less."

Olivia gathered her full skirt and settled in the dusty seat. Mary started with the obvious—the ignition, headlights and gas tank—then moved on to the rest. True to her word, in five minutes, Olivia was able to depress the brake, adjust the choke, start the engine and lower and activate the cutting blade, all on her own. With a smile of satisfaction, she switched off the motor.

"Gasoline's over there, oil's right beside it," Mary said with a gesture toward the corner. "I'd recommend a swimsuit and shorts so you can get a matching sunburn on your left arm and, if your hands are as lily-white as the rest of you, maybe a pair of Guthrie's work gloves so you don't get calluses or blisters."

She *wanted* calluses, Olivia thought grimly. She wanted her hands to feel as if she'd *done* something.

"Taking care of the yard will be a big help to Guthrie. He doesn't often have the time or the energy to worry about it." Mary leaned against the wall and gave a wistful sigh. "When his mama was still alive, it was her job—her hobby. She had the prettiest flowers—beds all along the porch and around the trees, irises and daffodils out by the gate, moss rose in pots all over. It was lovely. And her garden—tomatoes this big, and so wonderful." She gestured with both hands, then let them fall.

"You miss her," Olivia commented softly.

"Every day. She was my best friend. The two of us and Betsey Rafferty—Easy's mama—oh, we had some good times together." As she lapsed into silence, a look of sorrow crossed her face for old friends now gone.

"Are you all right?" Olivia asked gently.

"Just feeling my age today." Mary sighed, then brightened. "I came by to invite you to the next meeting of the Ladies' Auxiliary. It's tomorrow afternoon at my house. It's not a tea party, but it's the closest thing you'll find in Heartbreak."

"What do you do?"

"It started out fifty years ago as a church group, but now pretty much anyone can belong. Of course, pretty much everybody in Heartbreak goes to church," she said with a chuckle. "My husband says we're a bunch of nosy women.

My daughter calls us do-gooders. We're in charge of the Founders' Day barbecue—that's coming up at the end of the month—and we raise money for the library and the youth sports programs. We visit the old folks who can't get out much and help out at the school when we can. We see a need, we try to meet it. You think you might be interested?''

She thought it sounded like exactly the hands-on experience she'd avoided in Atlanta—like something else that *mattered*. "I'd have to bring the girls," she warned.

"Well, of course you would. Oh, hon, nothing happens in Heartbreak where kids aren't welcome. Everyone would be disappointed if you *didn't* bring them."

Olivia considered it. If she was going to live here awhile—maybe a good long while—she wanted to meet some people and make some friends. But how hard would it be to walk into a room filled with people who wondered why she was here or knew and resented her for it?

Understanding her hesitance, Mary squeezed her hand. "You think about it, hon. We'll get started at two o'clock tomorrow. The first mailbox headed back into town."

"I'll try. Thanks for the mower lesson." Olivia walked to the barn door with her, then returned to the stall and climbed back into the seat. The mower roared to life and, with her right foot tentatively on the pedal, crawled out of the stall and toward the door.

Emma looked up, her expression comical. Startled by the noise, the kitten fled to safety as Emma jumped to her feet. "Can I ride with you?" she shouted.

Olivia slowed the engine and lowered the roar a few decibels. "No, babe, sorry," she yelled back. "I'm going to the cabin to change clothes, and then I'm going to mow. You and Elly need to wait for me on Guthrie's porch, all right?"

Emma bobbed her head, then went to get Elly while Olivia waited. Elly stopped to beg a ride, then followed her sister toward the front of the house.

As soon as Olivia steered the mower into tall grass, she lowered the cutting deck halfway, then pushed the lever that set the blades spinning. Immediately clumps of grass clogged the discharge chute and the engine died. Chagrined, she restarted the engine, raised the deck and tried again, and it *worked*. The remaining grass was taller than she wanted and would require a second pass at a lower setting, but it worked.

She was delighted.

She cut a wide swath to the cabin, where she quickly changed into a tank top and shorts, liberally coated herself with sunscreen and traded sandals for tennis shoes. Back on the mower, she checked the girls' whereabouts—one on the porch floor with a coloring book, the other on the glider, reading—then marked off the third closest to the house and began working in ever-shrinking circles, watching with satisfaction as overgrown field gave way to some semblance of yard.

By the time she gave the entire area from driveway to tree line, house to road, the twice-over, she was hot, sweaty and hungry. Without a watch, she had no idea what time it was, but as she turned the mower toward the house, she hoped she had time to clean up and change before Guthrie returned—

He was sitting in the rocker nearest the porch steps, one ankle propped on the opposite knee, his hat balanced on the other knee, and he was grinning. And why shouldn't he be amused? Her hair clung to her damp skin, as did enough grass clippings to weave a skirt. She was dirty. She smelled bad. She looked bad.

She cut off the motor and listened to the quiet ring in her ears before summoning the energy to swing her leg over the steering wheel and step to the ground. A few hours of the mower's vibrations and sitting on a not-very-comfortable seat left her legs unsteady, her posterior numb and her gait graceless.

Gratefully she sank onto the top step and leaned back against the post. Without a word, he leaned forward and handed her his glass of soda. She took a long, icy drink, then gave it back.

"I asked you to take care of the house," he said evenly. "Not anything outside."

"You asked me to help you when you needed it." Her voice was just as even.

"I would've gotten to the mowing as soon as I had time."

"*I* had time today."

"And I appreciate it, but it's not necessary. It's hot work—"

"And I can handle both heat and work," she said sharply.

He gave her another of those steady, contemplative looks, then shrugged. "Whatever you say. What's for lunch?"

"Spaghetti." She'd made the sauce yesterday afternoon, simmered it all through dinner, then left it in the refrigerator. Though the rest of her cooking was average, spaghetti was one dish she did well.

"Oh. Spaghetti."

"'Oh' what?"

"Nothing."

Her brows drew together in a frown. "You don't like spaghetti."

Again he shrugged. "It's fine."

Wincing inwardly as her muscles protested, she got to her feet. "Give me fifteen minutes to clean up and I'll have lunch ready." Something *besides* spaghetti. But at least the big pot of sauce wouldn't go to waste. Given the opportunity, Emma and Elly would eat it for breakfast, lunch and dinner. "Kids, come on."

"We're busy, Mama," Elly replied without looking up from her coloring book.

"They can stay here with me," Guthrie said before Olivia had a chance to command their attention.

"That's not necess—"

He cut her off with a steely look. "I'm not an idiot. I can watch two five-year-olds for fifteen minutes. If they try to run off, I'll rope 'em and tie 'em to the rail."

Both girls' heads popped up, wearing identical startled expressions. Elly was the first to realize he was teasing, and she giggled as she returned to her picture.

Olivia relented gracelessly. "I'll be right back. You guys behave, or you'll have to deal with *me*."

"Such a threat, Olivia," Guthrie murmured to her back as she set off across the newly mown, wonderfully sweet-smelling yard to the cabin.

Though she tossed him a scowl over her shoulder, as she turned back, she thought that might be the only time he'd called her by her name, except when he'd introduced her to his lawyer. She couldn't be certain, of course—they'd had a lot of conversations—but she was pretty sure she would have remembered her name in his voice, with four distinct syllables and an Oklahoma drawl. She was downright convinced she would have remembered that little tingle quivering down her spine.

And how could she possibly have forgotten the corresponding panic tightening in her chest?

She felt like a schoolgirl in the first stages of a crush, only she wasn't a schoolgirl and, at her age, in her emotional state, a crush could be dangerous. Harmless infatuations were the territory of the young, carefree and easily healed. She was too smart, too responsible, too traditional—and too lonely—to think she could indulge herself in any relationship and walk away emotionally intact.

And she *would* walk away. She'd promised the kids. She'd promised herself. Come hell or high water, she *would* find her way home. There she could have all the crushes, infatuations and relationships she wanted.

Though she really wanted just one, with someone she would love the rest of her life, someone who would treasure her the rest of his life.

In Georgia.

Upstairs in the girls' bathroom, she showered and dried in record time, then pulled on the purple sundress she'd discarded earlier. She braided her wet hair, dabbed moisturizer on her face and aloe vera on her arms, then grabbed her keys and headed back to Guthrie's. She would've liked a few minutes to dry her hair and bring some order to it, a few more minutes to put on makeup, but he wasn't paying her to worry about her appearance. It wasn't as if she needed or even wanted to look good for him. She just liked looking her best.

"Gee, look at that," he remarked as she passed him on her way inside. "Seventeen whole minutes alone with your kids, and I didn't break them or lose them or anything."

She glanced at the girls, still quietly entertaining themselves, but didn't look at him. "Lunch will be ready soon."

In the kitchen, she put the sauce on the back burner to heat and a pot of hot water on high heat in front, then stood in front of the open refrigerator door. She could fix sandwiches for Guthrie, though she hated to. What did he need her for if that was the best she could provide? She had all the makings for an omelet, but that wasn't much of a meal for someone who'd been working hard all morning and would be busy all afternoon, too. If she defrosted a package of beef from the freezer, she could add it to vegetables for a quick stew—

A strong, brown hand grasped the refrigerator door above her head and pushed it shut. "We generally use the air conditioner when we want to cool the room," he drawled. "It's more efficient, you know."

"I was looking for something to fix you..."

"I said spaghetti's fine. It's just not one of my favorites." He gave a shake of his head. "Jeez, didn't your parents ever make you eat something you weren't wild about? Or did they order the cook to tailor the menu to your specifications?"

The look that came into her eyes was definitely one of hurt, and it made Guthrie silently swear. "Hey." He touched her arm and felt soft skin, still warm from the sun and faintly perfumed by lotion, then awkwardly shifted his hand to her shoulder, to the protection of purple fabric. "I was just teasing. I didn't mean... I'm sorry."

"Sure." Her voice sounded choked, and her movements were jerky as she turned away, treating the pans on the stove to her full attention. "Maybe it would be best if you give me a complete list of what you do and don't like."

That wouldn't be too hard. He was developing a troublesome fondness for blue eyes, pale brown hair and paler soft skin. He'd discovered quite a liking for a voice richly Southern and lushly feminine. For having someone here when he came in from work. For looking at her, talking to her, thinking about her.

Given the chance, he imagined he could discover a hell of a liking for touching her. *Really*, completely, intimately touching her.

And that was the last thing either of them needed. Their lives were already complicated enough.

"I like—" His voice was thicker than normal. With a scowl, he swallowed hard to ease the tightness in his throat. "I like just about everything but liver, carrots or spinach. Spaghetti doesn't come real high on my list, and neither does meat loaf or green beans."

She glanced over her shoulder at him. "You ate green beans the other night. You have jars of them in the pantry."

One corner of his mouth lifted. "Mary plants them in her garden. She babies them through the whole growing season, then spends an entire day canning them, and she gives me quarts and quarts, and I don't know how to tell her that I don't like them."

Slowly she faced him. "You could just throw them away, give her back the jars and tell her they were delicious."

"But that would be wrong."

"More wrong than pretending you like something you don't?"

He shrugged. "It doesn't hurt anyone."

She studied him a moment longer, then gave a slow shake of her head and began fitting fistfuls of spaghetti into the pot of boiling water.

"Why are you shaking your head?"

"I don't believe I've ever met a man who cared that much about not hurting someone's feelings."

The soft words sounded uncomfortably close to admiration, and they made him edgy. "Surely your husband—"

"No. Not my husband."

The flat, unemotional way she said it closed the door on any further discussion. Of course, it made Guthrie even more curious. How happy—or unhappy—had her marriage been? Had she loved Miles, hated him, tolerated him? Did she miss him? When she'd cried on the porch that first night, had it been for herself, the kids and the upheaval in their lives, or for him?

Did she need time to get over him, or was she ready for the next man in her life?

It didn't matter, because *he* certainly wasn't going to be the next man. Not unless she changed her mind about going home. Not unless she adapted a thousand percent to ranch life and Heartbreak. Not unless she forgot that Georgia even existed.

And that was about as likely as him pulling up stakes and making his new home in Atlanta.

She drained the spaghetti while he fixed four glasses of pop, dished it up while he called the kids in from the porch. Emma and Elly settled in at the table and ate with relish. He ate from hunger, though he had to admit, as spaghetti went, it was better than most.

He was leaving to go back to work when Olivia followed him onto the back porch. "Mary came by this morning."

He could have guessed that *somebody* did, because he'd been pretty damn sure that, along with all the other housekeeping chores she hadn't done back home, she hadn't mowed the lawn, either. He'd figured either someone had given her a quick how-to or she'd found the manual filed with the warranty papers in his office. Since his filing system was incomprehensible to anyone but him, a visitor was the better bet.

"She said they're having a meeting of the Ladies' Auxiliary at her house tomorrow afternoon. She asked me to go and take the girls."

He wondered why she was telling him. "And?"

"I just wondered... Should I?"

"Do you want to?"

"I—I think so."

"Then go."

"But I won't know anyone but Mary."

"Trust me. She's enough," he said dryly. "If you're going to live in Heartbreak, even just for a while, the women in the Ladies' Auxiliary are the people you should know."

"Then..." She shifted nervously. "You don't care?"

"Why would I?"

"Because if I'm there, then I'm not here."

He gazed down at her for a moment before finally catching on. "You mean, if you're there helping them, you won't be here working?" Slapping his hat on his head, he gave her an irritated look. "You don't need my permission. Olivia, we're *partners*. You do understand that word?"

Stubbornly she shook her head. "We're partners on the land and the cabin. You're paying me for the job."

He leaned close to her and immediately wished he hadn't, because her fragrance subtly perfumed the hot, still air and put him in mind of things better not considered. Forcing his attention back on track, he said, "Let me fill you in on a little secret. The pasture you're letting me use is worth a hell of a lot more than the cabin I'm letting you use. I should be paying you for that and doing *your* housework, cooking and laundry. Even then, I'd still probably come up short of what it's worth."

He straightened, put the width of the steps between them. "I'm not your boss. You don't owe me any set number of hours a day. If you want to go do something, go. Do it. I'd appreciate the courtesy of being told, but I certainly don't expect to be asked for permission. Okay?"

Slowly she nodded, but she didn't look too convinced.

"Then I'll see you at supper." He returned to the barn, where he'd left the tractor. He planned to finish spraying weeds this afternoon, then tomorrow he would borrow Jim

Stephens's bulldozer and try to get another small part of the land cleared. It wasn't an easy process. Once the trees were down, they had to be gathered into a pile and left to dry before burning.

While he had the dozer, he would get rid of as many rocks as he could—for all the good it would do. This part of Oklahoma sprouted sandstone the way Mary's carefully tended garden sprouted green beans—in great abundance. He could pick a field clean this week only to find a whole new crop next week. He used them where he could—in rock corners, a circle of wire filled with stone and supporting fence, or to fill in potholes in the ranch roads—and cursed them where he couldn't.

As he climbed into the tractor seat, he heard the screen door slam and looked back to see Olivia standing on the porch, hanging a dish towel over the railing there. There was a clothesline out at what had once been the back edge of the yard where his mother had always hung laundry on hot days like this. She'd claimed the sun would suck the moisture out of the clothes faster than the heat any gas-powered dryer could generate, and usually she'd been right.

Nadine would be appalled to see the shape her yard was in, but she would understand. There was too much to do here for one man and not enough profit to hire help and make it worthwhile.

But it wasn't too much for one man and one woman. He had to admit that he liked coming home to a house that smelled of food and polish and just plain *clean*. He liked seeing things the way they used to be—neatly kept, everything in its place, furniture gleaming. In the last week, the house had become a more comfortable place to be.

Thanks to Olivia.

As he started the engine, she tilted her face up to the sun, then took a deep breath. From this distance it was impossible to see the fabric of her dress tighten, he told himself. It was absolutely impossible to see the look of satisfaction—with herself, with the day, with this place—on her face. But he could imagine.

Oh, hell, yes, he could imagine.

Frowning, he drove through the gate and headed for the fields slated for spraying this afternoon. As the tractor reached the top of the first small hill, he looked back just in time to see a flash of purple disappear inside the house. But out of sight, unfortunately, was *not* out of mind.

He worked his way through the fields until finally, as the sun began to slide closer to the western horizon, he reached the last one. It was closest to the cabin, with only a barbed wire fence and a stand of trees separating them. It was a small field, with a ton of rocks, and for those reasons he'd long ignored it. Hell, right now it needed only a few more weeds to officially change its designation from field to wildflower meadow.

He sat on the crest of a rise, the engine idling, and gazed across the field at Indian paintbrush and Indian blanket, the state wildflower. There were purple and white coneflowers and black-eyed Susans, sweet William and jumping jacks and chigger weed with its bright orange blossoms. Nuisances, all—but not too bad to look at and easily contained with timber on three sides and the road on the fourth. Hell, what would it hurt to leave it alone awhile longer? It wasn't as if he could get much use from the field, not until he cleared the timber.

And those were excuses. Rationalizations. If he was going to be a sap and do something stupid, the least he could do was be honest with himself about it. He was leaving the flowers alone because Olivia liked them. There was precious little that was pretty in her life right now, and if five lousy acres of colorful weeds might bring her some pleasure... Hell, it was like Mary's green beans. Eating them didn't hurt him, even if he didn't like them, and sparing these flowers wouldn't hurt him, either.

Turning in a wide circle, he headed the tractor back toward the barn. By the time he got there and tended to the horses, it would be quitting time. He'd have time to clean up before dinner, and after dinner maybe they could take a walk. Maybe he would show her the field and she would give him one of those steady, appreciative looks, and *maybe*...

Maybe he'd get himself into more trouble than he knew how to get out of. Maybe he'd find out that sparing the flowers *could* hurt. Maybe he'd regret not giving them all a triple dose of herbicide.

Or maybe not.

Supper was over, the dishwasher was loaded and Olivia was about ready to take the twins and head home when Guthrie finally made his suggestion. Occasionally through the evening, he'd thought better of it, but each time that happened, he'd put the whole thing out of his mind and concentrated on what the girls were saying or what their mother was doing, and so he'd made it through the meal without being able to change his mind.

He walked down the hall to the front door with her as the girls ran ahead. "If you want..." Last chance, his self-preservation warned. *It's not too late.* "I'll show you a place where you can dig up those flowers you wanted to transplant."

After a moment's hesitation, during which she studied him as if he had ulterior motives, she smiled. "I'd like that."

"We'll stop by the cabin on the way. You and Emma need to change into tennis shoes." He locked up behind them, then he and Olivia followed the twins across the yard. Piles of grass dotted the space where she'd raked this afternoon. She'd worked damn hard and must be feeling it—the sunburn on her face and arms was showing it—and the knowledge made him feel guilty, because he *did* have ulterior motives for suggesting this walk. "Listen, if you're too tired—"

Her smile was twice as nice as the one she'd given him inside. "No, not at all. I mean, I am tired, but not too tired."

"My mom used to take care of the yard. She loved tending the garden, but she never cared much for mowing. She claimed she only did it because neatly cut grass made her flowers look prettier. She used to threaten to get a goat and let it keep the grass cropped, so one day my dad brought one home and turned it loose—and it ate every single flower she'd planted. She never complained about the mowing again, but I don't think she ever stopped complaining about that goat.''

She was giving him a sidelong look as they walked. ''You said you were six when your father died. Do you remember much about him?''

He took a moment to consider the answer, then finally shrugged. ''I have a lot of memories, but I don't know whether they're really my memories or my mother's. She talked about him all the time when I was growing up, always reminding me of things we had done together, lessons he'd taught me, things he'd said. I think I really do remember him teaching me to ride and going fishing and picnics at the swimming hole, but I don't know for sure.'' As they approached the cabin steps, he again took a moment to consider what he was about to ask, then went ahead. ''Are you afraid the girls will forget their father?''

''Not afraid, necessarily. Just…'' With a glance at the cabin door, she left the conversation hanging, climbed the porch steps and went inside with Emma. Elly waited with him, climbing onto the rail, balancing precariously as she walked from one post to the next.

''You're going to fall and break your neck,'' he commented as she maneuvered around the post and set off for the next one.

''I know how to fall. I took gymnastics back home.'' Confidence gave way to tomboyish scorn. ''Emma took ballet. She wanted to be a ballerina.'' Raising her arms above her head, she attempted a twirl and lost her balance.

Guthrie scooped her up without moving a step and settled her feet on the floor. ''What did you want to be?''

''An astronaut. A race car driver.'' She grinned slyly. ''President. Mama said I could be anything I wanted. Daddy said she was wrong, that I would be a wife and mother, just like Mama and her mama and his mama and all my friends' mamas. *Was* she wrong?''

"Nope. You can do anything, if you study hard enough and work hard enough and want it bad enough," he replied evenly, wondering as he did what kind of father David Miles had been. Not so good that the girls appeared to be in serious mourning. Guthrie had cried for weeks after his father's death. Emma had cried to go home, but as far as he knew, since coming here, neither twin had cried for her father. So bad, maybe, that Olivia not only wasn't afraid that the girls would forget him but hoped that they would?

She and Emma returned, wearing clunky tennis shoes and distracting him from his thoughts. He led the way around the cabin, through the trees and a makeshift gate in the fence.

"Oh, my gosh." Olivia walked a few yards ahead of them, stopped and turned in a slow circle before facing him again. "It's beautiful. I can't believe this is so close to the cabin and I hadn't seen it." Then she laughed. "I can't believe this is on your property and you haven't mowed it down."

"I considered it."

She didn't ask when or why he'd decided against it, though the look she gave him suggested that she knew—or, at least, suspected. "This is wonderful. Do you know what they are?"

Joining her, he pointed out the varieties he knew. She contributed the ones she was familiar with, then gave a sweet sigh. "This is amazing. Doesn't it smell wonderful?"

He breathed deeply and smelled weeds. He kept that impression to himself, though.

"Are there other places like this around?"

"Not on my ranch." There was a faintly offended undertone to his voice that made her grin.

"Don't worry, Guthrie," she teased. "No one's going to think you're a bad rancher for having a wildflower meadow."

Not bad, he agreed. Maybe just besotted.

Not sharing their mother's fondness for flowers, the girls settled on a large boulder square in the middle of the field while Guthrie and Olivia strolled through the flowers. He let her set the pace, stopping often as she bent to examine one flower or another. After a while, he broke the companionable silence to return to their earlier conversation. "How big a loss is their father's death in their lives?"

Olivia stooped to pick up a red rock. She checked the bottom for bugs, then wrapped her fingers around it. He knew from a lifetime's experience that it was still warm with the day's heat, that its surface was gritty, that a sharp blow would break it in half. He figured if he went looking for it later, he'd find it in some place of honor around her cabin.

"As you know, losing your father should be one of the most traumatic events a child could experience," she said at last. "For the girls, it's more the results of his death that have troubled them, rather than the actual dying. They miss him, of course, but losing their home, their friends and everything familiar—that's what's been really tough. Tougher for Emma than for Elly, but still not easy."

And toughest of all for Olivia. It'd been her home, too—her friends, her security, her future. "I take it he wasn't a big part of their lives."

"No." She glanced at her daughters as if making certain they couldn't hear. "David wasn't a very fatherly father. They did their best to love him, but he didn't make it easy."

And what about you? he wanted to ask. *Did you do your best to love him? Was his death a big loss in your life? Do you cry in your bed at night because he's gone and you'd give anything to have him back?*

But he didn't ask. Was he just not bold enough? Or was he afraid of the answers she might give?

"I have pictures of him in the house," she went on. "I promised myself I would answer any questions they have, within reason, of course. But the sort of memory-building your mother did with you... Heavens, I don't even have stories to tell. He never did much with them."

"If he gave them nothing of himself to remember, then let them forget him. It's not a great loss." For them, at least.

"That sounds cold."

He doubted she could be cold if she tried. He also doubted she would take his advice. She would probably dredge up forgotten memories to share with the girls, or maybe even make up new ones out of the air. With her help, David Miles would be a better father in death than he'd ever been alive.

And why not? It wouldn't hurt, and it just might help. After all, take him and Ethan. Guthrie had known all his life that his father loved him, while Ethan had *never* had his father's love. Who was to say that that difference didn't account in some way for the different men they'd become? Maybe Ethan would have been a better man if he'd ever had reason to believe that Gordon gave a damn about him. Maybe Guthrie would have been more like him if he hadn't had *his* father's love to live up to.

They reached the western edge of the field and turned back toward the girls. "Is the cabin the original house on the property?" Olivia asked, gesturing to the roof just visible through the trees.

"No, my house is. The cabin was built about twenty-five years ago, when Ethan's grandmother came to live with us. She was too damn mean to share a house with the rest of us, so Gordon built that place. It's the only worthwhile thing he ever did in his sorry life."

"That, and Ethan," she said softly.

"Ethan?" he scoffed. "He's about as worthless as they come."

She pushed her hands—and the red rock—into her pockets and let a moment or two pass in silence before commenting, "You're not a very forgiving man, are you?"

Her question made the skin on the back of his neck prickle. "I'm the nicest guy in the whole damn county. Anyone will tell you that."

"I'm sure they will. You take in widows, kids and strays, honor fraudulent promises that you didn't even make, go out of your way to be kind to others—and you hold a grudge to beat all grudges."

He glowered at her. "I've spent most of Ethan's life cleaning up his messes. I've forgiven every damn thing he ever did, even though he was never the least bit sorry about any of it. But some things are unforgivable.''

"Like selling your land." Her voice grew softer as she switched the focus from Ethan. "Stealing your girl. Breaking your heart."

She was good. Three little phrases, and she'd hit his three biggest betrayals dead center. His feet stopped moving of their own accord, and he stared hard at her back until she stopped, too, and swung around to face him. "Yeah," he said, his jaw tight, his voice sharp. "Like those things. And some things are off limits for discussion."

"You asked me Sunday if I had any questions."

"And you said no."

"I've thought of some."

"Too bad. I've forgotten the answers."

"Guthrie—"

He started to brush past her, but she blocked his way. "Okay, okay. I'll shut up. I won't say another word. Just don't go away angry."

Like last weekend, she was mistaking defensiveness for anger. She was a perceptive woman. She should know better. Did she think it was easy to admit that the only woman he'd ever loved—intensely, passionately, desperately loved—had preferred another man over him? That the best friend he'd ever had had betrayed him damn near every time his back was turned? That in losing both his fiancée and his best friend, he'd lost a part of himself?

His breathing was audibly uneven, and his face was warm. He stared at her a long time, and she stared back. There was interest in her expression, but not curiosity. Sympathy but not pity.

The tension that held his body rigid slowly drained away. His muscles relaxed, and his fingers that had formed subconsciously into fists loosened. "What do you want to know?"

"What happened?"

He shrugged, bringing relief to his shoulders and neck. "I'd say she decided she liked him better."

"It couldn't have been that simple," she chided.

"What do *you* know?"

"I've never had a best friend, but I know a man *you* would consider your best friend wouldn't get involved with the woman you were going to marry that easily. It must have been difficult for them."

"For them?" he echoed disbelievingly. "They ran off with each other to have their fun. I was the one left standing in the lurch with a pair of gold wedding bands and a surprised look on my face. And you think it was difficult for *them?*"

"Which was worse? The broken heart? Or the wounded pride?"

"I didn't *have* any pride," he said bitterly. "They saw to that."

"She came back," Olivia said softly. "Why didn't you forgive her then and go ahead with the marriage?"

"She didn't want to be forgiven, and she didn't want me. By then, I didn't want her, either."

"You must miss them incredibly."

He opened his mouth to deny it, then closed it again when he realized that she was right. He'd hated, resented and, yes, missed them for the last fourteen years. Even after Shay had come back, he'd still missed her because the damage had been done. She was a different person, and so was he. She'd come to the house one evening to apologize, but he'd refused to let her in, to talk to her at all. In the six years since, he'd rarely seen her, and on the occasions he had, they hadn't even managed to exchange civil hellos.

Shoving his hands into his pockets, he checked an outcropping of stone for snakes, then leaned against it. He was facing west, where the sun was beginning to color the sky in delicate golds, pinks and purples. "We were going to be partners—Easy and me," he said at last. "He would have his folks' place, and I was taking over this place as soon as I graduated from high school. We were going to raise cattle here and horses there—paints, like Maverick. He had a way with horses—never met one he couldn't sweet-talk into doing anything he wanted." He'd never met many women, either, who were immune to his charm. Guthrie had thought Shay was the only one.

He'd been so incredibly wrong that it would have been funny if it hadn't damn near killed him.

"We needed money to get started, so after graduation, he went out on the rodeo circuit. He did pretty good—won some championships, got some cash. And he found out that rodeo cowboys, especially the ones finishing in the money, draw women the way honey draws flies. He started spending more time on the road and less time at home. I was spending all my free time with Shay so it didn't matter much."

Olivia found the boulder's only flat surface and used it as a seat, drawing her knees up, smoothing her skirt down and watching the sunset without looking at him. He looked at her, though only from the corner of his eye, searching her expression for anything he might not like. He found nothing— just carefully schooled and lovely features.

"Easy came home two weeks before the wedding. He was in a bad mood—looking for trouble. A week and a half later he took off with Shay. I found out when neither of them showed up for the rehearsal. Finally, two weeks after that, she contacted Mary. They were somewhere in the Dakotas, everything was fine, sorry about the way things happened, but this really was for the best."

When Mary had passed on the message, he'd been furious. What could be *best* about getting jilted mere days before the wedding? What could possibly be *best* about the woman he loved beginning an affair with the man who was closer to him than any brother could ever be?

And he'd been hurt. These were the people, along with his mother, who were supposed to love him most, and yet they hadn't thought twice about betraying twenty years of friendship, love and dreams. And for what? So they could have a few years' fun together and then split up?

Now, after fourteen years of anger, hurt and betrayal... Now he just felt drained. Weary. As if, for this one moment, none of it mattered so much anymore.

And he suspected that the reason was seated beside him.

She sat so still, as if the sunset were the most important thing in her life. Then she gave a small sigh, blindly reached out and wrapped her fingers around his. That was all she did—take his hand and hold on tightly—but it was enough.

It was exactly what he needed.

## Chapter 7

It was a quarter to two Saturday when Olivia faced her image in the bathroom mirror. She was wearing a sleeveless dress in a soft floral print that fitted snugly to her waist then flared just the tiniest bit to midcalf. Her hair was pulled back in a French braid, and her makeup was expertly applied. She smelled of her favorite perfume, and her hands... Well, she hadn't had a manicure in weeks and had done a lot of physical work lately, and her hands looked it, but she was meeting other women who most likely had no time for manicures, either. They probably wouldn't notice.

In the living room, Elly was complaining loudly about being made to take a bath in the middle of the day and putting on clean, *nice* clothes. Emma, dressed for an elegant garden party, was sitting quietly, probably playing with her doll—no doubt dressed equally elegantly—and ignoring her sister. It didn't matter, though. When she was feeling put-upon, Elly never required an audience for her rants.

But she had one this afternoon, Olivia realized the instant she walked through the bedroom door. Guthrie was standing near the door, hat in hand, and listening seriously as her elder daughter carried on. His gaze shifted to *her,* and she swore, for one unguarded moment, she saw appreciation and something else in his dark eyes—something more, something intimate. The certainty warmed her cheeks and tightened her throat, making her voice husky when she spoke. "I didn't know you were coming back early."

"I thought I'd ride over to the Stephens place with you. I'm picking up Jim's dozer to do some clearing. You can bring the truck back when you're done."

"We can take my car."

He glanced out the door at the old, beat-up station wagon that had sat in the same spot for more than a week now and almost smiled. "Are you sure about that?" Without waiting for a response, he went on. "The truck's air-conditioned. When Elly's gone to such trouble to look good for her neighbors, the last thing she needs is to show up hot, windblown and sweaty."

Olivia knew he had substituted her daughter's name for her own—knew it without understanding how. "Does she? Look good, I mean."

His gaze moved slowly from her braid all the way down to her sandals, then back up. "Very good."

"Thank you. On Elly's behalf, of course."

"Of course." He opened the door, and Olivia ushered the girls out. She settled them in the truck's back seat, then fastened her seat belt while Guthrie did the same.

It took only a few minutes to reach the turnoff for the Stephens ranch. Guthrie pointed out the beginning of their property, marked by pipe fence painted white, bisected by a matching pipe gate. A gravel lane ran between pastures, then split, turning left for the ranch buildings, right for the house. A half-dozen cars were parked beside the low, sprawling stone house, and another recent arrival was climbing out of hers as Guthrie shut off the engine.

He murmured something that sounded obscene, causing Olivia to look first at him, then follow his gaze to the other guest. She was about Olivia's age, and she was female, but that was where the similarities between them ended. She was tall, slender and every inch of her exposed skin was tanned dark gold—and with a skirt that couldn't possibly be both one inch shorter and decent, and a tank top that couldn't get any skimpier, that was a lot of skin. She had blond hair— long, thick, lots of it—and painted nails—on both hand and foot—and was, quite simply, gorgeous.

Olivia didn't need to ask. This was Shay Stephens, the woman who'd broken Guthrie's heart. The woman he'd loved long after, the woman he still felt *something* for.

She shifted uneasily. Was it too late to back out? Could she remember some reason she needed to return home? Could the girls *please* launch into one of their rare, full-fledged, absolutely-not-to-be-tolerated tantrums, requiring punishment in the privacy of the cabin?

But she could think of no reason to run back home beyond cowardice and shaky self-esteem, the girls were behaving extraordinarily well at the moment, and Guthrie was already coming around to open the door for her. She reluctantly unfastened her seat belt and slid to the ground, then helped the girls out. By the time they got to the front of the truck, Shay was waiting.

"So...you're the new part-owner of Harris Ranch." Her voice was as utterly feminine as her appearance, with a charming hint of an Oklahoma twang. She gave Olivia and the twins—Elly in a chambray shift, Emma in ruffles and ribbons with matching hat, and all three of them with their hair in matching braids—up and down looks, then offered a cynical smile. "*Too* cute. I'm Shay Stephens, the fool-minded daughter and the lying, faithless bi—" With a glance at the girls, she broke off.

Olivia could feel the hostility radiating from Guthrie beside her and the tension from the girls in front of her. She swallowed hard, ordered herself not to tremble and extended her hand. "I'm Olivia Miles. This is Emma and this is Elly."

As they shook hands, Shay gave Olivia another long look,

then responded in a mock, sugary-sweet Georgia drawl. "Goodness me, I didn't know honest-to-God, bona fide Southern belles still existed, but here you stand before me. Mercy me and fiddle-dee-dee."

Guthrie took hold of Olivia's arm. "Come on, Olivia. I'll take you inside. I want to say hello to Mary before I go."

As they walked away, Shay called, "How about saying hello to *me*, Guthrie? It's only been fourteen years."

He ignored her, but his fingers tightened around Olivia's arm. After a moment, she murmured, "Ease up a bit, will you? That's my arm, not Shay's throat."

He looked at her, flushed, then gentled his grip before letting go completely.

"She's beautiful," Olivia remarked evenly as they stepped from grass to flagstone walkway.

"I suppose. If you like that type."

She laughed softly. "Young, beautiful and sexy? Oh, honey, *every* man likes that type. I can see how Easy forgot she was yours—and why you haven't forgiven him for it." She paused before commenting, "You two still have something in common—your opinion of Southern women. Or, at least, *this* Southern woman in particular."

They'd reached the covered entry, with its small relief from the sun, big pots of hostas and heavily carved double doors. "What opinion?" he asked as he pressed the doorbell.

"That I'm useless. Pampered. Good for adornment but not much else."

He turned to stare at her. "I never said—"

"Not in so many words."

"Not in *any* words," he said heatedly.

Before she could respond, one door swung open and Mary started to greet them. Guthrie interrupted her. "Elly, Emma, go inside and see Miss Mary's dogs," he directed, and as soon as they obeyed, he gripped the knob, pulled the door from Mary's grasp and closed it again. He folded his arms across his chest and scowled. "I *never* said you were use less."

She knew it was in her own best interests to let the subject drop, but something wouldn't let her. Maybe it was the helplessness she'd felt since finding out that David had left them broke. Maybe it was the inadequacy she'd become so intensely aware of since then. Maybe it was frustration at having her entire future in limbo, at meeting Shay Stephens, at knowing that, after everything, Guthrie still felt something for the woman. Whatever the reason, she couldn't politely agree with him, then go inside to spend an afternoon with a bunch of strangers and the woman he'd loved.

"You made fun of my life in Atlanta because I enrolled the girls in private school, because I didn't clean house or scrub floors or do laundry, because I went to parties and the club and paid people to do things I didn't want to do myself. You called me a snob."

"I did not—"

"You said Southern people with money don't mingle with common folk, that they stick to 'their own kind.' If that's not another way of saying *snob,* then I don't know what is."

He stared at her and, mimicking his folded-arms position, she stared back. Finally he eased the tension in his jaw long enough to ask, "Isn't it true?"

"I'm *not*—"

"Did you ever have any friends who didn't have money? Who didn't live in the same expensive neighborhoods and belong to the same exclusive clubs and hire the same less fortunate people to clean up after them? Did the kids ever know a single child who wasn't enrolled in the same fancy private school?"

She didn't need to answer—he already knew—but she grudgingly forced the word out anyway. "No."

"When you go back, you won't be able to live in those neighborhoods or belong to those clubs. The kids won't be able to go to that fancy school. Under the circumstances, how many of those people will still want to be friends with you? How many will want their kids to play with yours?"

When she didn't answer, he gestured impatiently. "It

shouldn't be a difficult question, Olivia. We're talking *friends* here—people who are supposed to care about you no matter what. Will they ask you to their parties, to their club? Will their kids invite your kids to sleep over? Or will they forget they ever knew you?''

Though she knew it was wasted breath, she tried to excuse her old friends—and the woman she'd been before coming here. ''We'll be living in a different part of town. The girls will be going to a different school.''

''But you'll still be the same person. The kids will still be the same kids. The only *real* difference will be that you don't still have money.'' He paused before quietly finishing. ''If that's not snobbery, I don't know what is. And it doesn't even make you angry, does it? These people measure your worth— your kids' worth—by your bank account, and you accept it as the way things are because that's the way *you* are.''

The silence that settled between them was less than comfortable. Olivia stared out across the yard as a pickup rumbled down the dusty road. She'd already been forced to admit to herself that she'd been pampered and useless back home. Now there was no way to avoid facing the fact that, like everyone she'd called friend, she'd also been a snob—at least, until David's death had taken that luxury from her.

She should have left well enough alone. She'd known it.

Swallowing hard, she asked, ''Do I have any other character flaws you'd like to point out before I walk into a room filled with strangers?''

''Olivia—'' He reached out but apparently thought better of it and drew back without touching her. ''I didn't mean to offend you.''

''Then what did you intend?''

His expression turned wary and defensive, and he took a step back. ''*You* brought the subject up.''

''Oh, I see. And that made you feel perfectly comfortable insulting me. So if you ever mention Shay again, then I'll be perfectly free to remind you of the fact that she dumped y because she wanted a tawdry affair with your best friend far more than she wanted marriage with you."

The color drained from his face, and his eyes turned as dark and cold as a frigid winter night. Turning on his boot heel, he stalked away.

Panic and shock stabbed through her. "Guthrie, wait—"

Ignoring her call, he disappeared around the corner of the house. Though it was too late to undo the damage, she covered her mouth with one hand and silently muttered every curse she'd ever heard.

"That's called hitting below the belt. Around here, it's considered unfair."

Hating the oh-so-feminine sound of that voice, Olivia slowly turned to face the woman. "And leaving him at the church to run off with his best man was?"

Shay strolled to a bench near the door and sat down, crossing her incredibly long legs. "You're right. I have no room to criticize."

After a moment, Olivia sat at the opposite end of the bench.

"You know, the best way to deal with getting your feelings hurt *isn't* seeing if you can hurt the other person more."

"I know."

"I'm sorry I was rude with you in the driveway. Just seeing Guthrie makes me feel so damn guilty that I go on the defensive. Kind of like you."

Except that Olivia didn't feel guilty for anything she'd done to him—well, at least, not until a minute ago. She felt guilty for her whole damn life before meeting him, for not having been a better person until circumstances left her no choice.

She wanted him to think she was a good person.

She wanted him to think she mattered.

Keeping her gaze focused on a hummingbird fluttering over the lavender blooms of the largest hosta, she flatly asked, "Does he still love you?"

"Is that what you think? And that makes you jealous?" Shay's voice grew richer, lovelier, with laughter.

Olivia scowled, and her fingers knotted to match the nerves deep in her stomach. "I'm *not* staying here."

"And that has what to do with being jealous?"

"I can't be jealous if I'm not involved, and I can't get involved when I'm going home to Georgia the first chance I get."

Shay laughed again. "Right. You're practically living with the handsomest, nicest, sweetest, most honorable man in the county, and from what I understand, you won't be going home for a good long while. Tell me just how you plan to stay uninvolved when you already care too much what he thinks of you."

Still staring at the bird, Olivia ignored her request and forced out her next question. "Do *you* still love *him?*"

She knew just from the change in the atmosphere that the other woman had gotten serious. When she couldn't resist any longer, she sneaked a peek and saw a sad, wistful expression on Shay's face.

"After my family, Guthrie was the most important person in my life for more years than I can count. He was a huge part of who I was—the brother I never had, my best friend, my lover, my first love. Losing him—leaving him—damn near destroyed me. It did destroy Easy and me." Giving Olivia an uneasy glance, she went on. "I love him for everything he was, but not the way a woman loves a man. I wish I did. It would be easier than—" Clamping her mouth shut, she looked away and left the sentence unfinished.

Easier than what? Olivia wondered, but she didn't probe.

After a still moment, Shay unfolded from the bench in one long, graceful, sensual move. "We'd better get inside before Mom comes looking for you. If she'd realized I was here, she would have already rescued you."

Reluctantly Olivia followed her inside and to the family room at the back of the house where tall windows looked out on a flagstone patio and pool. Back in the distance were the barn and several other buildings, and grouped in front of the barn were a half-dozen men. She wondered if Guthrie one of them, or if he'd already taken the bulldozer and headed for home. She wondered, if he *was* out there, if he would talk to her, accept her apology, forgive her.

She didn't have the nerve to find out.

Mary introduced her to everyone present, and Emma and Elly eagerly showed off their new friends, a pair of pampered poodles, good for nothing but wearing bows in their hair and yipping. Olivia disliked them on sight.

The afternoon dragged. She listened, smiled a lot and pretended to have a good time. When the meeting finally broke up, she was relieved to gather the children and go home. There she got dinner started, made a cake for dessert and left it to bake while she took the girls to the cabin to change into play clothes. By the time she got back, Guthrie had returned. She could feel it in the air.

He'd also left again, evidenced by the absence of the pickup out front and the note on the kitchen counter. *Gone out.*

She stared at the words so long and so hard that her vision blurred, that she was convinced she could close her eyes and reproduce an exact copy, from the top loop on the *G* to the abbreviated cross on the *t.*

He was so angry that he couldn't bring himself to sit down across from her at the table and eat food she'd prepared, so angry that he felt he had to leave his own home to escape her.

As a single tear slipped free, she crumpled the paper, then tried to surreptitiously wipe away the tear. She wasn't sneaky enough, though.

"What's wrong, Mama?" Emma asked from her seat at the table.

"Nothing, darlin'."

"You're crying," her daughter stubbornly accused.

"No, babe. I just got something in my eye."

"Yeah, tears."

Elly twisted in her seat to face the kitchen. "Where's Mr. Guthrie?"

"He won't be having dinner with us tonight."

"Why?"

"He had to go somewhere." Olivia pulled the cake from the oven and left it on a rack to cool, then served up dishes of sautéed chicken and sauce, vegetables and rice.

"Where'd he go?" Emma asked.

*Out.* For a drive to cool down? To have dinner someplace else—with someone else? On a last-minute date? "I don't know, Em. He didn't say."

"Why didn't he tell us he wasn't gonna be here?" Elly's indignation would have been comical if Olivia hadn't felt so shaken.

"Sweetheart, this may come as a surprise to you, but grown-ups don't have to clear things through you first."

Elly smiled winningly. "*You* do."

"That's because I'm your mother and I'm responsible for you. Guthrie doesn't owe you any explanations." Or her, either, she acknowledged, but that didn't keep her from wondering.

It didn't keep her from taking a chair out on the cabin porch once the girls were tucked in bed and snoring softly and watching, waiting, for his return.

It didn't keep her from wishing…

The night was quiet and cooled by a breeze out of the west that carried with it the faint fragrance of wildflowers. Stars dotted the night sky, more than she'd ever seen above Atlanta, with its ten-million-watt glow. Occasionally a soft whickering from the horses or the distant yip of a coyote broke the stillness, and once a pickup truck rolled past, sending up a cloud of dust in its wake. Long after it was gone, she could smell the dust and fancied she could feel it on her skin.

It was a perfectly peaceful setting. Too bad she felt only uneasiness.

Her eyes were growing heavy when suddenly she became aware of tires crunching on gravel. An instant later headlights stabbed through the darkness, swinging across the yard, the cabin and her as they turned through the gate.

When Guthrie turned off the engine, silence settled again, then was broken by the slamming of his door. She followed the shadow that was him as it moved onto the porch, then stopped in front of the door—merely stopped and stood there. Just when she thought that he would surely go inside, he turned away from the door, left the porch and started her way.

Now it was *her* turn to go inside, but her body refused to obey her brain's command. She watched him come closer and knew she owed him major apologies, but all she could think was how good he looked, how easily he moved, how glad she was that he was home—and alone.

He stopped at the foot of the steps, then eased onto the top one, sitting sideways so he could see her. She watched him settle, leaning his back against the carved balusters, stretching his long legs out in front of him, crossing them at the ankles. He wore jeans and a dark T-shirt, and his hat was nowhere in sight. Dressed like that, he could be any man doing any job in any part of the country, but she couldn't quite place him anywhere but here. He belonged here, as surely as she didn't.

The faint smell of cigarette smoke drifted across the few feet that separated them, and she ran through a mental list of places he could pick up the odor. At the home of a friend who smoked. In a restaurant. In a convenience store. At a bar. With a woman who counted more than cigarettes among her vices. Maybe even lighting up one of his own when the deed was done.

The image was so clichéd that it made her silently groan—and so unwelcome that it made her wince. She didn't know the first fact about his sex life in the last fourteen years, but she preferred to think it was on the *occasional* side. She liked to think he had too much respect for women, for the act, for himself, to indulge indiscriminately.

She wanted to think that when he thought about that, he thought about *her*.

Heaving a sigh, she opened her mouth, and they both spoke at once. "I'm sorry—" They both broke off.

After a moment, she began again. "I'm sorry for what I said. It was mean and uncalled-for. I'm sorry you felt you had to leave the house this evening to get away from us, and I'm sorry I was so sensitive, and I'm really sorry—" *really,* she repeated to herself in hopes of believing it "—that things didn't work out between you and Shay."

"I'm not." He tilted his head back and closed his eyes as the moon crept free of the cloud cover. One side of his face was touched with its clear, soft light. The other remained in shadow. "I think I finally figured out what I was supposed to say when that whole conversation got started."

"What?" she asked warily.

Opening his eyes only slightly, he turned toward her and smiled. "You said Shay and I had something in common— that we both thought you were useless, pampered and not good for much besides looking at."

That wasn't exactly the way she'd put it—*Good for adornment but not much else*—but his version was true, too. For much of their marriage, she'd been just one more aspect of David's image, and not much else. Just as he'd required a beautiful house in the right neighborhood, built by the right contractor and decorated by the right designer, he had also required the perfect wife—impeccable breeding, pretty if not drop-dead gorgeous, flawlessly put together, intelligent enough to know her place. He'd shown her off with the rest of his possessions, as if he had created her.

She was sorry to say he hadn't. Her parents had done that, and their parents before them. She'd been the tenth generation of women bred to be good marriage prospects.

"Not that there's anything wrong with looking at you," he remarked. "I enjoy it. But I think you wanted me to say that I had nothing in common with Shay, that I didn't think you were useless at all, that I admire the way you've coped with the changes in your life in the past month. It would be hard for any woman to wake up one day and find out that she'd lost everything, but it was especially hard for you because you had so damn much to lose. No one would have blam you if you crawled off somewhere and cried for a while, but instead you've made the best of it. You've done what needs to be done, even though it has to be done in a place and life as foreign to you as your old life would be to me, and I do admire you for it.''

Olivia flushed—with embarrassment? No, pure pleasure. But she wasn't sure which of his words were responsible for it. That he wasn't sorry things didn't work out with Shay? That he had nothing in common with her? That he liked looking at *her*—thin, pale, frazzled mother of two and no picture of pure, feminine sexuality like Shay? Or that he admired her?

Any of the above, she decided. *All* of the above.

"I think," he finished, "you just wanted a little reassurance, and instead I found something to criticize. Am I right?"

"Maybe. Probably." If he'd stood there, after running into gorgeous Shay, and told her he admired her, she would have felt all warm and fuzzy inside instead of insecure. Inadequate. Frightened.

Leaving the chair, she crouched near him and tucked her long skirt modestly around her. "So you don't think I'm a snob."

"No. Not at all." The moonlit side of his mouth quirked in a half smile. "I think you *used* to be a snob. But what you used to be doesn't matter much here. I mean, hell, you *used* to be rich and indulged and happily married, but your life has changed—"

"No." Her interruption was quiet and lingered between them on the night air. He looked at her, and she looked back, aware that he could read more on her face than she could on his.

"No to which part?" His voice was only a note or two lower than before, but suddenly it seemed more potent. More masculine. Incredibly intimate. "Rich?"

She shook her head.

"Indulged?"

Another shake.

He hesitated as if it mattered. "Happily married?"

Guthrie watched her wet her lips with the tip of her tongue, watched her nod in the shadows, and he settled in to consider her silent confession. Across from him, she moved, too, sitting on the floor, the wall against her back, waiting for him to speak.

He'd wondered about this practically from the beginning—whether she'd loved her husband, whether she cried for him at night, whether he should feel guilty for wanting her when she was so recently widowed. Now he had the chance to find out, if he could swallow the lump in his throat, if he could form coherent thoughts and sentences. "How married were you?"

"We had been separated for nearly a year. We had just decided to file for divorce when he died."

Separated nearly a year. Almost divorced. His first thought should have been regret that the divorce hadn't gone through before Miles died. Then maybe she would have had no claim on the ranch. But instead he found himself thinking, *Separated nearly a year, almost divorced. A green light for whatever fantasies he wanted to indulge. He could want her without guilt.*

Not that the guilt had stopped him from wanting her anyway.

"What went wrong?" he asked quietly, evenly, as if they were just making conversation and not talking about something vitally important.

"Everything. David and I never should have been anything more than a—a fling. I was twenty. We'd been dating four or five months when..." She took a shaky breath. "I got pregnant. My parents thought we should marry. David thought I was as suitable as anyone else he might find, and an association with my family could only help his career. So...we got married. Two months later I lost the baby."

"I'm sorry." The words felt inadequate—what could possibly ease the pain of losing a child?—but they were all he had to offer, and she accepted them with a nod before going on.

"David was happy to continue with the marriage. It was all I could do to get out of bed in the morning, to face each new day without wishing it were the last, so we let things continue. We weren't happy. We weren't unhappy. We just *were*."

Off to the west, lightning sparked across the sky, and he realized that the wind had picked up and the temperature had dropped a few degrees. Thunder rumbled, but it was distant, more an impression of sound than an actual sound. He listened to it until it disappeared, then asked, "Why didn't you end the marriage then?"

A thick, black cloud crept across the moon and blocked the stars, making the night darker, more familiar. With her heavy sigh, she seemed to find some comfort in the closeness. "It was easier not to. Ending it would have meant one of us moving out, finding a place to live, starting a brand-new life. We wouldn't have been part of a couple anymore. We would have lost friends, wouldn't have had someone to share dinner or movies or weekends with. Instead of being Olivia Miles, David's wife, I would have been just Olivia."

*Just Olivia.* His smile was thin. Married or divorced, rich or poor, she would never be *just Olivia*. It simply wasn't possible.

"So you drifted along," he said, "and you got pregnant again, and after the twins were born, you drifted apart." Even *further* apart. "What made you finally decide to divorce?"

Lightning illuminated her slight smile. "I literally woke up one morning and thought, 'There's got to be more to life than this.' I wanted... Passion. Commitment. Devotion. I wanted to be wanted for myself, not because I was pregnant, not because marrying me would accomplish some goal. I wanted the girls to expect to marry for love, to never settle for less. I wanted them to *feel*. *I* wanted to feel." Her voice softened with faint self-mocking. "I wanted to matter."

And he'd made her feel as if she didn't. Though there was no way he could have known that such a beautiful, intelligent woman could possibly feel insignificant, he felt like a bastard anyway.

She continued, an unsteady quaver underscoring her words. "David could have replaced me—did replace me—with any of a half-dozen women. I wanted someone who might consider me irreplaceable." She glanced in his direction. "That's not so much to ask, is it?"

His voice didn't want to work. It came out thick, hoarse, barely recognizable. "No. That's not so much." It was no more, he suspected, than he could offer. If she would stay. If he could convince her to stay.

The lightning flashed again, followed by thunder. On the freshening wind, he could smell badly needed rain. He hoped that was all they got—no hail, high winds or tornadoes. Just sweet, life-giving rain.

"I love storms," she murmured. "I used to sit on the porch, where I'd stay dry under the roof, and watch them move in with all their power and fury, then ease on out, leaving everything little the worse for wear—usually."

He shifted to sit beside her, the logs rough against his back, her bare arm warm against his. No sooner had he settled, though, than a cry came from inside.

"Mommy?"

She called through the screen door. "I'm out here, babe."

Elly came outside, wearing her nightgown and dragging a stuffed dog by its ear. Her hair stood on end and she looked extremely ill-tempered as she crawled onto Olivia's lap. "I'm not scared," she announced, talking through a yawn. "It's just that the storm waked me."

"Before you can count to five, Emma will be here," Olivia said softly as she settled Elly more comfortably. "And she's not the least bit shy about being scared."

Sure enough, in seconds Emma's shriek, accompanied by running footsteps, split the quiet. "Mommy, Mommy, it's a tornado, a tornado's coming and we're all gonna be blowed away and we'll never see Atlanta again! Mommy! Elly! Where are you? Did it already get you? *Mommy!*"

Elly lifted her head from Olivia's shoulder. "We're out here, Em. Don't be a scaredy-cat. It's not a tornado, is it, Mr. Guthrie? It's just a little ol' thunder and lightning storm, and nobody's scared of it but great big ol' crybabies."

Emma burst through the door just as lightning flashed with the brilliance and ear-shattering crack that indicated a nearby strike. Guthrie hoped it hit one of those oaks he hadn't gotten to with the dozer this afternoon and split it right down to the ground.

Emma leaped over Olivia's legs and dived into the few inches of space that separated her from Guthrie. Her small body was trembling uncontrollably and her wails were pretty damn ear-shattering themselves. He lifted her, intending to pass her over to her mother, but she wrapped her thin arms around his neck, pressed her face against his chest and held on for all she was worth.

He wasn't sure what to do. He'd never had to comfort a hysterical five-year-old before and, if asked, he'd say he didn't have a clue. But his arm just naturally went around her tiny waist, and his other hand found its way to stroke her hair. "It's okay, Emma," he murmured, ducking his head so his mouth was near her ear. "It's not a tornado. It's just a little wind and rain, and it'll be gone in no time."

"It'll blowed us all away!" she whimpered.

"No, it won't. I've lived here all my life, and I've never been blowed—blown away once. It's just wind and rain—nothing to worry about."

Lightning crackled from one edge of the sky to the other, leaving a faintly acrid odor behind, and the entire porch vibrated with the subsequent thunder. Still clinging tightly to him, Emma was whispering frantically. He strained to make out the words.

"Just a little wind and rain…nothing to worry about…gone in no time. Just wind and rain…but wind can blow you away, and rain can drowned you."

He lifted her chin, brushed her hair back. Her face was

pale, her eyes wide, frightened shadows. "Do you want to go inside?"

Her panic increased. "Oh, no! What if the cabin blowed away with us inside?"

"Like in *The Wizard of Oz!*" Elly said excitedly. "And then we could land on the yellow brick road, and the cabin could fall on that wicked woman at the thing today, and everyone would say, 'Hooray, the witch is dead!'"

Emma sneaked a peek at the silly faces her sister was making and softly, almost inaudibly, giggled. Her tears forgotten, she plopped down on Guthrie's lap and unselfconsciously pulled his arms closer around her. "She wasn't a witch," she disagreed. "I liked her."

"Of course you liked her. She told you you were—" Elly shifted into a falsetto and bobbed her head from side to side "—such a pretty little girl. She told *me* I was a stinker."

"You *are* a stinker," Olivia pointed out. "You work hard at being one. If Sha—if she had told *you* you were pretty, you probably would've kicked her or something."

"I'd've popped her in the nose."

"I'd've liked to have seen that," Guthrie murmured, then he grunted as Olivia's elbow found its way into his ribs. "Hey, what's that for?"

"Don't encourage her. She's got enough mischief in her as it is. Look, kids." She gave him a glance that included him among their number. "Here comes the rain."

They heard it first, pushed by the wind, then felt the immediate temperature drop that preceded it. It fell in sheets, advancing over the trees, across the grass, hitting the far end of the porch seconds before continuing to their end. It puddled and splashed, blew under the eaves, dampened their clothes and saturated the ground, and it made quiet conversation impossible.

The lightning and thunder moved on with the leading edge of the storm, and, as quickly as it had come, the rain followed. One moment it was a torrent. The next it was reduced to drips.

After a time, Olivia stirred. "I think it's safe for all little girls to go back to bed, don't you?"

Elly scrambled to her feet. "All right, Olivia dear. But, you know, you should get to bed soon, too. Morning comes early 'round here. G'night, Mr. Guthrie."

"Good night, Elly."

Emma got to her feet, straightened her gown, then gave Olivia a hug. "Good night, Mama. I love you."

"I love you, too, babe. You, too, El."

Emma started to join Elly at the door, but abruptly she turned back to face him. She looked so serious—but then, she usually did. "Mr. Guthrie, if you had a little girl who was afraid of things, would you tell her she's nothing but a big dumb coward who deserves to be scared?"

Beside him, Olivia stiffened. He thought of their conversation last night—*David wasn't a very fatherly father. They did their best to love him, but he didn't make it easy*—and thought how incredibly lucky the bastard was to be dead. If he weren't, and Guthrie came face-to-face with him, he just might have to kill him.

"No, I wouldn't, Emma," he said quietly.

"Why not?"

"My mother was a lot older than you, but she was afraid of storms. Miss Mary is afraid of horses. My father was afraid of the doctor giving him shots. But none of them were cowards. Everyone's afraid of something."

"Mama's afraid of frogs and lizards and toads," she said solemnly, "and Elly's afraid of the dentist. What are *you* afraid of?"

*This.* This coziness with Olivia and the kids. This feeling that they could be a family. This *desire* of his to turn them into a family.

But no, he admitted. That wasn't right. Those things didn't frighten him at all. He suspected that he and Olivia and whatever babies they might have could make one hell of a family for Emma and Elly.

He was afraid of wanting it, needing it, coming to believe

he could have it, only to find out that he couldn't. That whatever passion, commitment and devotion he could offer Olivia wouldn't be enough to make her forget about going home. That whatever love he could give wouldn't be enough to make her stay.

He was afraid he might come to find her—all three *hers*—irreplaceable and lose them anyway.

"Mr. Guthrie?" Emma prompted.

His smile was taut and thin. "You have to promise not to tell anyone, okay?" When she nodded, he leaned closer and whispered, "I'm afraid of mice."

Her big eyes rounded. "*Mice?* But they're so little and you're so big."

"I know. Silly, isn't it?"

"No. No sillier than bein' afraid of anything else. Good night, Mr. Guthrie." She swiftly bent, pressed a kiss to his chin, then scampered inside with Elly.

"I'd better get them tucked." Olivia got to her feet, dusted her skirt, then stopped at the screen door. "I'll be right back."

He sat motionless, feeling strangely... He didn't know *what* he felt. Just that it was sweeter than anything he'd felt in a long time. And dangerous. Undeniably dangerous.

The upstairs lights cast distorted reflections across the wet ground. It was easy to imagine Olivia settling the girls into their beds, giving them kisses, making them feel safe. Any minute now she would turn the lights off and come back downstairs, come back outside and maybe sit beside him again, close enough to touch, close enough to entice, close enough... Too close.

Abruptly he got to his feet and left the porch. His strides were long, his pace quick, as he moved—hell, damn near ran—across the yard to his own house. He didn't have a clue what she would make of his disappearing act. He only knew it was for the best. Because if he'd stayed, if she had come near him, if she'd touched him or even looked at him, by the time the sun came up in the morning, they would have moved this partnership of theirs to a whole other level. And that would have put him one giant step closer to the kind of future he'd always wanted…

Or given him three times the sorrow that he'd always lived with.

# Chapter 8

Sunday was unforgivably hot. Olivia stood at the kitchen sink, mindlessly washing pans from this morning's breakfast, and dreamed of a place with cool water, cooler shade and a few hours of unbreachable privacy. If she could transplant herself and Guthrie to such a haven, she would guarantee that this time he wouldn't slip off without so much as a goodbye.

This time, since it was her fantasy, she would give him no place to escape to. There would be just him and her, cool shade and water, and no consequences.

That was what she needed—a hot, greedy, no-strings affair. The sort of affair David had indulged in through the last years of their marriage. The sort of affair neither she nor Guthrie seemed to have the capacity for. Oh, but if they did...

She gave a great sigh as he walked into the kitchen. He left his glass on the counter next to the sink, then took up position a few feet away. "Why so blue?"

"I'm not blue," she lied even as she answered herself honestly. *Because I'm not easy. Because you're honorable. Be-*

*cause we're both forever sort of people and, damn it, our forevers are in different states.*

"As soon as you finish up there, let's go into town," he suggested. "I'll show you around, and we can have dinner, pick up groceries and maybe swing by Miz Wilson's on the way home."

Miz Wilson. Though Olivia hadn't connected all the names to the proper faces at Mary's house yesterday, she was fairly sure Wilson hadn't been one of them. But why else would it sound familiar? She hadn't met anyone else besides Guthrie's lawyer, who was certainly no *Miz.*

Then the name clicked. *Where do you go to buy a dog?* she'd asked last week, and he'd replied, *You don't. You go by old Miz Wilson's in town. She's Heartbreak's unofficial animal shelter.*

"Why would we want to go by Miz Wilson's?" she asked suspiciously.

"Just to see what kind of animals are looking for a home."

"You've got three barn cats, four horses, five bulls, 140 mama cows, plus the calves. You don't need any more animals around here."

"I don't," he agreed, "but Elly does. She wants a dog more'n anything in the whole world, except a pony and maybe a four-wheeler."

Olivia turned back to her pot scrubbing. "I can't afford a dog right now. There are vet bills and food bills and—"

"He won't need a vet unless he gets sick. I can pick up the vaccines at the feed store and give them myself. And a bag of dog food every week or two isn't going to make much of a difference on the grocery bill."

"What about when we leave here? I don't know where we'll be living. They may not be allowed to keep him, and having to give him up would break their hearts."

Suddenly he found the wood floor so incredibly interesting that the words he mumbled practically got lost down there. "So don't leave."

Her heart slid into a faster rhythm and a quivery feeling

settled in the pit of her stomach. She very carefully rinsed the pot and set it in the dish drainer, then dried her hands and faced him. "Don't leave?" she echoed in a breathy voice.

He scraped his boot toe back and forth along the seam joining two planks. "You don't have to."

Was he actually suggesting that they stay? Did he *want* them to stay? The possibility was staggering.

"I—I promised the girls. I promised myself."

"You made that promise before you ever saw the place. You made it assuming that you wouldn't like it here—that the girls wouldn't like it here. But they might. Elly does. Emma might learn." Finally he met her gaze. The expression in his dark eyes was equal measures wariness, shyness and something she couldn't quite identify. Something fierce. Something that warmed her and frightened her, that made her feel secure—and *in*secure as hell. "You have a place here, Olivia. You have property, a house, people who want to be your friends—*real* friends who won't turn their backs when you need them. You have nothing back in Atlanta."

Did *he* want to be her friend—or something more? Did *she* want to be *his* something more?

Yes. No. For a while. She wanted that steamy, no-strings affair. She wanted his affection, his passion, his body. But she didn't—did *not*—want to fall in love with a man whose place would never be *her* place. She didn't want to be forced into a choice between the man she loved and the home that was a soul-deep, through-and-through part of her. She couldn't begin to even imagine living the rest of her life so far from home or raising her daughters as anything other than by-the-grace-of-God Southerners. She didn't *want* to imagine it.

"It's our *home*."

"Someplace else can be home if you give it a chance."

She shook her head numbly. "It would never be the same. You know what I'm talking about. You feel the same connection to this place that we feel to Georgia."

With a grim nod, he acknowledged that she was right.

Some small traitorous part of her was sorry he did. Some part wanted more arguments, wanted to be convinced.

Resting his hands on the edge of the counter behind him, he returned to their original conversation. "So we'll tell the kids the dog is mine. That way they won't expect to take him with them when they leave."

She needed a moment to refocus her thoughts, to ease the anxiety settled in her chest. "And what will you do with him once they're gone?"

"Give him a home." He gave her a hard, unflinching look and a promise. "*I'm* not going anywhere, Olivia. I'll always be here."

Most definitely a promise.

After letting his words sink in, he pushed away from the counter. "I'll be in the office. When you're ready to go, let me know."

She watched him until he disappeared through the office door, then slowly turned back to the sink. The girls were playing in the backyard—at least, Elly was, galloping an imaginary horse across the grass. Emma was curled in the corner of an old metal glider, once painted green, and talking to her doll.

Elly likes it here, Guthrie had said, and Emma might learn. He was right about Elly, probably right about Emma, but they were kids. They were adaptable. The question was, could *she* learn to like it here?

She could. The weather was hot, but she was used to that in Georgia. There was a certain beauty to the rolling countryside, the stands of timber interspersed with pasture. While a big city like Atlanta offered all the conveniences, a little place like Heartbreak had a charm of its own. The people she'd met so far were genuinely friendly and welcoming, and Guthrie... Too often when he was around, she found herself short of breath and in need of something cool. Enough said.

But whether she could learn to like it wasn't really the question, either. Could she live here forever? Could she *not* live in Atlanta forever? Could she ever learn to appreciate scrub oaks over sugar pines? Honeysuckle instead of wisteria? Country twangs over soft Southern drawls? Could she ever walk into the cabin and feel as if it were her home rather than temporary lodging? Could she ever go to sleep without missing Atlanta, ever wake up without expecting to see magnolias, live oaks and Spanish moss outside her window?

Could she ever go one day—just one twenty-four-hour day—without wishing she were back in the South where she belonged?

She honestly didn't know. All she could say was it hadn't happened yet. Her homesickness was as strong today as it'd been her first night out of the state. She *wanted* to go home.

Finishing with the dishes, she dried her hands, rubbed in a dollop of lotion, then went to the office. Guthrie had left the door open and was sitting at the desk, entering figures into the computer. He glanced at her, but didn't interrupt his work. She didn't speak, but instead moved to the wall where a group of photographs hung.

After a moment, he saved the file, then came to stand beside her, identifying each photo. "That's my great-grandfather. He came from back east—somewhere in Pennsylvania and settled this land. That's my grandparents. My parents right after they got married, just before I was born, with me when I was two years old. That's my dad just before he died, and that's the last picture of Mom before she died."

"You look like your father."

"With my mother's eyes."

After giving each photograph its due, she quietly asked, "Why no photos of Ethan?"

Immediately he stiffened and his mouth formed a thin line. "I've got some."

"But not on display anywhere. I've cleaned every room in this house. I would have seen them."

He stared at her, and she stared back, keeping her gaze level and steady. After a time, he turned away, opened the bottom desk drawer and began pulling out framed photos one at a time. "That one went in the drawer when he got arrested

the first time. This one came off the wall when he got arrested
the tenth time. I put this one away when he took off the
summer after his junior year and never bothered to call even
once and let Mom know he was all right. I put this one away
when he took off again after he graduated, and this one when
he disappeared after she died, and this one when he came
back only to ask for money because he was in trouble, and
this one—'' he picked up the last frame, then tossed it on the
desk ''—when you showed up.''

The last was a family photo—Guthrie and his mother as
dark as Ethan and his father were fair—and one was a high
school graduation picture. The others were shots of the two
brothers together, some professional, the rest snapshots. In
several of them, Ethan was gazing up at his older, bigger
brother with something close to hero worship in his blue eyes.

And now that same brother wanted him out of his life forever.

She gathered the frames and carefully returned them to the
drawer, then forced a cheerful smile. ''I'm ready for that tour
of Heartbreak, if your offer still stands. I just need to get my
purse from the cabin.''

''I'll get the kids and meet you at the truck.''

It took her only a moment to cross the yard to the cabin,
then return. Elly was already buckled into the back seat, and
Guthrie was helping Emma with her lap belt. What a difference, Olivia thought as she settled in. Little more than a week
ago, her younger daughter had ordered him to keep his distance. Now she accepted his assistance as if it were the most
natural thing in the world. Last night she'd turned to him for
comfort—something she'd learned at a tender age to never
expect from her father—and had even given him a kiss, something else she'd learned didn't go over well with David.

When the opportunity to return home arose, how hard
would it be for her to say goodbye to him?

How hard would it be for Olivia?

The drive into town that had seemed interminable last week
was pleasurable today. Guthrie pointed out the occasional

neighbors, mentioning a few names she remembered from the Ladies' Auxiliary meeting, and he talked to the kids with an ease that seemed as old as it was new.

It was an all too enjoyable way to pass the miles.

"Where did Heartbreak get its name?" she asked when they stopped at the intersection of Cody and Main Streets.

"About a hundred years ago, a fellow from South Carolina came out here to make his fortune in oil, leaving his fiancée behind while he built a house, a town—named Flora in her honor—and an empire. When he'd accomplished all three, he brought her out here for the wedding. She stayed two days, declared that she could never live so far from the comforts of home and all things civilized, and boarded the next train headed east. With the love of his life *out* of his life, he lost interest in the house, the town and the empire, and before long he lost it all. Folks decided to rename the town Heartbreak in his memory."

"So he died of a broken heart. How romantic."

"Not exactly. He took up cowboying for a while, acquired some cattle and some land and started a ranch. He had eight children with his first wife and six with the second, and was working on the first with his pretty young third wife when he died—" he glanced at the girls in the rearview mirror "—in the saddle at the age of eighty-three."

Olivia smiled dryly. "Charming story."

"Most folks around here think so, though not Jim Stephens. His granddaddy was the oldest of those fourteen kids."

"So you almost married into the founding family of Heartbreak." She kept her voice steady, her tone conversational. If he could learn to talk about Shay and their near-marriage as part of a normal conversation, then maybe they would lose some of their power to hurt him. Maybe he could accept what had happened, deal with whatever he felt and find some sort of closure.

She wanted him to find some closure.

His fingers tightened around the steering wheel, and for a time he said nothing, did nothing but drive. Finally, though, he pulled to the side of the road, eased his grip and said, "Yeah. Almost."

But instead he'd joined that first Stephens's other family—men whose loves of their lives left their lives.

While she reflected unhappily on that, he turned his attention to the kids. "Emma, Elly, this is where you'll be going to school this fall. You'll be in Miss Gardner's class or Miss Barefoot's. Their rooms are on the end right there." He gave Olivia an oblique look. "They're good teachers."

"I'm sure they are," she blandly agreed. "With college degrees and everything."

With a faint smile, he pushed his hat back. Two simple acts, and they made him look younger, handsomer, more charming. Like a brash young cowboy sure of himself and his world. "Smart ass," he murmured so low the girls couldn't hear.

Looking out the side window as he pulled onto the street again, she gave in to the smile that tugged at her lips.

The tour didn't take long. After all, Heartbreak *was* a small town. But there was more to it than she'd realized—blocks of neat houses with tidy yards and neighborly porches; a nice park with a stream running through it, picnic tables and playground equipment; playing fields for football, baseball and soccer, kid-size and regulation; and more churches than she'd imagined a small town could support.

They wound up back on Main Street, claiming the only available space in the block where two of Heartbreak's three restaurants were located. The diner across the street, where they'd gone for ice cream after meeting with the lawyer, appeared packed. The Heartbreak Café, a few doors down from their space, was almost as crowded.

Guthrie held the door for them, and Emma and Elly raced inside to the only available booth. They slid in on the same bench, Elly on her knees, craning her neck to look around, Emma on her bottom, ankles crossed, hands folded on the tabletop.

The girls' choice had been automatic, Olivia knew. On the

rare occasions David had accompanied them to a restaurant, he'd made a point of sitting far enough away that they couldn't spill anything or touch him with grimy hands. Still, it left her with one rather cozy bench to share with Guthrie.

And the mere prospect sent a tingle down her spine.

She slid in all the way to the wall, he stayed on the edge, and they still met in the middle. His shirt was soft, his arm muscled, his skin warm. She felt…ah, jeez, damn near giddy. Like a teenage girl with an adolescent crush.

Like a full-grown woman with starry-eyed dreams.

A waitress brought menus and ice water and angled for an introduction. Guthrie gave a simple one. *This is Olivia Miles and her daughters, Emma and Elly.* He didn't mention that they were partners, or friends, or anything else.

Once they'd placed their orders, a half-dozen other customers stopped by for hellos and introductions. Small-town living, Olivia reminded herself even as she wished for a little privacy.

"Do you know ever'body in this whole town?" Elly asked after their last visitor retreated to his own table.

"I guess I do," Guthrie replied. "I've lived here all my life."

"That's a lot of people. I lived all my life in Atlanta, but I don't know near that many people."

"You can meet 'em when we go back," Emma pointed out.

"I don't wanna go back. I like Oklahoma."

Olivia ignored the subtle shift of Guthrie's elbow against her ribs.

"What's not to like about it?" he asked with an innocent look. "It's a nice place with nice people and—"

"And it's not Georgia," Emma finished for him. "We're going back to Georgia. Mama promised, and she *always* keeps her promises. Only bad people make promises and don't keep 'em."

"Well, I guess we know what category that puts me in,

don't we?" Shay Stephens asked brittlely as she delivered the girls' burgers and fries.

Olivia was surprised to see her. Guthrie had told her that Shay ran a café, but it hadn't occurred to her that it was *this* café. After all, he'd chosen of his own free will to come here. "Hello, Shay."

"Welcome to my humble establishment. It's not much, but it's—" she gave the place a look, then smiled tautly "—shabby. And it's all mine—well, mine and the bank's."

It wasn't much to look at, Olivia privately agreed. The benches were covered in turquoise vinyl patched with black duct tape. The chairs were mismatched, the wood floor scarred, the walls in bad need of a paint job. The menus were grease stained and torn, and judging by the temperature, the air conditioner was losing its fight against the summer heat. But... "If the food tastes half as good as it smells, it must be fantastic. Are you the cook?"

Beside her Guthrie made a noise that might have been a choked-off snort. Shay acknowledged it snidely. "That's his less-than-eloquent way of saying that you could give me a pot full of water and a blazing fire and I still couldn't make it boil right. Of course, he thinks I can't do much of anything right, don't you, Guthrie?"

Guthrie felt the heat creep up his neck. You hold a grudge to beat all grudges, Olivia had told him a few nights ago, and she was right. He'd held this one for fourteen years—and why? Because Easy and Shay had betrayed him? Because he'd loved them both and they'd ruined his life?

Both were true in the beginning. When they'd run off together, he'd lost everything that was important to him—his soon-to-be-wife, his best friend, his whole damn future. He'd been hurt, angry, humiliated. He'd felt betrayed and abandoned, and all the pity heaped on him by well-meaning friends hadn't helped.

He'd gotten over loving Shay and Easy, but somewhere along the way he should have gotten past losing them. He should have let all that hostility go. He didn't want to be friends again, didn't want to trust them again, but he didn't need to hate them. Doing so only made Olivia think less of him.

He was coming to care way too much what Olivia thought of him.

Drawing a deep breath, he raised his gaze from the tabletop. "I imagine there are a number of things you do right." His voice was steady, his tone not friendly but not overtly hostile, either. It wasn't a great start, but it was a start.

Then he ruined it with the next sharp, sly words that just sort of popped out. "But not *right* enough to hold on to Easy."

She stood motionless for a heartbeat, maybe two, then walked away. Next to him Olivia sighed. "For a moment there you were almost civil."

"I was trying."

"I know." She laid her hand over his, gave it a reassuring squeeze. "Have you ever considered…" She waited until the waitress served their dinners—roast beef with all the trimmings—and was gone again to finish. "That maybe they didn't run off to have their fun? Maybe they were in love."

He watched as the kids dipped fries in ketchup, both rolling them counterclockwise, nibbling almost daintily, then reaching at the same time for another. He didn't need the distraction to consider her question. The answer was no, plain and simple. He'd always believed Easy had seduced Shay away from him, that maybe she'd had cold feet about the wedding and his best man had taken advantage of it. He'd thought they had hurt him deliberately, thought they were selfish and self-centered, that they'd thrown away twenty years of friendship for a little sleazy sex.

Had he been wrong?

Olivia apparently thought so. He didn't know what he thought.

*Have you ever considered that maybe…they were in love?* Part of him wanted to deny it. He and Shay had been together since they were fifteen. Easy had been nothing more than a brother to her.

But hadn't his own relationship with her been nothing more than brotherly until that summer their hormones had come to life with a vengeance? And if he could fall in love with her, why couldn't Easy? And why shouldn't she love him back?

Because she'd sworn she loved Guthrie. But if she could love him, she could love Easy, too. And if she'd discovered she did after she was engaged to *him*, what would she do? Try to deny it? Pretend it didn't exist? Redouble her devotion to Guthrie?

And what would Easy do? Leave town? Remove himself from temptation? Risk his fool neck in every rodeo that came along?

He took an uneven breath. "Hell."

Olivia's smile was gentle. "That possibility changes everything, doesn't it?"

It didn't make what they'd done all right. It didn't excuse the fact that they didn't come to him and explain what had happened. It sure as hell didn't excuse the way they'd run off together like cowards. But—if it was true, if Olivia was right—it made it, if not forgivable, then understandable.

Except that it wasn't easy being understanding, not after fourteen years of nursing a grudge. "If they were in love—" he gave the last two words an ugly twist "—it sure as hell didn't last."

"They were together eight years. My marriage didn't last that long. Besides, how *could* it last? You would have been a terrible burden for them."

"Gee, thanks."

"Don't get sarcastic. We're aiming for civility here, remember?" Then she went on. "What I meant was they would have felt terribly guilty over what they did to you. Every time they looked at each other, they would have been reminded that the only way they could be together was to hurt you. You were his best friend. You were one of the men she loved. It couldn't have been easy for them."

Why did she care so much whether it'd been easy for *them?* he wondered as they turned their attention to their meal. At least they'd had each other. *He'd* been left alone to cancel the wedding, return the gifts, endure the whispers and comments and outright pity. *He* was the one who'd spent what was supposed to be his wedding night trying to drown his sorrows in a bottle of champagne, while they'd been *enjoying* their way to the Dakotas.

Now they had all wound up alone. Easy had never come home again, and Guthrie and Shay couldn't even speak. So much for twenty years of loving each other like family.

"I know it was tough for you, too."

He glanced at Olivia. She'd already finished eating and was watching him as he toyed with his carrots. Laying the fork aside, he turned slightly on the bench to make looking back easier, and then he did just that—he looked. For a long time. Just looked.

And wanted.

She'd been fragile-flower pretty the day she'd tracked him down behind the barn and announced that she was the new owner of Harris Ranch. In the short time since, she had changed. Her pale porcelain skin had a bit of color now, just a pale wash of gold from her hours in the sun. The desperate, panicked look was gone from her eyes, and he hadn't seen that thin, heartsick smile in days. She was more than pretty now. She was closer to beautiful than he'd ever been.

She folded her hands together—nails clipped short, unpainted, incredibly soft skin starting to show the first calluses of hard work. Pampered hands that were slowly turning into capable hands. "At least Shay and Easy got to be someplace else, where no one knew what had happened. You had to deal with it here, where you know everyone—where everyone knew what they'd done."

He gave her half a dry smile. "I wondered when I was going to make the list for your sympathy."

"I didn't know you wanted my sympathy."

"Among other things."

"What other things?"

He stared at her. "Ask that question again when we're alone, and I'll show you." His voice came out low, barely a whisper of sound to each word, but she understood. He saw it in the widening of her eyes, in the flush that tinged her cheeks.

Slowly, dazedly, she shook her head from side to side. "I'm leaving here as soon as I can."

"It can't be soon enough to stop me from wanting..." In the very next heartbeat was already too late.

They stared at each other, one long still moment sliding into another, until Elly's voice broke the spell. "Can we go now? We're all done eating, and there's nothin' to do. Let's go home and go swimmin' or something. Can we, Mr. Guthrie?"

*Or something.* For damn sure.

He left a tip on the table, then took the check to the register while Olivia herded the kids to the door. Even stiffer and more awkward than before, Shay announced the total, counted out his change and started to turn away. Feeling pretty damn awkward himself, he spoke her name. When she stopped, he quietly asked, "Do you ever hear from him?"

The look she gave him was sharp and startled. For an instant there was such pain in her brown eyes—such heartache. Olivia was right, Guthrie acknowledged grimly. At some point, Shay had fallen in love with Easy, and with an intensity that she'd never felt for *him*.

The knowledge should sting, should refuel fourteen years of resentment and anger. All the times she'd professed undying love to him, it had really been Easy she wanted, Easy she loved. All the lies she'd told, all the pain she'd caused, all the trouble and heartache and pity...

But it didn't stir his anger. In fact, he found some comfort in knowing that she hadn't left him on a whim, that there'd been more to her running off with Easy than just sex.

Noticing that her hands were unsteady, she folded her arms across her chest and tucked her fingers tightly against her body before giving his question a wary answer. "No. Not in six years."

He suspected she could be more exact than that—years, months, days, minutes. He knew the exact hour when he'd realized that he'd been jilted. He remembered looking at his watch and thinking that his entire life had been ripped apart at eleven minutes after seven on the nineteenth of April. "Why did you leave him?"

The tension that held her rigid increased a degree or two. "I didn't. *He* left *me.* For a pretty little barrel racer from Hermosa, South Dakota. Before that, it was a pretty little redhead from Bonham, Texas. And before that it was a pretty little rodeo queen from Pima, Arizona. He left often, for any woman who didn't remind him of me. He got to where he couldn't even bear the sight of me, because I reminded him of *you.*"

"I—" He hesitated, thought of Olivia waiting at the door, then forced the words out. "I'm sorry."

"You would be." Her laugh was dry and mocking, and it disappeared as quickly as it came. "It's not your fault. We have no one but ourselves to blame."

That was a statement not even Olivia would expect him to argue. With a nod, he pocketed his change and started toward the door. He hadn't gone more than a few paces when she spoke.

"Guthrie?" Her gaze slid past him to the door. "Ethan did you a favor. This one's worth keeping."

He glanced at Olivia, smiling down at the girls, all womanly and soft and beautiful, and his body responded. His breath quickened, his chest tightened and a hard knot of pure, sweet lust formed deep inside. "I know," he agreed quietly.

He just didn't know if he *could* keep her. She had nothing in Atlanta, he'd pointed out this morning—no family, no friends, no man. No place to live, no job, no guarantee that she'd be happy.

But what did she have in Heartbreak? A cabin that hadn't been built for luxury. A menial housekeeping job. A share in a ranch that was just barely self-sustaining when times were good.

And him.

It wasn't a whole lot more than the nothing Atlanta had to offer. Heartbreak, Harris Ranch and Guthrie Harris himself, all combined, weren't much of a prize, especially to a woman accustomed to so much more. But he could give her things all the money in the world couldn't buy—respect, affection, devotion. He could be a good father to her daughters. He could be a good husband to her.

He could love her.

And she could give him a whole new meaning for *heartbreak*.

And this time, he acknowledged as he followed her and the girls outside, he might not recover.


Wednesday was the hottest, stillest day Olivia could recall. Not even the slightest breeze ruffled the air. With no wind to help them along, a line of thin, insubstantial clouds seemed stuck in the sky in air too thick to simply drift. The birds were silent in the trees, and the horses were lethargic in the pasture. Emma and Elly had declared it too hot to play outside and, last time she'd checked, had fallen asleep in a heap on the living-room floor with the puppy they'd named Skippy snuggled between them.

All in all, it was an eerie afternoon.

Olivia used the cuff of her work gloves to wipe the sweat from her brow, then reached for another tomato plant. Mary had delivered a truckload of plants this morning, fresh from her own greenhouse—tomatoes and bell peppers, plus flowers of every variety imaginable. After investing much of Monday and Tuesday to cleaning out overgrown flower beds, Olivia had intended to invest a few of her hard-earned dollars on bedding plants this weekend, so she'd been grateful for their neighbor's generosity. She just wished the day was better suited for working. She wasn't sure which was going to wilt faster in this furnace—the plants or her.

The sound of a roughly idling engine drew her attention to the road that circled behind the barn. Guthrie had gone out to check cattle after lunch. She hadn't expected him back for several hours, but maybe something had come up—some vital portion of the fence was down or he'd found some cow that needed doctoring. If there was one thing she'd learned, there wasn't a lot of *routine* to a rancher's routine.

The one-ton truck came to a stop beside the barn, then silence settled again as the engine was cut off. Absently tamping dirt around the base of a nice, bushy plant, she watched as he climbed out, took his hat off to wipe his forehead, then started toward her.

A slow smile began forming in spite of her efforts to stop it. It was a smile she found herself wearing every time he came around lately, sweet with appreciation and awareness and plain old pleasure. She *liked* looking at him, liked being around him and daydreaming about more. Looking at more of him. Being a part of him.

He crouched on the opposite side of the plants. She offered him her glass, and he took a long drink of cool water before setting it between them. "It's too damn hot to be working outside today."

Her gaze moved slowly over him. His face was flushed and damp. His T-shirt was stained with sweat, and his arms gleamed with it. All that moisture made her throat go dry when she tried to swallow. "Are you knocking off early because of the heat?"

"Because of the weather. Some of the animals are antsy, and I don't like the way the sky looks."

She tore her gaze away from him for a glance at the sky. It was a thin, pale blue, as if the heat had leached the color right out, leaving only the lightest of washes behind. "Doesn't look like much," she remarked.

"Look behind you."

Twisting, she obeyed, then her eyes widened. The clouds in the northwest stretched upward thousands of feet and ranged in color from dusky gray to pure, brilliant white.

Though fat and puffy as they climbed, they were virtually flat across the bottom, and the front edge formed an impressive wedge.

"I wouldn't recommend planting any more of those," Guthrie said. "If that anvil cloud doesn't change direction, we're liable to get a hell of a storm with enough hail to destroy your whole garden."

"Should I dig up what I've already planted?"

He looked at the five plants, then at the clouds, then her. "If you don't want to risk losing them. Where are the kids?"

"Asleep in your living room." She moved to her knees and carefully worked the nearest plant free of the ground and its metal cage and returned it to the pot it had come in. Leaving her, Guthrie carried the remaining plants into the laundry room, then came back to collect the cages and tools while she took the last two pots inside.

When she would have turned into the kitchen, he touched her arm. "Let me show you the storm cellar," he said. "Just in case."

They went back into the yard, past the garden and the old faded glider, to a grass-covered mound. Four steps led down to the door, set at an angle and facing southeast. It creaked in protest when he opened it. He went in first, ducking his head to clear the door. She went as far as the bottom step and stopped.

The space wasn't large—maybe six by eight feet. The walls were made of concrete blocks, the floor of hard-packed dirt, and two wooden benches lined the sides. Though it smelled musty, what she could see of the space was free of cobwebs or any other signs of creepy crawlies. Still, the cellar made her skin crawl.

"Come on in," Guthrie invited.

"I don't think I can."

"Are you claustrophobic?"

"I might be now."

"This is no joke, Olivia. If you think there's even a possibility of a tornado, you need to bring the kids in here. It's the only place you're guaranteed to be safe. But you'll never get Emma in here if she sees that you're scared. Come on. There's nothing to be afraid of here."

He was right about Emma. She would be reluctant to enter the cellar under the best of circumstances. If she saw that Olivia felt the same way, they would have to drag her kicking and screaming. And there *was* nothing to be afraid of. The place was clean and, with the door propped back, well lit.

Ducking her head, she stepped through the doorway and automatically wrinkled her nose. "You could use some air freshener in here—maybe some of those scented candles."

Guthrie's chuckle was dry. "I'll remember that next time I go into town."

She walked to the opposite end of the cellar. The cooler air felt good on her skin—though she was pretty sure being underground in what was essentially an oversize burial plot wasn't a worthy trade for a little relief from the heat.

At the sound of a creak, she whirled around just in time to see Guthrie pulling the door toward him. It closed with a solid thunk, and then she could see nothing—not the white fabric of her dress, not her fingers trembling in front of her face, *nothing*. "Guthrie?" In a panic, she headed for the door and walked right into him. She stumbled, and his arms automatically went around her, supporting her while she caught her balance, quite possibly taking away her emotional balance for good.

The pitch-black was forgotten, and the weather outside, and the fact that she was underground and going back to Atlanta as soon as she could. Every thought, every protest, every bit of sense, disappeared from her mind, leaving her only with variations of one thought. This was good. She wanted this. She needed this. She just might wither and die without it.

His arms were around her waist. His body was hard and strong against hers. His heartbeat was reassuringly steady, the rate flatteringly fast. His breath brushed her forehead as he murmured, "Don't you have something to ask me?"

She was hot, achy, dazed and in serious need, and he

wanted her to think? To talk? To make sense? But she didn't have to think. She merely needed to remember. Sunday. In the café.

He gave her the opening words. "I wondered when I was going to make the list for your sympathy."

"And I didn't know you wanted—" He slid one hand to her bottom, drew her against his arousal, and she gasped. Rational thought fled. "I didn't know…didn't…you wanted…"

"Your sympathy. Among other things." He brushed his mouth across her temple, made his way by instinct and feel along her jaw to the corner of her mouth. There was something she was supposed to ask—*What other things?*—but asking would mean thinking. It would mean talking, and if she was using her mouth to talk, then he couldn't be using it for kisses, and she so desperately wanted his kisses.

She slid her arms around his neck, turned her head a fraction of an inch to bring his mouth where she wanted it, then gave a soft whimper of need as he kissed her. He wasn't shy. He didn't tease or play. He simply, deeply, hungrily kissed her. It was achingly sweet, sweetly needy and it made her want to cry.

Ending the kiss was a slow process. He pulled back, thought better of it and returned for another slow exploration of her mouth with his tongue, then pulled back again. He nibbled her lower lip, came back for another taste, then finally lifted his head. Even in utter darkness she knew he was looking at her. She could feel the intensity, the passion, of his gaze as surely as she could feel it in his body. "I want you, Olivia."

Words simple and blunt, leaving no room for misunderstanding. Words that made her blood hotter, her body softer. Words that made her forget that they were underground, that creepy crawlies existed, that a storm was brewing outside. The most potent tornado this summer heat could spawn couldn't begin to compare to the tempest whirling and building inside her.

He kissed her again, and she kissed him back, with recklessness, greed, hunger. Her hands sought his body, sliding underneath his shirt, finding his nipples and making his breath catch, then searching lower, rubbing with rough caresses, making him groan.

Trapping her hands in his, he lowered her to the floor and followed her down. The earth was hard, cool, dry, underneath her. He was hard, hot and demanding above. With his leg between her thighs, his arousal against her hip, he left a line of kisses down her jaw and throat to the neckline of her dress. He kissed there, too, his tongue moistening fevered flesh, while his fingers made short work of the buttons.

The instant her breasts were exposed, he sucked one nipple into his mouth, drawing hard on it, sending waves of tiny shocks through her system. She reached for him, but he pinned her wrists to the ground—writhed beneath him, but he pressed her down with his body. She was hot, frantic, not above begging. "Please, Guthrie..." *Please make the ache go away. Please make me ache more. Please give me pleasure. Please want me. Please take me. Please please me.*

But instead of enticing, her whimper had the opposite effect. He drew back, the air cooling her skin where his mouth had moistened it, then turned away. She couldn't see it, but she felt it—felt the loss of connection, the loss of passion—and she heard the scuffing when he got to his feet.

Slowly, her body throbbing, her face burning, she sat up. She brushed one hand over her hair, coming down from its braid, then turned her unsteady hands to fastening the buttons that left her exposed to the waist. Finding the task impossible, she gave up and instead climbed to her feet.

"Well, that was quick." Her voice sounded thick, choked. "It took David nearly four years to decide he didn't want me. It took you only minutes."

The air shimmered with heat and tension when he came close. "Not want you?" His own voice was pretty damn thick as he unerringly located her hand. He drew it to the part of his body she'd intimately caressed just moments ago—still swollen, still impressively rigid. "Does that feel like I don't want you?"

It didn't. It felt tempting, enticing, promising. "Then why...?"

"Not here. Not in the dirt. Not without someone watching the kids."

Shame flooded her. In those few moments when she'd forgotten everything else, she'd also forgotten the girls—forgotten that she was a mother and remembered instead that she was a woman, with a woman's needs. A woman's heart.

Guthrie's fingers gentled as he lifted her hand to his mouth, pressed a kiss to her palm, then held it tightly. "I want you, but I can wait until the time—and the place—is right. Understand?"

She nodded, and he chuckled softly. "I can't see you in the dark, darlin'."

Rising onto her toes, she pressed a kiss to his chin. For such an innocent gesture, it damn near sizzled. "I understand."

With a sigh that sounded regretful, he released her and went to the door. Light filtered in as he eased it open, then spilled in, blinding them both, as the wind caught the door and flung it against the frame.

The sun was still shining, and the heat was still intense, but the threat of the storm was increasing. The clouds were closer now, and the wind had picked up, sending dust clouds dancing just above the ground. When Olivia moved from the steps to the grass, a gust caught her full skirt, whipping it around her legs with a sharp crack, and yanked her hair from its tired braid.

Guthrie pulled her close and fastened the buttons she'd been too clumsy to manage, then pushed against the wind to close the door once more. "Make sure the cabin's closed up, then go wait with the girls. I'm going to take care of the horses, then I'll meet you inside."

She hurried across the yard to the cabin, where she closed every window, then took a moment to secure her hair in a ponytail and to change into a clean dress. She didn't want to explain to the girls—experts at noticing things they shouldn't—how she'd gotten dirt stains on her back.

Emma and Elly were still asleep when she let herself in Guthrie's front door. Skippy raised his head, saw that she didn't come bearing food and lowered it again with a sigh.

"Disappointment's tough to deal with, isn't it, Skip?" she remarked as she headed for the kitchen. When Guthrie had stopped kissing her, stopped touching her, the disappointment had threatened to consume her. She'd been alone so long, had had nothing but fantasy and distant memory for so long—and distant memories of David didn't begin to approach the reality of Guthrie. If she'd ever felt so desperate, so womanly, so *alive* with David, she couldn't remember it.

But then, she'd never come close to loving David. She'd lived with him for seven years, had been married to him for eight, and even in the best of times, he'd never touched her the way Guthrie did.

But she was going back to Atlanta...wasn't she?

She always kept her promises...didn't she?

As she walked into the kitchen, a sudden rushing outside made itself heard over the air conditioner, along with a pinging that seemed to come from everywhere. She stood at the window, hugging herself, and watched the rain come down, watched the small chunks of hail dot the yard and bounce off the porch. Out back, Guthrie did the same thing in the open door for a minute or two, then abruptly took off for the house at a run.

Olivia opened the back door as he took the steps in one leap. "You should have waited out there," she chided as he took off his hat, then peeled off his wet T-shirt.

"Why would I want to be in the barn with the horses when I could come in here with you?" he asked with a grin before taking the dish towel she offered to dry his face.

"How are the horses?"

"They're okay. They're all in the barn."

"What about the cows?"

"They won't fit in the barn," he teased. "They'll huddle together under the trees. As long as the hail doesn't get worse and the winds don't carry them off, they'll be fine. What about the kids?"

"Still sleeping." Unable to resist, she let her gaze drift from his face to his chest—broad, heavily muscled, lots of smooth brown skin dotted with goose bumps. "Why—" She had to clear her throat. "Why don't you go up and change into dry clothes and I'll make some coffee to get you warm."

He leaned back against the washer, his hands braced on the edge of the machine, his legs spread just enough that she could slide between them. "Why don't you come over here and kiss me? I guarantee that'll get me warm. That'll damn near make me steam."

The invitation tempted her even more, she thought, than he could imagine, but thunder, followed by a pitiful whine, kept her at a distance.

"Was that Emma or Elly?"

She gave him a dry look. "That was Skippy. If you've helped them pick out a dog who's scared of storms, too, *you* get to cuddle with him."

"Nope, that's the girls' job. My cuddling extends only to two-legged creatures—and their mother." He pushed away from the washer and made it through the kitchen door before turning back.

"Olivia." He said her name in four distinct syllables, as if savoring every one, then waited for her to meet his gaze before he quietly, earnestly continued. "Don't ever judge me by David. He was a fool. *I'm* not."

And with that, he left her standing in the utility room with a storm raging outside and a silly, warm, incredibly satisfied feeling inside.

# Chapter 9

The storm entertained them for most of the evening, finally ending sometime around nine. Guthrie walked home with Olivia and the girls, got good-night kisses from the twins, then waited on the porch for a sweeter, more satisfying—and, yes, less satisfying, too—version from their mother. It didn't give him a good night at all, but rather a restless one, filled with tossing and turning interrupted by occasional erotic dreams.

After breakfast Thursday morning, he hooked up the box blade to the tractor and spent the next six hours repairing the damage his already-rutted roads had suffered from the torrential rain. It wasn't his favorite job—the mindless work gave him far too much time to think—but it was the only job that was absolutely essential today. When it was finished, he could knock off without feeling guilty and follow more pleasant pursuits for the rest of the day. A phone call to Mary after breakfast had ensured that.

After removing a grimy blue-and-white gimme cap from the local feed store, he used the tail of his shirt to wipe the sweat from his face. After last evening's storms had passed, the night had been unusually cool, but today was as hot, humid and still as ever. When he was a kid, he'd hardly even noticed the heat. Of course, once his chores were done, the time he'd spent outside had been in play with Easy and Shay—riding horses or bikes, exploring in the woods, picnicking by the swimming hole, fishing in the pond Easy's dad had kept stocked. It had rarely registered that they were living in a giant outdoor oven, sometimes as humid as a steam bath, others as dry as the desert. They'd had too much fun to care.

Like Elly, he thought with a grin. She climbed the fruit trees, talked to the horses, explored the barn and searched for small creatures who would fit for an hour or two in her pocket. She was happier than she'd ever been, she had announced last night at dinner, and hoped they never, ever left.

He'd added his own silent hopes while Emma had protested, reminding everyone that Mama had *promised* they would go back home. While she'd had complete faith in that promise, Olivia had looked the slightest bit uncertain before awkwardly changing the subject.

He intended to play on those uncertainties for all he was worth.

Lowering the blade to the ground, he set to work on the downside of the last rutted slope on the place. There were a couple of spots—at the bottoms of hills where temporary creeks gave the runoff a place to go—that would require more work, including rocks hauled in from the pasture to use as fill, but he would take care of those later. This slope was the last job he needed to do today.

The blade dragged over the ground, smoothing high spots, pushing the excess dirt into the low spots. He worked back and forth, the blade scraping each time with a metallic clang across the top of a chunk of sandstone buried deep in the earth, leaving a ridged, white scar across its surface. When the roadway had finally been smoothed to his satisfaction, he maneuvered the tractor around, then headed for home.

When he walked into the kitchen, Olivia was working at

the counter next to the sink and the girls were already in their seats. Emma sat quietly, with one strap of her swimsuit showing under the fussy dress she wore. Her hair was in a neat braid, and she smelled of coconut-scented sunscreen.

Elly sat on the back of her chair, her sandaled feet on the seat, and wore nothing but her swimsuit. Her hair was pushed back in wild spikes from her face with a hot pink headband, and lime green sunglasses covered her eyes.

When he came close, she stood up and twined her arms around his neck. "Hey, Mr. Guthrie, guess what? Miss Mary's bringing us to her house so's we can go swimmin' in her swimmin' pool. Ain't that neat?"

"Don't say 'ain't,'" Emma said as she applied another dab of sunscreen to her already-greasy nose. "And you didn't even give him a chance to guess. You just went right ahead and told him."

Leaning against him, Elly sighed heavily. "We're wearin' our swimmin' suits, Em. You think he didn't see?"

"Not mine. If you put on your cover-up like Mama told you to—"

"Then I'd just be wearin' a swimmin' suit with a cover-up. He'd still see." She gave an exaggerated shake of her head. "You're so pissy, Emmy."

Olivia turned from the counter where she was making sandwiches. "Elly! Don't call your sister that!"

"Well, Daddy did."

"Daddy called her *prissy*—and don't call her that, either. Let Guthrie wash up—and for the last time, sit down in that chair on your bottom, or you won't be going anywhere this afternoon except to your room."

After smacking a kiss on his cheek, Elly obeyed, settling in her chair. With a grin, Guthrie joined Olivia at the sink and began scrubbing up. "Swimming at Mary's," he murmured. "How'd you manage that?"

"She called this morning and offered. She said I probably needed a break." She glanced at them, then lowered her voice even more. "I love them dearly, but I hadn't realized how much I'd come to count on those few hours a day when they were at day school.''

"They'll be gone all day once school starts in August. You won't know what to do with yourself."

"I'll be able to help you. What do you do around here in the fall?"

"We round up the cattle and get 'em ready to sell, deliver the fall calves and breed the spring, do the branding and the castrating." He watched her from the corner of his eye. "Considering your experiences with David and Ethan, you might enjoy that last part. I know a few women around here who are damn good at it. Then you cook 'em up and—"

"Wait a minute." She gave him a narrow-eyed look that didn't disguise her amusement. "Cook what up?"

"Let's see, what would be a polite way to describe the portion of the bull's anatomy that's removed in a castration?"

Distaste replaced amusement. "And you *eat* it?"

"Slice it thin, bread it in a mix of cornmeal and flour and fry it till it's crisp. Serve it up with fried potatoes, corn on the cob and beer—"

"Lots of beer, I imagine," she said dryly.

"When you're hot, tired and hungry, it's a damn good meal."

She handed him a dish towel to dry his hands, then carried the kids' plates to the table. "Gee, and all I fixed today was ham sandwiches, pasta salad and deviled eggs."

He watched her come back toward him, smiling, lovely, looking as at home in his kitchen as she seemed in his life. What would he have to do to make her *feel* that way? To make her realize that her *home*—the one place where she belonged, to the exclusion of all other places—was right here with him?

He didn't know yet. But whatever it was, he would do it. He had no choice, because without her, this would never again be much of a home for him.

They finished eating just a minute before a horn sounded outside. Elly leaped from her chair and ran for the front door.

Emma stood more slowly. "If you want, I can stay here and keep you company, Mama, so you won't get lonely."

Olivia smiled gently. "I appreciate the offer, but you need to keep Elly company. I've got Skippy. I won't get lonely."

Damn straight, Guthrie thought.

Elly returned to the kitchen, pulling Mary by the hand. Taking off her floppy sun hat, she gave Guthrie a wicked grin, then greeted Olivia. "I appreciate you loaning me your two critters for the afternoon. Jim's gone off to Texas to look at some stock, so it's been awful quiet around our place."

"Well, they'll liven things up for you. In fact, if they get too lively, just give me a call." Olivia gave each girl a kiss, made sure they had their towels and sunscreen, then walked to the door with them.

Guthrie cleared the table, put the leftovers in the refrigerator and rinsed the dishes to later load in the dishwasher. When he turned, he saw Olivia leaning against the doorjamb, watching him with a smile.

"I like a man who knows his way around the kitchen."

He leaned against the counter. "That's not all I know, darlin'."

"I know. You know your way around the horses. The cows. The ranch." She came a few slow steps closer. "You even know how to get a few hours free from the kids."

"Mary told you," he said sheepishly.

"Not in so many words. But I saw that grin she gave you when she came in."

"Do you mind?"

She came even closer, so close that not even a deep breath separated them. "Mind? I only wish I'd thought of it myself. So…I take it you're not going right back to work."

"Not unless you want me to." He swallowed hard as she touched the tip of her index finger to a button square in his chest. "Do you?"

She unfastened that button, then the ones above it, and pressed a kiss to his chest. It was all the answer he needed.

He swallowed hard to make his voice work. "Let me take a shower."

"You do that." She stepped back—way back—giving him clear passage to the hallway.

"I'll make it quick."

Her smile was sweet and serious. "Take your time. I'm not going anywhere."

With a pang, he wished she really meant those last words—not just for this afternoon, but for forever. He wished she would embrace living here not just today and next month but next year and the next fifty years. He wished she would make this place home—for herself, for her kids, for him.

Persuading her to do just that would be his job. His pleasure.

As he pushed away from the counter, he gave her a long, lazy, intimate look that warmed her face, then quietly repeated, "I'll make it quick."

Olivia watched him go, then, when his footsteps had disappeared into the bathroom upstairs, let out her breath in a deep, deep sigh. When was the last time a man had looked at her like that?

Never.

When was the last time no more than a look had made her feel like that?

Never, ever.

Was she making a mistake in allowing their relationship to proceed to the next natural step? Was she setting herself up for heartbreak? After all, she had more to consider here than herself, her own needs, her own feelings. She had to do what was right for the girls, too. There was a time when she'd known exactly what that was.

Right now she didn't.

All she knew was that she wanted Guthrie more than she'd ever wanted anything for herself in her life. Maybe she *would* get her heart broken. Or maybe she wouldn't. Either way, it was a chance she had to take.

She loaded the dishes into the dishwasher, checked on

Skippy, asleep under the table where Elly had been slipping him food, then slowly went down the hall. At the bottom of the stairs, she wiped her palms down her dress, touched a hand to her hair, then took a reassuring breath.

The sound of water running in the shower grew louder the higher she climbed. The thought of Guthrie naked, his hair slicked back, all that marvelous brown skin exposed and wet, was intriguing—and terrifying. She'd never been with any man but David—who, in the end, had turned to other women. She wished for a few meaningless affairs, if only for the experience, then chided herself for it. Experience didn't count. Emotions did, and she was feeling all the right ones. Anticipation. Desire. Affection. Lust. Longing.

Love.

Ignoring that last, she went into Guthrie's bedroom. She spent a few minutes in the room every morning—dusting, making the bed, picking up the occasional laundry left out of place. Those few minutes were work. These next few hours would be pure pleasure. It changed everything about the room. She didn't notice things to be done—dust she'd missed, windows to be washed, a coffee cup forgotten.

She noticed instead what a comfortable room it was, with well-used furniture, a quilt of puffy squares in colors that matched the large braided rug, with sheer curtains at the windows that allowed a clear view of the buildings out back. There was nothing fussy about the room—no doilies atop the furniture, not a lot of pictures on the walls, no clutter anywhere. It was simply a wonderful, welcoming place to spend a night...or a sweetly sinful afternoon.

She was folding the quilt when the water shut off next door. She imagined him stepping out of the tub, naked and dripping and aroused, and for a moment, her hands trembled. Her entire body trembled.

With a deep breath for steadiness, she folded the quilt to the foot of the bed, then folded it again before moving it to the easy chair. His sheets were easy-care white and smelled fresh from the laundry she'd done this morning. She folded back the top one, smoothed a wrinkle, then fluffed pillows that didn't need fluffing.

And then he was there. He'd made no noise, but she sensed him—felt him in the heat that rushed through her, in the nervousness and anticipation and pure, sweet lust that claimed her.

Slowly she straightened, then turned to face him. He stood just inside the door with his hair slicked back, the way he combed it after every shower. Water droplets he'd missed dotted his shoulders, and he wore a pair of clean jeans that fitted oh-so-snugly. Faded denim, swollen flesh. She swallowed hard at the sight. "I expected a towel. Maybe less."

"I thought it'd be less intimidating."

Her voice turned husky. "I'm not intimidated. I'm impressed."

"Actually, I meant for me—what with you being fully dressed."

She smiled at the idea that a man as handsome, as strong, as downright sexy, as Guthrie Harris could be intimidated by *her*. "That can be easily fixed." She was wearing one of her favorite sundresses and very little else. Kicking off her shoes took care of half of the *little else*. A bit of maneuvering underneath the long, full skirt removed the other half.

Now all she wore was the dress, with a long row of tiny white buttons down the front that she usually ignored in favor of just pulling the thing over her head. This afternoon she began unfastening, but the buttons were stubborn and the progress was slow.

Moving with such grace, such power, he crossed the room to stand in front of her. He brushed her hands away, then slid his arms around her waist and pulled her hard against him. "I couldn't sleep last night for thinking of you here," he murmured.

"I was lonely, too." Her bed had seemed empty—*she* had felt empty—and she'd considered more than once creeping outside and across the yard to knock at his door. But the good mother in her wouldn't let her leave the girls alone in the cabin while she slipped off to his bed, wouldn't let her bring him into her bed while the girls slept innocently unaware upstairs. And so she'd resigned herself to wanting and not having for the time being.

She was going to like wanting and having a whole lot more.

Holding her with one hand, he slid the other up her spine to her hair, removed the rubber band, gently worked her braid free. Then he slid both hands into her hair, holding her head, tilting it just so for his kiss. It was a sweet kiss—wonderfully, innocently sweet—and yet full of wicked promise. She knew how easily it could change, knew that in a heartbeat, instead of pleasing, it would be pleasurable. Instead of innocent, it would be erotic. Instead of promising, it would deliver all that she wanted, more than she could bear, exactly what she needed.

He backed her up until the bed bumped her knees, then laid her down as his tongue claimed her mouth. He tasted deeply of her before ending the kiss, rolling to one side, supporting his head on one hand while looking down at her. "Unbutton your dress."

Her gaze locked with his, she raised her hands once more to the buttons. The first slipped loose, then the second, the third. Somewhere around seven, she lost count, but after a time, groping blindly, she found no more.

He leaned forward to give her another long, intimate kiss before issuing his next command. "Let me see you."

She pushed back the fabric on either side, felt the cool air in the room skim across her skin.

"You're beautiful," he murmured.

The laugh that escaped her was soft, womanly, sexy—a laugh she had surely never laughed before because she would swear on what was happening here that she'd never felt this way before. "You haven't even looked."

He gave her half a grin that was wicked and sly. "You want me to look? Darlin', I'd be happy to oblige you."

She watched his gaze move lower, felt it slide across her

skin, knew each place it touched. Her jaw. Throat. Breasts. Ribs. Stomach. Hips. Thighs. Calves. Feet. Then back up, lingering partway. It created heat, fed the need, making it sharper, more potent, more killing. Just that long, slow look, and she was desperate for relief, for his body, for *him*.

She knew he was going to touch her before she saw his hand move, before she became aware of the heat radiating from his skin, before she felt the tender touch between her breasts. He stroked her, smooth skin and rough calluses sending the most enticing sensations racing through her, and he followed the caresses with kisses, long lines of wet kisses across her ribs, her abdomen, over her hip and down her thigh. As he traced a new path on the return trip, he moved over her, straddling her hips, sliding both hands to her shoulders as he took her nipple in his mouth.

With a gasp, she arched against him, but his hands and hips left her little room to move. As he suckled hard, she lifted both hands, tangling her fingers in his thick, dark hair, torn between pushing him away for a momentary respite from the torment and holding him tightly so the torment would never stop. In the end she simply held on, and when he lifted his head, she let him, too dazed, too breathless to protest.

"Beautiful," he murmured, and for that moment she believed him.

He kissed her mouth, tickled and teased and stroked her body, cast aside her dress and, with her less-than-competent help—oh, but she enjoyed the trying—removed his jeans. She waited, quivering, needy, anxious, in his bed that smelled of fabric softener and heat and *him*, but he didn't take her immediately. Instead, the mattress shifted, followed by the soft rubbing sound of old wood against wood, then the rustle of plastic. She opened her eyes, forced them to focus on him.

He was kneeling between her thighs, dealing with the birth control that she'd given no thought to. His body was strong and impossibly hard. A faint flush bronzed his cheeks, every muscle was achingly taut and the look in his eyes was hard and fierce until he noticed her watching him. Then it became tender—breath-stealingly tender—and fierce. Finished with the condom, he leaned over her, bearing the brunt of his weight on his hands, and gave her a frantic, desperate, devouring sort of kiss as he slowly filled her, until she could take no more, until he had no more to give.

Guthrie broke the kiss and dragged in a badly needed breath filled with the scents of her and him and sex. He'd dreamed about this last night, but the hottest dream imaginable couldn't match the reality of Olivia in his bed, underneath him, a part of him, holding him, gloving him, clinging to him. Nothing could match this—except exactly the same scene, minus the condom. Except the right to take her with no barriers, to fill her with the possibility—the hope, the expectation—of creating another life with her.

She caressed his back, and his body convulsed against hers. His skin was burning, his blood pumping hot, and his muscles were trembling and weak. He'd never experienced such discomfort, pain and need. He'd never felt so damn good.

Tentatively he withdrew, then filled her again, and caught her soft gasp with his kiss. He stroked her once more, deeper than before, and felt her body tighten. He did it again, again, his easy rhythm increasing, until he was filling her hard and she was meeting him, encouraging him with her soft, wordless pleas, the greedy thrust of her hips, the restless, intimate touches of her hands.

She came before him, and the helpless clenching of her body around his was exactly the torment he needed to reach his own climax. His vision went dark. His blood rushed in his ears. His heart, he thought, stopped beating. Spasms of pure sexual pleasure burst through him, making it impossible to breathe. He held tightly to her, filling her, groaning her name as a prayer that might save him, and then, when he could bear no more, he collapsed heavily against her.

After a time, his heart started beating again. One ragged deep breath filled his lungs with the scent of her—the very essence of her—and the dark, blinding veil lifted from his eyes so he could see her. As he focused on her, her face flushed, her hair curling damply, her lips parted, her body slick and trembling everywhere they touched, he knew that he'd been right. She *was* the woman who could save him.

If she would only try.

If she would only stay.

He touched her cheek with one unsteady hand, and she opened her eyes. She looked as if she might cry.

He understood the feeling.

With a shaky smile, she hugged him tightly. He felt the fierceness of it most where her body still held his. "Oh my gosh," she whispered.

That was all. It was enough.

Shifting onto his side, he turned her with him, her thigh lifted high onto his hip so he could remain inside her. He stroked her hair from her face, dried a drop of sweat that trickled across her forehead, then simply looked at her.

He'd never felt such tenderness that he couldn't express it. He wanted to tell her what he was feeling, but the only words he could think of—*I love you*—were inadequate. They might frighten her, sadden her. They might be a risk he couldn't afford to take.

And so he would say nothing. He would do nothing but look at her. Touch her. Maybe make love to her again.

And having made that wise decision, he opened his mouth anyway and foolish words rolled out. "If I got you pregnant, would you stay?"

Her blue gaze darted to his, and he would swear, that first fleeting emotion in them was hope—wishful, wistful hope—before anxiety took over. "But I thought you used—"

She tried to pull away, but he clamped his hand to her knee, keeping it hooked over his hip, and he held her shoulders with his other arm. "I did. The only way you're getting pregnant from what we just did is with a little divine intervention. I'm talking about in the future. Other times. If I got you pregnant, would you stay?"

She rested her fingertips along his throat. He could feel the steady beat of his pulse throb against her. "If I were pregnant," she began slowly, and he interrupted her.

"If *I* got you pregnant. If *we* were going to have a baby. If *you* were going to have *my* baby." His grin just barely qualified as cocky, as it was meant to be. "That's the only way it's going to happen, sweetheart. As long as you live here, it's me or nobody."

For a long still moment, she looked at him with such gentleness that he knew he wasn't going to like what she was about to say.

He was right.

"Would you really want that to be my only reason for staying? Not because it was right. Not because it was what I wanted. But only because I was pregnant?"

He wanted her under *any* circumstances. Miles had gotten *eight years* with her only because she'd gotten pregnant, and he'd been a fool who hadn't even truly wanted her. Why should Guthrie have to be better?

Because she wanted better. She wanted passion, commitment, devotion and love. She wanted to be irreplaceable. She deserved it.

And he could give her all those things. If she would just stay here to accept them.

She was looking at him, waiting for him to answer, to say no, he wouldn't want her to stay for any reason other than her own desire, and although it was a lie, he gave her the answer. "No. I guess not." Then, grudgingly, he asked, "Do you miss it? Atlanta? Really?" He rarely saw any signs of homesickness when he watched her, but wasn't that the sort of thing a person would feel most when it was quiet, when she was alone and her mind was idle to drift where it would?

"I do," she replied softly. "At night. Early in the morning. There was a live oak in our backyard, with Spanish moss hanging from its branches and wisteria growing around its trunk. It was the first thing I saw every morning when I woke up. Every morning after the kids left for day school, I'd have coffee outside under that tree. Everything was always so lush and green, and when the wisteria was in bloom, or the magnolias or the crape myrtles or the azaleas, it was so beautiful and peaceful."

She slid her hand from his throat to his shoulder, massaging away the tension that had settled there. "I miss the voices. There are a thousand and one Southern accents, and I loved every one. Here I sound strange to my own ears. After only a few weeks, Elly's already losing her accent."

"Elly wants to be a cowboy. She's adapting." He swallowed hard, then offered with a sense of wasted hope, "But Emma will never lose hers. She could live here twenty years and still sound like the quintessential Southern belle."

Her acknowledging smile was faint and bittersweet. "There's a feel to Atlanta—a sense of history, a graciousness, a rightness. I miss that. I miss the connection. I've had family in Georgia since before it *was* Georgia. It's a part of who and what we are. Without it I feel incomplete."

Too bad no one in all those generations of family had been a pioneer, willing to push westward and give her some precedent to follow. But, hell, it shouldn't be a place, he thought resentfully, that made her whole. A place couldn't make her happy, couldn't fulfill her, couldn't give purpose to her life. People could. A man—the right man—could.

He pulled away from her and rolled onto his back, stuffing a pillow under his head. There was a *feel* to Heartbreak, too. It had history—though nowhere near as extensive or illustrious as Atlanta. It was sorely lacking in graciousness, too. Life here was tough, with little time for tea parties, charity balls and socials. The only breeding that mattered around here was the livestock's, and social standing did nothing to protect against low market prices, bad weather and bad luck.

But in spite of that, it felt right for him and everyone else who'd sunk their roots here.

But not for Olivia.

She turned onto her stomach, leaning on one elbow, resting the other hand on his stomach. "I'll be here a long time," she said quietly.

Months, at least, and a lot could change in months. Hell, look at what a few weeks had done for him. She could fall in love with Heartbreak, with the ranch, with him. Atlanta could lose its hold on her. She could discover, to her surprise, that those roots she thought buried in Georgia clay had, in fact, sunk in right here, and Emma could discover that being a prissy rancher's daughter was every bit as satisfying—if not quite as expected—as being a prissy Georgia belle.

She just might become the first pioneer in her family's Southern-born, Southern-bred history.

He stroked her hair, his fingers gliding over it like pale brown silk, then rubbed his thumb over her jaw. "Olivia," he murmured, then shortened it. "Liv."

She did something akin to a full-body shrug, rubbing against him from shoulder to ankle, striking little sparks all the way. "No one's ever called me Liv."

"And lived to tell it?"

She shook her head. "My mother was Katherine—not Kate, Kathy, Kitty or Kat. And my father was Richard—never Rick, Rich or Dick. And I've always been just Olivia." Her smile was sweet, shy, womanly. "I like Liv."

He liked it, too, because it was just between them. Because using it somehow made her his. Because it was sweet and endearing. Because it was an acceptable substitute—just one sound away—for what he really wanted to call her.

Abruptly he groaned—because he'd gotten sappy there? Or because, in the last moment, her hand had slid below his waist, past his hip and was touching him in indecently intimate ways?

Closing his eyes, he let her play until teasing became a demand, until his body was hard, his muscles knotted, his tolerance for sweet pain worn thin. Then he caught her wrist, forced her hand away, forced some semblance of normalcy to cloak the wild need in his voice. "Reach in the drawer, Liv, and grab one of those condoms, then come over here and show me some of that famous Southern hospitality."

With a sensual smile accompanying a heavily overdone accent, she replied, "Why, Mr. Harris, I'd be delighted."

The instant her torturous caresses stopped, he wanted to grab her back. Instead, he opened his eyes and watched as she so graciously followed his directions, neatly tearing open the packet he would have savagely ripped. He clenched his jaw and his fists and every muscle in his body as she carefully, meticulously and oh-so-slowly rolled the latex sheath into place, and he broke out in a cold sweat when she moved so gracefully to sit astride him, taking him deep inside the shelter of her body.

For a moment she sat motionless, her spine straight, her head back, her eyes closed. Her body tightened, eased, relaxed to fit him, then she gave a deep, satisfied sigh that he felt within himself. He touched her breast and she shuddered, touched her belly and she moved in an enticing rub.

Before they went any further, there was one thing he had to say. Resting his hands on her thighs, feeling the muscles taut underneath his palms, he quietly spoke her name. "Liv?"

She lowered her head, opened her eyes, gazed down at him with a dazed, aroused, erotic look.

"No matter what you do, no matter where you do it, you could never, ever be *just Olivia*. Not even if you tried."

It was five-thirty when a horn sounded on the road out front. Olivia lifted her head from Guthrie's chest to look blankly out the nearest window. The late-afternoon sun was blazing, and in the pasture the horses were grazing. It was a lazy, contented scene—and she was one lazy, contented woman.

She laid her head down again, let her eyes drift shut, then abruptly remembered that Mary had promised to have the kids home in plenty of time for dinner. She'd started to scramble up when Guthrie sleepily trapped her with one arm.

"Where are you going?"

"Mary's here with the kids." The sound of a car door slamming made her wriggle free and grab her clothes, wiggling into her panties, thrusting her arms into her dress and fumbling with the buttons. While she fastened enough to be decent, she looked for and found the rubber band he'd pulled from her hair, stepped into her sandals and headed for the door.

"Liv?"

She looked back to see him leaning on one arm, impressively naked, and her chest tightened around her heart.

"Thank you."

A knock sounded at the door, sending up a chorus of barks from Skippy, but she took a moment to return to the bed and give him a kiss. "No. Thank *you.*" Grinning, she touched her fingers to his jaw. "You're the best time I've ever had." Then she fled out of the room, down the hall and down the stairs.

When she opened the door, she was fairly sure she looked presentable enough that the girls would never guess anything was different. Mary would—but Mary had known what Olivia would be doing this afternoon before Olivia had known it. Other than a sly grin, she would ignore the unbuttoned buttons, the French braid that was now a ponytail, the look of incredible satisfaction that Olivia couldn't hide if she tried.

"Mama, Mama, look what Miss Mary gave us! Mine's a dinosaur—"

"And mine's an elephant!" Elly and Emma tumbled over each other with their towels, cover-ups and big, brightly colored inflatable swim toys.

"Now, girls, remember—the toys stay on the porch," Mary reminded them. "At least until they're dry."

"Yes, Miss Mary," they responded in unison, backing up to settle the toys on the glider at the far end of the porch.

"Would you like to come in?" Olivia asked. "I've got some fresh tea." If lunchtime constituted fresh.

"I can't stay, hon. Thanks anyway." Mary glanced at the girls, then stepped closer. "Where is Guthrie?"

A blush heated Olivia's cheeks. "He—um, he's upstairs."

"I need to talk to him. I've got news…" She looked worried. "Would you ask him to meet me out at the pasture?"

"Sure." Before Olivia could say anything else—could ask if everything was all right, if something had happened to Shay or Jim—the older woman walked away, her stride long and purposeful. "Come on in, girls," Olivia said absently, holding the door for the kids. Once they were settled in the living room, she headed upstairs, walking into the bedroom just as Guthrie pulled a pair of faded denims over his hips.

"Did the kids have fun?" he asked, catching her hand, pulling her close.

"Mary's still here. She wants to talk to you out by the horses."

He turned to look out the window, and together they watched as Mary approached the fence. The horses moved to meet her—Buck stopping a respectable distance back, Maverick, Dusty and Mustang trotting right up to the fence. Like Buck, Mary stopped a few yards short of the fence. She simply stood there, her hands in her skirt pockets.

"Did she say about what?"

"No."

He released Olivia and fastened his jeans, then pulled on a T-shirt from the top drawer. He shoved his feet into thick white socks, then work boots, then combed his hair with his fingers as he started toward the door.

Olivia stayed by the window and listened to his progress by the sound of his footsteps. At the bottom of the stairs, both girls called greetings. He returned them without stopping but headed for the back door. A moment later she could see him through the window, his long legs eating up the ground.

He laid his hand on Mary's shoulder, and she turned, slid her arm around his waist and leaned against him. Obviously something bad had happened. Olivia wanted to turn away, as if doing so would magically make things better, but she couldn't move. She stood there in front of the window and watched them talk, watched Guthrie walk the few remaining yards to the fence, watched him pet the horses, then shrug away from Mary's comforting touch. They talked a few minutes longer—at least, she did. He didn't seem to have anything to say.

After a while, Mary patted his back a time or two, then walked away, her head down. A moment later came a car door slamming, then an engine that revved, then faded into the distance, and still Guthrie stood motionless with the horses.

Feeling worried and confused and unsure what to do, Olivia forced herself away from the window. She picked up a pillow that had fallen to the floor, then busied herself with the bed. She smoothed the sheets, fluffed the pillows, spread out the quilt, and still he hadn't moved.

Downstairs she warned the kids not to leave the house, then followed the path he'd taken. Her sandals made no noise on the grass, but the horses alerted him to her presence. Ignoring the huge creatures—not the easiest task she'd ever done—she leaned against the warm pipe so she could face him.

"Could I interest you in dinner in town with three charming females?" she asked in her best sugary-sweet, flutterylashed, Scarlett O'Hara imitation.

"No." He didn't even spare her a glance. He simply stared at Buck.

She reached for his hand. His fingers remained limp, his thoughts distant. "What's wrong, Guthrie? What happened?"

He was silent long enough for a puffy white cloud to drift over the sun, casting its shadow over them and most of the pasture, then just as lazily drift away. Then, abruptly, he clasped her fingers tightly enough to make her wince, as if he desperately needed the connection.

"My horse, Buck…" With a nod, he pointed him out. "He was a wild one—hated everyone, couldn't be controlled. The guy who owned him over in the next county was threatening to put him down, but he wound up giving him to Easy just to get him off his hands. Easy took him home, worked with him, gained his trust, gentled him, then gave him to me for my birthday. He's the best horse I've ever had."

Maverick pushed close to the fence and nuzzled him. Guthrie obliged with a scratching before he went on. "Easy was talented that way. He never met a horse he couldn't handle. He related better to them than he did to people—except women. He loved horses and women, and they loved him right back."

"And you," Olivia whispered, feeling a chill in spite of the searing heat. "He loved you, and you loved him."

After a moment's silence, he glanced at her. His face was expressionless, but his eyes… There was such emotion in his eyes. Anger. Confusion. Regret. Sorrow.

When he spoke again, his jaw was hard. So was his voice. "An old friend of Shay's was passing through town today. He stopped in at the café and mentioned that, about a month ago, Easy was on his way from one rodeo to another when he was in a wreck. Some people thought he'd been drinking. Some thought he just fell asleep at the wheel. Whatever…"

Please don't let him be dead, Olivia silently prayed. For his sake, for Shay's, for Guthrie's, he *couldn't* be dead.

"He was hurt pretty bad. The doctors didn't know if he would ever walk again, but it's for damn sure he'll never rodeo again and maybe never work with his horses again." He looked at her then and gave her a bleak smile. "If he can't work with his horses, he'd rather be dead."

Any assurances she offered would be nothing more than empty words. She didn't know Easy Rafferty and couldn't begin to guess how he would react to such devastating, life-changing injuries. Never having had a great passion in her life—besides Guthrie—she couldn't imagine how it would feel to lose it, to have to face the rest of your life without it. How much worse to know that it was due to your own foolishness or carelessness.

So she didn't offer any words at all. She simply pushed away from the fence, stepped right up to him and wrapped her arms tightly around him. For a moment he stood stiff and unyielding, then slowly he relented, holding her close, bending his head to rest his cheek against her hair. A shudder ricocheted through him, then another, and then he drew a great rejuvenating breath.

"I hated him for so long," he murmured, his breath stirring above her ear. "I wanted bad things to happen to him. I wanted him to suffer the way he and Shay had made me suffer."

She rubbed between his shoulder blades, where tension knotted his muscles. "Of course you did. *I* wanted bad things to happen to him, wanted him to suffer, just from hearing what he did, and I don't even know the guy."

"But I never meant— God, I never really wanted—"

"Guthrie." With both hands, she forced his head back, then cupped her palms to his cheeks. "You know what Shay called you the other day?"

His laugh was harsh and choked. "I can imagine."

"I doubt it. She said you were the nicest, sweetest and most honorable man in the county. No one would ever believe that you wished harm on anyone else, particularly Easy." She hesitated, then asked, "Where is he?"

"The accident happened in New Mexico. Shay's trying to find out where he is now."

Poor Shay, Olivia thought. The woman obviously still harbored feelings for the man she'd once run away with. How difficult it must be for her to know that he was hurt and there was nothing she could do to help, to not even be able to visit or call him. "What about his folks?"

"They left Heartbreak years ago. They didn't keep in touch with anyone."

"If Shay finds him…" She moistened her lips. "Will you go to see him?"

The look he gave her was sharp and startled. Its intensity didn't ease until he pulled away and went to lean on the fence. "I—I don't—"

"Knowing that you don't hate him might mean a lot to him."

"It might mean a lot to me, too—*if* it were true."

Olivia didn't believe for an instant that he hated Easy—

really, truly *hated* him. At the café Sunday with Shay, he'd tried to find less hostile ground for, if not friendship, then a polite association they could both live with. Given the chance, she was convinced he'd do the same with Easy. "You don't hate him," she said, her voice soft and just the slightest bit chiding.

"I've hated him damn near as long as I haven't. I could never trust him again. We could never be friends again." He laced his fingers together, squeezing them so tightly that they turned white. "I don't know exactly *what* I feel for him, beyond sorry. I'm sorry as hell that things went so wrong for him—but, believe me, he'd rather that I hate him than feel sorry for him."

She stepped up beside him, resting her arms on the pipe again. Maverick sidestepped to a point in front of her, demanding her attention. The paint was a beautiful animal, playful and huge and could crush her without even trying, but all he seemed to want was the same scratching Guthrie had given him, the same scratching she'd watched Elly and Emma give him. Drawing a deep breath, she lifted one hand from the pipe to accommodate him, but suddenly he was no longer there. Buck had shouldered him aside and now blocked them completely.

She transferred her attention to the giant creature Guthrie usually rode—the best horse he'd ever had. He was as gorgeous as the others, though usually more than a tad standoffish. She wondered whimsically if it was her defense of Easy that had brought him near today. She'd heard of camels remembering former owners who'd mistreated them years earlier. Could this horse remember the man who'd saved his life, who'd gentled him and given him the best home any animal could want?

"Fold your fingers over like this." Guthrie smoothed her hand into a loose fist. "Now extend your arm down here. Give him a chance to smell you. Once he's done that, scratch him right under here. But watch his mouth. If he starts to bare his teeth, back off."

She followed his instructions. "After this afternoon, I smell like you."

"Good. Buck likes me."

"I like you, too," she said with a grin as she cautiously stretched closer to scratch under the horse's chin. Keeping one eye on him, she returned to the conversation. "No one expects you to be friends with Easy again, Guthrie. Certainly no one expects you to trust him again after the way he betrayed you. But you can forgive him. Holding a grudge is hard work, and it hurts you more than him. Besides, you're a better man than that."

"You think so?" he asked dryly.

"I know so."

He moved to stand behind her, trapping her between his body and the fence, and pressed a kiss to her cheek. "Want to go for a ride?"

She looked at Buck, who looked back, his brown eyes so big and solemn. Getting this close was one thing. Petting him was another. But climbing on his back, giving him both the motive and the means to do her some serious damage? That was a risk she wasn't quite prepared to take.

Then Guthrie moved closer, nuzzling her ear, pressing his arousal against her bottom, and she realized that the ride he had in mind required neither horse nor saddle nor courage. Laughing, she tilted her head to one side so he could nuzzle more. "Are you trying to distract me?"

"Is it working?"

His hands moved to her waist, then slid up to cover her breasts, and she gave a soft, dreamy sigh. "Oh, yes," she whispered. "I'm distracted." And attracted. Aroused. Enticed. Beguiled.

"Can I interest you in a roll in the hay? A back seat rendezvous? A tumble in the tack room?"

She turned in his arms and clasped her hands behind his neck. "The kids will be tired after swimming all afternoon. They'll want to go to bed early. If we're quiet..."

"I can be quiet," he boasted. "*You* were the one doing the heavy-duty pleading."

Instead of reminding him that he'd done some pleading of his own, she simply, sweetly—and with great satisfaction—smiled. "Yes," she agreed. "I was. And I'll do it again. Tonight."

# Chapter 10

Olivia was right. Emma and Elly were subdued through dinner, and by eight o'clock, they were falling asleep on their feet. Guthrie made a trip upstairs, then locked up the house and walked across the yard to the cabin with them, with Skippy running in circles around them. When he stopped on the porch to wait while Olivia settled them in bed, Emma tugged his hand, then gestured for him to crouch to her level.

"You can come up and kiss us good-night if you want," she said solemnly.

"Thank you," he replied equally solemnly. "I'd like that." And he would. He would like to do all the fatherly things in their lives—including going to bed with their mother every night and waking up beside her every morning.

"So would we. We'll get our teeth brushed and our nighties on and call you."

Rising to his feet, he suppressed a smile at her formality. As Olivia brushed past him, he murmured, "You can put *your* nightie on, too."

She gave him an unintentionally seductive smile, then followed the girls inside. When the screen door closed, he turned to gaze toward the road.

If he followed it a half mile to the west, it would take him to the turnoff for the Rafferty place. Once it had been a prosperous ranch, but the Raffertys had sold all but thirty acres and the buildings to Jim Stephens when they'd left. According to Melva in the tax assessor's office, money arrived promptly every January to cover the property taxes on that remaining thirty acres, but no one knew who was paying it, or why.

*He* knew. For the kind of top-quality horse operation Easy had always wanted, thirty acres was more than enough. But would he ever have come back to get it started? Would he ever have found the nerve to move back home as if nothing had ever gone wrong?

About a year ago, when he was feeling particularly down, Guthrie had driven that half mile down the road. The mailbox that marked the turn had laid on the ground, courtesy of a drive-by bashing. The fence had been down in places, and the driveway had been grown over with weeds. It traveled a straight shot between pastures gone wild to the house, barely habitable, and the barn, in even worse shape.

Everything had been run-down, grown out of control and neglected—such a contrast to the shipshape operation Bud Rafferty had run. It had saddened Guthrie to see how badly things had deteriorated—had reminded him that his life wasn't in much better shape.

But whatever happened next, whether Olivia stayed or forced him to let her go, he was better off now than Easy.

That saddened him, too.

Closing his eyes, he rubbed his face with both hands. He truly was sorry for Easy's bad luck. Even when he'd hated him most, he'd never *really* wanted anything bad to happen. But regret had nothing to do with forgiveness. He could regret Easy's injuries from now until he died, but it wouldn't make him forgive his old friend.

But Olivia could.

Oh, not that she'd force the matter. She would never issue

an ultimatum. Now that she'd presented her case, she wouldn't even argue it with him. She would just expect him to do what was right, and because he would hate like hell to disappoint her, eventually he would do it. He had little doubt.

Upstairs there was a creak, then Elly called through the open window, "Mr. Guthrie! You can come up now."

His grim mood eased with the sound of her voice. He went inside and took the stairs to the only bedroom with lights on. The kids were already in bed, Emma with her doll at the head of the bed, Elly with a ragged stuffed dog at the foot, and Skippy curled up on his own bed—a quilt folded in fourths— near the window.

"How about a story, Mama?" Emma asked.

"You've had a story, Emma." Olivia turned off the overhead light, leaving only the bedside lamp burning.

"Yes, but you told it to us while we were brushin' and flossin' and undressin'," Elly protested. "We couldn't pay 'tention."

"I thought you paid 'tention quite well." Olivia bent to kiss first Emma, then Elly. "I love you, babe. Sleep tight."

She traded places with Guthrie at the door. He sat down on the edge of the bed, then looked at her. "Do you mind?"

"Not very well," Elly said, and both girls burst into giggles.

Olivia made a face at them all. "Since I'm obviously not needed here, I'll be downstairs."

A good-night kiss had sounded simple enough when Emma asked for it. Now that it was time, though, he felt awkward.

"You don't kiss many little girls good-night, do you?" Elly asked as she scrambled out from under the sheet and switched ends.

"No, I don't."

Emma scooted over to make room for her sister. "Do you kiss Mama good-night?"

"I plan to."

"Betcha kiss lots more grown-ups than little girls." Elly propped her stuffed dog under her head for a pillow, then folded her hands over her stomach. "You like our mama, don't you?"

He swallowed hard. "Yes, I do."

"Are you gonna marry her and be our daddy?"

Emma studied her doll, fussily combing its hair with her fingers. "We had a daddy, but he died. He wasn't a very good daddy. He said we were brats. He told Mama to keep us out of his hair."

Elly poked her. "Hush! We wasn't supposed to be listenin' when he said that." She shrugged for Guthrie's benefit, as if to emphasize that their father's comments weren't important. "Miss Mary says you're gonna be a fine daddy someday. Me and Emma thinks so, too, except... You couldn't be our daddy if we was in Atlanta, could you?"

At an absolute loss for how to handle the turn the conversation had taken, Guthrie settled for numbly shaking his head.

Once again Elly poked Emma in the side. "See? I told you."

"Why couldn't you come to Atlanta with us?" Emma asked. "We got a big house. There's lots of room. Can't you come, too?"

"But what would he do with the cows and the bulls and the horses and the cats and Skippy?" Elly's voice took on a strained quality, as if she'd explained this before. "He's a *rancher*, Emma Rae, and he can't be a *rancher* in Atlanta. He gots to stay on his *ranch*. 'Sides, we don't got a big house there. We don't got any house at all. 'Member?"

A sad look no five-year-old should ever wear slid over Emma's face. "I 'member," she whispered. She slid lower in the bed, then held out her arms. "G'night, Mr. Guthrie."

"Good night, Emma." He hugged her, pressed a kiss to her forehead, felt her kiss lightly brush his cheek, then repeated the process with Elly. Feeling more than a little choked up, he switched off the lamp, and immediately a light-activated night-light cast its eerie green glow over the room.

In need of fresh air, he went downstairs and onto the porch, where he gripped the rail and stared into the darkness. Life wasn't fair. The kids had deserved better than a first-class bastard for a father. Olivia deserved better for a husband. But she'd married him, had children with him, stayed with him— while all she wanted from Guthrie was to make her time away from Georgia a little more bearable. Damn it—

The screen door opened and closed quietly behind him, then she came to stand a few feet away. "Hey, cowboy."

Pale light filtered out the living-room window, falling across her. As he'd requested, she'd changed into her night-gown—the long, thin, fitted garment that'd given him more than a little discomfort the morning Elly had sneaked over to the barn. It was utterly plain—white, of a fabric soft as a T-shirt that draped and clung as snugly as a T-shirt. There was no adornment on the scooped neck, no ribbons nor buttons, not even one tiny bow. It was essentially a calf-length tank top, and it was sexy as hell.

Especially now that he intimately knew the body it draped and clung to.

She wrapped her arm around one rough post that supported the porch roof. "Did you kiss the girls and make them sigh?"

"I believe it's 'kiss the girls and make them cry.'"

"Not my girls. They know good kisses when they get them."

"How would they know? Did their father ever kiss them?"

Her sweet smile faded. "Not if he could avoid it."

"Why did you stay with him so long, Olivia? If you didn't care for yourself, why didn't you leave him for their sakes?"

She released the post and folded her arms across her chest. "Are you looking for a fight? Because if you are, I think I'm a tad underdressed—and a whole lot not in the mood."

He took a deep breath and smelled honeysuckle and pine and, closer, subtler, the exotic fragrance of her perfume. "I don't want to fight. I'm just... Annoyed."

"With me?"

"With the jerk you married."

She came a step closer. "He's dead, you know."

"That doesn't change the fact that he was worse than

worthless as a father.'' He touched her hair lightly with his palm. ''He wasn't much of a husband, either, was he?''

For a long time, she simply looked at him, then she sighed. ''No, he was neither a good husband nor a good father. He was emotionally distant with the girls, but I tried to make up for it. I tried to rationalize it. *I* was the primary parent. *I* was the one who taught them, who influenced them. It was *my* love that mattered. I told myself that living with a distant father couldn't be worse than living with no father at all. He didn't hit them. He didn't mistreat them. He just ignored them.''

''But being ignored can hurt, too.''

''They're happy kids,'' she replied, her tone defensive. ''They're well adjusted. They're smart. They're confident— well, Elly's confident. Emma likely would have been timid with or without a decent father.''

She was right. The kids were remarkably normal. But how much happier they could have been with a father who loved them—and how much sadder they would be now, he admitted. As it was, Miles's death provided an occasional sorrowful moment. But losing a good father, a loving father… He knew from his own experience how devastating that was.

Sliding his hand around the back of her neck, he drew her near. She came willingly, but maintained the protective pose even when his arms were around her. ''Did I tell you how pretty you look in your *nightie?*''

''No.'' Her answer was mumbled to give the impression of pouting, but he could see the beginnings of a smile tugging at the corners of her lips.

''You are.'' He brushed her hair back from her ear. ''That morning I brought Elly over, when you were sitting out here drinking a cup of coffee… I thought then what a pleasure it would be to start the day with you looking like this—all soft and sexy and womanly…'' He liked the sound of that last word. *Womanly.* It embodied every ideal that fueled his fantasies.

*She* embodied those ideals, those fantasies.

Ducking his head, he brushed his mouth where his fingers had just been, making her shiver, persuading her to relax, to slide her arms around his waist. "And how much better it would be to end the day the same way."

She tilted her head back to meet his gaze. "A soft woman in a plain nightgown. You're easy to please, aren't you?" Her soft tone was meant to tease, but instead it enticed. Seduced.

"No, not at all. In fact, I'm rather greedy. I want it all, Liv."

She blinked, swallowed hard, wet her lips. "All?"

He answered her with a kiss that was hot, selfish, demanding. She responded with one that matched. Then, just when he was about to discover how sweetly painful a kiss could be, she ended it and slipped away to the door. There, with an innocent smile, she offered a wicked invitation. "Come inside, cowboy. I want to give you pleasure."

Who was he to turn a lady down?

With a glass of iced tea in one hand and a folding fan in the other, Olivia settled into the rocker on the front porch with a sigh. It was Tuesday afternoon, the temperature was hovering around ninety-four degrees, the humidity was only a tad lower, and—after sweeping, dusting, vacuuming, mopping, washing, drying and putting away laundry, cooking breakfast and lunch and getting a start on dinner, and watering all the flowers and plants she'd finally gotten in the ground—she was ready to rest her feet for a while.

In the yard Elly and Emma were playing in the sprinkler, shrieking with laughter and making up games as they went along. For a while, Skippy had played with them, but then the heat or the excitement had gotten to him. Now he lay curled up in the shade of an apple tree, occasionally lifting his head to watch, mostly just conserving his energy.

Olivia sighed again. It was amazing how much contentment a good day's work, two happy kids and a man like Guthrie could bring a woman. She hadn't felt this satisfied in...well, she didn't know. She couldn't remember if she'd *ever* been so satisfied. Certainly not with David.

Of course, she'd never been in love with David.

Shying away from the obvious implication of that statement, she opened the fan case. The two wooden halves folded down to form a handle for the paper picture that fanned out with them. She'd found it in a kitchen drawer, and Guthrie, after simply looking at it a long time, had given it to her. She suspected it had belonged to his mother, and she'd returned it to the drawer. She would be happy to use it, but she wouldn't take it with her.

She shied away from that thought, too, and concentrated instead on the here and now. The sky was pale blue, the clouds thin and white, the sun merciless in its heat. When she'd first come here nearly three weeks ago, it had seemed the quietest place in the world to a city girl. This afternoon she heard all the sounds she'd missed then—the birdsongs, the hum of insects, the bees buzzing around the flowers, the soft rustle of wind through the trees. This was a peaceful quiet, the kind a person could grow used to. After living here, the city would seem unbearably noisy with its millions of people, millions of cars and constant intrusion into her life.

However, speaking of cars… She became aware of the sound of an engine and wondered—hoped—for a moment if Guthrie was returning from work. She couldn't think of a better way to spend a lazy hot afternoon than with him. Almost immediately, though, it became apparent that the engine ran much too smoothly to belong to the one-ton truck, also that it was coming from the direction of the road out front, not the ranch road out back.

She shifted her gaze to the road as a small silver car turned into the driveway. Though she couldn't see the driver yet, she recognized the car from her visit to Mary's house as Shay's. Both girls waved when she passed, then raced to greet her as she parked and climbed out.

"Hey, look, we're all wet!" Elly said excitedly.

"I see that. Are you having fun?"

"Oh, yes," Emma replied. "It's much too hot today to not play in the water."

Shay murmured something appropriate, then eased past both girls as if afraid they might suddenly grab her and transfer their soaked, muddy, ragged look to her. Was she one of those women who didn't like children—didn't want to ruin her figure, didn't want the mess and the hassle and the bother and the eighteen years of putting someone else's needs above her own?

Or maybe she liked them too much. Maybe she'd dreamed of having her own babies—Easy Rafferty's babies—and couldn't quite deal with the fact that that would probably never happen.

Or maybe, when she'd taken such care with her appearance, she simply didn't want two five-year-olds destroying it.

"Hey, Shay," she said lazily as the woman came onto the porch. "Have a seat."

She looked at the rocker, with its thin coating of dust, then her tiny white denim skirt and her snug white tank top, and chose instead to lean against the railing.

"How are you?"

Shay's smile was brittle. "I've been better."

In spite of her perfectly applied makeup, just-so hair and flattering clothing, she'd looked better, too, Olivia thought. There were shadows under her eyes and stress lines bracketing her mouth, and she wore a rather haunted, tormented look that aged her. "Any word on Easy?"

"I found the hospital in Albuquerque where they took him after the accident. Once he was stable, he was transferred to another hospital in Houston, then to a rehab hospital down there. Apparently he got his fill of that pretty quickly, because they went to wake him one morning and he was gone." She gave a scornful shake of her head. "Sounds like something he would do. He never could stand to be tied down or to have someone fussing over him."

"He's been in three hospitals in a month?" And was able to walk—to sneak—out of the third one? That didn't sound nearly as ominous as Mary's initial report. Maybe the seriousness of his injuries had been exaggerated. Maybe—

"Two months," Shay corrected her. "Troy—the guy who told me about it—was wrong about when it happened. It was two months ago. I was painting my house that weekend. I'd just gotten my taxes taken care of—and only four days late—and I celebrated by painting the house because I was sick to death of white walls, and so I found this great pale yellow and dusty rose and royal blue, and I painted every damn room in the house a different color, and he—" Choking up, she broke off, looked away, then whispered a heartfelt, *"Damn."*

Olivia put her tea and fan down, retrieved one of the beach towels the girls had left on the swing and draped it over the other rocker, then took Shay by the shoulders and guided her into it. "Can I get you something to drink?"

"You have any whiskey?"

"Not unless Guthrie has it hidden in his desk drawer."

With a dry smile, Shay shook her head. "Nah, he never drinks anything stronger than beer, and not even that very often."

"I have iced tea and cold soda."

"Pop, Magnolia," Shay corrected her once again, but there was no edge to her voice. "If you're going to live here, you're going to have to learn to call it pop."

"But I'm not going to—" Olivia broke off. How many times had she reminded herself and others that she wasn't staying here, that she was going home just as soon as she possibly could? And why couldn't she say it now? Why had the words caught in her throat and refused to come out?

For a moment, interest replaced distress in Shay's eyes. "Sit down here, Magnolia, and tell your Aunt Shay what's going on."

"I never had any aunts, but if I did have one, she'd have to be a whole lot older than you," Olivia remarked as she sank into the rocker again.

"All right. Big sister Shay."

"You're not old enough—"

"I'm thirty-four—same age as Guthrie. And you're...?"

"Twenty-nine."

Shay nodded to prove her point. "So what's this nonsense about you're not going to live here?"

Olivia closed the fan, then immediately reopened it and used it to stir the sultry air a bit. "It was always my intention, even before we got here, to return to Atlanta," she said, feeling awkward and uneasy and a bit queasy.

"But that was before you met Guthrie. Before you two..." She finished with a shrug and a knowing grin that made Olivia's cheeks warm. "How could you even think about going back now?"

Olivia thought of all the reasons she'd explained to Guthrie and especially to herself so many times that they made her tired, and offered only the single, most important, unarguable one. "Atlanta is our *home*."

The noise Shay made was rude and obnoxious. "Atlanta's not your home. It's where you're from, where you lived. *Home* is where you make it."

Just a little miffed, Olivia made an effort to control it. "That's easy enough for you to say, when you just happen to make your home where you're from."

"Honey, for eight years I made my home in cheap motels across the western half of the country. We rarely stayed anywhere longer than a week, except in the few months Easy had off each year. I never had a kitchen or a yard or a chance to have kids. I never even got to think about settling down. But none of that mattered, because I was with Easy. He was all I needed to be *home*."

Olivia softly asked, "Then why did you come back here?"

"Because after a while, he decided that he could have a better home with other women. He didn't want me anymore, and I had no place else to go, so I came here."

"I'm sorry."

Shay stared off into the distance—in the general direction, as Olivia understood it, of the Rafferty place. "Yeah," she murmured. "So am I." After a moment's silence, she looked at Olivia. "Have you ever had a broken heart?"

"No."

"I didn't think so. You were married most of your adult life, and that was no love match, since you're obviously no grieving widow. Take my word for it—they're best avoided. You have no reason to go off and break your own heart— and for damn sure no reason to break Guthrie's heart. You pull up stakes and move these kids back to Atlanta, it'll be the biggest mistake you ever made. You'll find out for yourself that it's not *home*. It's just a place where you used to live."

Olivia wanted to argue the point with her—wanted to insist that there was something so special and unique about Atlanta, something that was a very part of her. But she didn't feel like arguing, not when, just a short while ago, she'd felt more contented than she'd ever felt before.

On a hot, dusty ranch.

Outside Heartbreak, Oklahoma.

After another short silence, Shay spoke again. "I actually had a reason for coming out here that had nothing to do with Easy or Guthrie or Atlanta. I was at Mom's, and she asked me to remind you that the Founder's Day barbecue is this Saturday." She grinned. "What she *really* wanted me to do was twist your arm until you volunteered to work in one of the Ladies' Auxiliary booths for an hour or two."

"I'm not much of a salesman," Olivia warned.

"Right, Magnolia. The men around here are simple cowboys. Just wear one of those garden party dresses, sweeten up that Georgia-peach accent, flutter those Southern-belle lashes, and you could sell hot sauce to the devil."

There was no such thing, Olivia thought, as a simple cowboy. Not judging by Guthrie and Easy. "Where and when does she want me?"

"The crafts booth is in need from ten to eleven and the concessions booth from two until three. Which one or both would you like?"

"Mama, Mama, look at us!" the girls called in unison. They were standing on their heads in waterlogged grass, legs open wide, toes wiggling as the sprinkler doused them.

"Amazing what two years of gymnastics and ballet will teach a child," she murmured before absently answering Shay's question. "Sure. Both sound fine."

Shay popped to her feet. "I know a distracted answer when I hear one. I'm getting out of here before you come to your senses. See you Saturday."

"Wait a minute." Olivia left the chair and followed the woman as far as the steps. "Hey, wait. What did I just agree to?"

At her car, Shay turned back with another big grin. "Two hours. Saturday morning, Saturday afternoon. See you there!"

As she drove away, Olivia's frown slowly turned into a smile. She'd never been to a small-town Founder's Day festival before—had never manned a booth or been a part of a community celebration. Back in her old life in Atlanta—not *home,* according to Shay—such things weren't done. Any celebrations they'd taken part in, others had been well paid to do the planning and the manning.

She was looking forward, she thought with serious satisfaction, to experiencing the difference.

Friday night storms brought a break in the heat Saturday morning. Olivia lay on her side in bed, gazing out the open windows, smelling the sweet, rain-clean fragrances of the grass, the air, the world in general.

On the chest, an old fan stirred the cooler air. Behind her, Guthrie's body provided enough heat to balance it and make the temperature just exactly right.

He stroked her breast, and shivers tingled through her, strongest where his body was still joined with hers. He'd awakened her before the sunrise with hot touches and hotter kisses, and he'd brought her the laziest, sweetest, softest climax imaginable—and then done it again.

Now she sighed regretfully. "The girls will be up soon."

"I've already been up," he teased just above her ear. Drawing a soft whimper from her, he withdrew from her body, made a quick trip to the bathroom next door, then returned to nuzzle her neck. "You know, we could just tell them the truth and move you guys into my house and quit sneaking around."

She rolled onto her back to look at him. "Tell them the truth? Guthrie, they're five years old. They don't understand about sex."

The instant she said the last word, she regretted it, because his entire face tightened. "Maybe I don't, either. Is that what we're doing here? Just having sex?"

Wrapping her arms around his neck, she ignored his stiffness and pulled him to her. "No, of course not. We're having *great* sex. Fabulous sex. Wonderful, passionate, hot, sweet, tender, toe-curling, amazingly perfect sex. Sex so incredible that a person might call it making love, or heaven on earth...or the best thing that's ever happened to her. What we call it doesn't matter. What we feel, what it means—that's what's important."

"And what do you feel?"

She touched his face, using her fingertips to gently smooth away the frown lines that marred his features. "I feel better than I've ever felt. I feel... For the first time in my life, I feel as if I matter."

The frown disappeared, and tenderness replaced annoyance in his eyes. "Liv, I—"

A cry from upstairs interrupted him. "*Woo-hoo!* Em, it's morning! Wake up! Today's the festival in town, and Mr. Guthrie's gonna take us and let us pet the animals and ride the rides and eat whatever our little hearts desire! Get up, sleepyhead, so we can go!"

He raised his gaze to the ceiling, listening to the sound of tiny feet pounding first to the window, then to the bathroom. With a grim smile, he left the bed and quickly dressed. "I'll see you at breakfast," he murmured, then leaned across the bed to kiss her one last time.

She watched him go, heard the quiet click of the front door behind him, then found her nightgown where he'd tossed it last night. After giving it a thorough shake, she shimmied into it just as Elly started down the stairs.

"Mama, are you up?" Her older daughter stuck her head around the corner and her eyes widened comically. "Why's everyone sleepin' late today? I even had to wake Skippy. We gotta get goin'. Today's the festival, 'member, and I'm all ready."

Olivia stuffed Guthrie's pillow behind her—and swore she smelled his scent seeping out of the cotton and foam to surround her—and gave Elly a head-to-toe look. "I don't think so. Not dressed like that."

Elly climbed onto the bed and twisted from side to side so she could see herself in the dresser mirror. "What's wrong with the way I'm dressed?"

"For starters, blue and purple stripes and yellow and green polka dots do not go together. You can't wear Emma's dress as a shirt, and it's going to be much too warm today for jeans and boots."

Continuing to admire herself, Elly grinned. "But look at it this way—you won't lose me in the crowd."

"I won't lose you anyway. Hang Emma's dress back up in the closet and put on shorts—blue denim shorts—and sandals or tennis shoes. Then you can wear any shirt—of your own—that you want."

"Oh, Mama," Elly said with a great sigh. "You're almost as prissy as Emma Rae."

Two hours later, as they stood near the makeshift pen that enclosed the pony ride at the Founder's Day festival, Olivia repeated the comment to Guthrie, followed by her own incredulous question. "Do you think I'm prissy?"

"Hell, yes," he replied with a big grin. Then he slid his arm around her waist and pulled her close. "Lucky for you, though, I happen to like *prissy*."

"But I—I am not—" Scowling, she watched the girls, on the backs of a pair of ponies who were almost as identical as their riders. Though the ponies were docile and less likely to run off than *she* was, the kids were having a ball. No doubt, as soon as the ride was over, the pleading would begin—of Guthrie, to teach them to ride, and of her, for a sweet little pony all their own. Why, not one of them was much bigger than a large dog. It wouldn't eat much and could live in the yard and, even if they went to Atlanta, hey, it would get used to apartment living in no time.

*Even if they went to Atlanta.* She closed her eyes for a moment, summoned an image of their hometown and waited for the homesickness to wash over her. It didn't. Oh, there were a few twinges close to her heart, but that was about it. Of course, she was distracted now, what with all the voices around her, the sound of a band tuning up a few spaces away, the cheery music of the merry-go-round, the delighted giggles of her own kids, and Guthrie, holding her close in front of the kids, his neighbors and friends and people they didn't even know.

The longing would come back. Tonight, when she went to bed, when everyone was asleep and the quiet settled in… But she hadn't gone to bed alone for more than a week, and there was rarely a minute when everyone else was asleep and she was awake. If one happened, by chance, to come along, she never used it to think about Atlanta and all she'd left behind but instead found herself dreaming about Heartbreak and all she'd found.

Maybe Shay was right. Maybe Atlanta was merely where she came from. Maybe Guthrie was all she needed to be home.

*Maybe.*

"All right," he murmured in her ear. "I take it back. You're not prissy. Now don't pout."

Opening her eyes, she found him standing so close that not touching him—even in front of the kids, his neighbors and friends and people they didn't even know—seemed unnatural. Lightly she brushed her fingertips across his jaw, then softly, curiously asked, "What were you about to say this morning when Elly woke up?"

A blankness slid over his features. "I don't remember."

"Yes, you do. I said that, for the first time, I feel as if I matter, and you said, 'Liv, I…?'"

"I think you matter a lot? I think it's time for the kids to wake up?"

She shook her head. She had thought—had *known*—in that instant before Elly's wake-up shout that he was going to say something important, something intimate, something she needed to hear as much as she was afraid of hearing it. She'd thought he was going to say something that neither of them could back away from, that would change them forever.

Something sweet. Like *Liv, I love you.*

# Chapter 11

*Liv, I love you.*

That was what he'd been about to say, Guthrie silently, somberly acknowledged. And *You matter more than life to me.* And *I want to spend the next sixty years with you.* And *Marry me, Liv. Stay with me. Now and forever.*

But those weren't things he could blurt out in a rush, or in a crowd, or standing next to the pony ride. They weren't words she would be real happy to hear, not with her heart set on going back to Georgia.

"How about, 'Liv, I'm hungry?'" he suggested. "Or, 'Liv, I want you?'"

She gave him a pretty, pouty frown. "We'd just made love—twice."

Ducking his head close to hers, he murmured, "Do you think being inside you twice keeps me from wanting to be there again?"

He was saved from further discussion by a hearty greeting from Pete Davis, who owned the feed store. The interruption was gratefully received, because he wasn't about to profess undying love at a carnival, nor was he going to embarrass himself by getting turned on at nine-thirty in the morning in a very public place—which would undoubtedly happen if he didn't get his mind out of her bed and off her body.

A few minutes into the conversation, Olivia laid her hand on his arm. "It's time for me to find the Ladies' Auxiliary booth. You're sure you don't mind watching the kids?"

"I'm sure."

"If it's the crafts booth you're looking for, it's right over there." Pete waved toward the booths under the trees. "I imagine it's gonna be the best-manned—or should I say womaned?—booth this morning. People're anxious to meet you."

Two weeks ago, Guthrie thought, the idea would have made her nervous. This morning she simply smiled one of those gorgeous, make-a-man-weak-in-the-knees smiles, then took her leave.

Both he and Pete watched her go, then the older man sighed as she disappeared from sight. "I swear, boy, you are the luckiest son of a gun alive. Any other man around here lose half his ranch to some city slicker, it'd be an ugly old hag who'd sent her husband to his grave with her whining and her nagging. But not you. No, sir, you get the prettiest woman these old eyes have ever had the pleasure of looking on."

He was pretty damned lucky, Guthrie agreed. But if he was going to hold on to her now that he'd gotten her, he was going to need a whole lot more than luck. He just might need a miracle.

He and Pete talked about market prices and cattle woes until the pony ride finally ended and Elly and Emma raced over. Emma held her arms up to him, and he picked her up as Elly climbed the rails of the pen, swung one leg over the top and grinned brightly. "Mr. Guthrie, I *like* ponies. Doncha think you might need one at the ranch? You know, just to keep the big guys company when you're not around?"

"I don't know, Elly. I didn't realize the big guys were lonely when I'm not there."

"Well, of course, they are. But a pony'd maybe give 'em something to keep 'em busy."

"And, of course, if the pony ever got lonely, you and Emma would be there to cheer him up, wouldn't you? And you'd probably have to take long rides to do it."

She nodded solemnly. "Prob'ly."

Pete chuckled at her earnest reply, drawing her attention and another big grin. "Hey," she said, sticking out one hand. "I'm Elly Miles, and this here's my sister, Emma Rae Miles, only no one calls her that 'less she's in trouble or whinin'. Mostly she's just Emma. We live with Mr. Guthrie, but not really *with* him. We gots a cabin by his house, and he stays at his house and we stay at the cabin, 'cept sometimes he stays at the cabin, too, don't you, Mr. Guthrie?"

As Guthrie's face burned crimson, Pete burst into raucous laughter. "Never can hide anything from the little ones," he said gleefully. "You'd better learn that lesson now, before you up and marry that pretty little girl."

Guthrie's first impulse was to remind the old man that he'd said nothing about marrying Olivia. The last thing he needed was a rumor like that going around. But such a reminder, especially when Elly had just announced that he was spending the night with her mother, would be less than gentlemanly. Besides, whether he'd said anything to anyone about marrying Olivia, it was true. He wanted it more than he could begin to say.

Pete offered his hand to each girl in turn. "Elly, Emma, it's a pleasure meeting you. Son, I'll see you around." He slapped Guthrie on the back as he walked away.

"Elly." Still embarrassed, Guthrie spoke her name in two distinct syllables.

"But, Mr. Guthrie, 'member when the storm came? And you was there when we woke up and you stayed there till after we went back to bed?"

Emma took up her sister's side. "And ever' night for the last week, you gave us good-night kisses, so you stayed there after we went to sleep."

Guthrie was relieved that the incidents they were talking about were purely innocent—though that relief was short-lived.

"And, of course," Elly said matter-of-factly, "I seen you leaving this morning when I was waking Skippy. It's okay, Mr. Guthrie. Emma and I use to have sleepovers all the time back in Atlanta. It's okay for mamas to have 'em, too."

"Listen, honey…" He settled Emma on one hip, then lifted Elly to the other. Their thin little arms immediately looped around his neck, creating a warmth of a whole different kind. "It would probably be best if this is our secret, okay? You can keep a secret, can't you?"

Both girls nodded solemnly. "We won't tell *anyone*, Mr. Guthrie," Emma solemnly promised, and Elly agreed with a bob of her head.

The girls wriggled to the ground and, with each tightly claiming one of his hands, they set off through the festival grounds. They listened for a moment to the band as they kicked off their show with a bluegrass favorite, then Elly blew a dollar on the ring toss. They visited the local version of the petting zoo—Miz Wilson's collection of child-friendly animals, including a pig, a rabbit, a goat and a llama. And every few yards, it seemed, they were stopped by someone he knew, wanting introductions to his girls and fishing for gossip about their mother. He obliged with introductions to the kids but remained closemouthed about Olivia.

When they claimed a bench under an oak to drink the pop he'd bought, Elly remarked, "You sure know lots of nice people, Mr. Guthrie."

"Yes, I do," he agreed. Sometimes, when he was really busy on the ranch, he didn't see anyone but the Stephenses for weeks at a time, and sometimes he got annoyed with everyone knowing everyone else's business, but they *were* nice. They were good friends. He couldn't imagine living without them hovering in the background, every single one.

"We don't know nice people in Atlanta," Emma said, sit-

228 *Cattleman's Promise*

ting beside him with her hand resting so lightly on his knee that he hardly felt it.

"Aw, come on. You must have known someone who was nice," he teased.

"Well, Amber Lynn's stepdaddy was kinda nice, but they divorced and he moved away, and he was the only one."

"If there was only one nice person in all of Atlanta, then it must not have been a very good place to live."

"Two," Emma disagreed. "Mama's nice."

"Three," added Elly. "*I'm* nice."

"And me. That's four." Emma's ponytail swayed as she sorrowfully shook her head. "Mr. Guthrie? If we didn't go back to Atlanta, could we stay here? I mean, not here, but at the cabin."

Guthrie swallowed hard. "You could stay as long as you want."

"Forever?" Elly asked.

"Forever and ever."

"And would you always be here?"

"Always," he said.

Giving his knee a reassuring pat, Emma repeated his answer softly, confidently, to herself. *"Always."*

"Aren't you guys the picture of the perfect family? All you need is Miss Magnolia Blossom, and you'd be all set."

As the girls edged closer to him, Guthrie looked up at Shay. It was the first time he'd seen her in fourteen years that he'd felt nothing—no anger, no resentment, no hostility. No lust, no desire, no love, no hate. For the first time in fourteen years, he felt free—thanks to Olivia.

"Shay." His tone was neutral, guarded. He knew how easy it was to slide into old habits if he wasn't careful.

"Hi, Emma, Elly."

"Hey, Miss Shay," both kids chorused.

"Have you found out anything more about Easy?"

The mention of his name made her look weary. "The rehab hospital assumes he went home when he left there—but, of course, they can't give out his address. I tried calling every

Rafferty in the Houston area. If anyone knows him, they're lying pretty well.''

''Why do you think anyone there would know him? I don't remember the Raffertys having any ties to Houston.''

''The woman I talked to at the Albuquerque hospital said he was transferred to Houston because he had family there. I assume Bud and Betsey wound up there after they left here.''

Or maybe Easy had other family—a wife, maybe kids— that Shay didn't know about. Guthrie didn't voice the possibility aloud, though. She didn't look as if she could handle it. ''Didn't you guys keep in touch with his folks when they moved?''

A pained look crept across her face as she hugged her arms to her chest. ''He did. I didn't. They blamed me for seducing their sweet, innocent boy. They didn't want to see me, talk to me or even hear my name. As far as they were concerned, I no longer existed. When he visited them, I stayed with a friend. He dropped me off, disappeared for a week or so, then came back to get me. I never asked where he'd gone, what they'd done, how they were, and he never mentioned it.'' Her voice dropped lower. ''For that week or so, I no longer existed for him, either.''

Easy had been neither sweet nor innocent since he was fifteen, Guthrie thought with a scowl, and he'd been the most muleheaded person around. Shay at her most seductive—and that was pretty damn seductive—couldn't have persuaded him to do anything he didn't want. *He* had decided to get involved with her. *He* had decided to run off with her. He deserved at least half the blame—or credit or responsibility—for their affair.

''Why don't you write to him in care of the hospital?'' he suggested. ''Surely they would forward a letter to him.''

''That's what they said.''

''But?''

Her smile was painfully sad, her eyes suddenly damp. ''I've spent a lot of time trying to reach Easy. Most of the time he didn't want to be reached—at least, not by me.''

He didn't know what to say—didn't know how to offer comfort to someone he'd once loved, then hated, and now felt nothing for. Fortunately, distraction arrived in the form of Olivia, approaching from the direction of the booths. The twins jumped up from the bench and ran to meet her, wrapping their arms around her waist, talking excitedly at the same time. For a moment he forgot about Shay and simply watched the three most important people in his life—at least, until she spoke.

"Tell her you'll take her to Atlanta every year after the fall roundup and the spring calving. Tell her you'll build a steam bath so she doesn't miss the heat and humidity, and you'll plant wisteria and magnolias and eat nothing but Southern foods. Tell her you'll play *Gone with the Wind* nonstop on the VCR and fly the Confederate flag. Tell her whatever it takes to make her stay here." Her thin smile was bittersweet. "Tell her you love her and want to marry her and will devote the rest of your life to keeping her this happy."

He looked at her a moment before shifting his gaze back to Olivia. "You think that would work?"

"I can't believe it wouldn't."

The kids returned to their seats on the bench. Olivia slipped behind them, rested both hands on his shoulders and murmured, "Hey," near his ear before shifting her attention to Shay. "Good morning."

"Hey, Magnolia," Shay drawled, then held up both hands as if framing a portrait. "The perfect family. Can I call it or what?" She gave them a flippant smile and a wave as she walked away. "Don't forget—steam baths and flags and the VCR."

As she disappeared into the crowd, Olivia asked, "What was that about?"

He pulled her hands from his shoulders and clasped them tightly. "It wasn't about anything, darlin'."

Just his future.

Maybe his life.

* * *

Once she finished her shift in the concession booth, Olivia left on a leisurely search for Guthrie and her children. She took her time, examining items for sale in various booths, listening to a song or two from the band, passing a few minutes in conversation with this new friend, a few minutes more with that one. She saw Shay, running a kids' game that involved fishing poles, paper sacks and goldfish, and listened to her patter for a moment but didn't interrupt. She let Pete from the feed store try to sweet-talk her into parting with a dollar for three chances at winning a stuffed bear.

"But I can't throw worth a darn," she protested as he bounced a bright yellow tennis ball enticingly in front of her.

"Give it a try anyway, girl. You just might win a bear."

"I've got *twins,* Pete. One bear wouldn't cut it at my house."

He brushed off her argument. "Guthrie's already won his girls a bear each—well, at least one of 'em's got a bear. Elly, she took hers and traded it to the pastor's boy for a cowboy hat and a six-shooter. This one would be just for you. He could keep you company…if you're ever in need of it."

That last was accompanied by the same sly grin that she'd seen at least two dozen times today, usually preceded or followed by a seemingly innocent comment. *How's Guthrie? How are you two getting along? Heartbreak's a fine place to raise a family. Do your girls like Guthrie? A father's important to little girls. Are you planning to get married again?*

Heavens, was everyone in town as matchmaking happy as Mary Stephens? Did they always jump to conclusions like this? Or were they all simply eager to see Guthrie—clearly one of their favored sons—happy?

"All right," she said at last, digging in her pocket for a dollar bill. She traded it for three balls, took aim for the holes cut out in plywood and lobbed the first one. It missed, bounced and dribbled to a stop near Pete's feet. The second did the same. The third landed in the hole above the one she was aiming for, then bounced out again.

"You weren't kidding, were you, girl? You really cain't

throw worth a darn." Pete grinned. "But then, Guthrie ain't interested in your pitchin' arm, is he?" He laughed delightedly, as if he'd said something hilarious.

Olivia gave him a wary look. "No, I guess not. Do you know where I can find him?"

"Last I saw, they was headed for the pony ride—again. His girls have really taken a liking to them little horses."

*His* girls? she thought as she thanked him and started in that direction. What was that about?

When she got to the corral, she spotted the kids immediately. Seated in kid-size saddles on kid-size ponies, they were taking a lazy ride to nowhere and loving it. Emma clutched an electric blue teddy bear in one arm, and Elly wore a red-and-white vinyl cowboy hat that fastened under her chin with red cord. In her right hand she held the reins, in her left a silver six-shooter. No doubt, in her mind she was chasing desperadoes at a gallop across the plains.

Smiling tenderly, Olivia turned her attention to the crowd circled around. Searching for Guthrie's cream-colored Stetson wasn't an option. Half the men around wore them. Giving up her spot by the rail, she began threading her way through, greeting people she knew, responding to the greetings of people she didn't.

She reached the other side with no sign of Guthrie, but she didn't worry. He would no more go off and leave her kids than she would. He was here somewhere. She just hadn't located him yet. When the ride was over, she would simply follow the girls and find him when he came to collect them.

She settled in the shade of a tall oak. On the opposite side of the tree was a bench, occupied by a half-dozen men, all wearing straw hats, Wranglers and boots, smoking cigars and chewing tobacco, talking the ranch business that was their lives. Jim Stephens had bought himself two longhorn bulls down in Texas, and Marlon Wallace had a calf come unexpectedly and lost its mama. The price of hay was holding steady, and, damn, this heat sure did wear on a man.

She listened with half a mind until a familiar name entered

the conversation. Then, though she never took her gaze off the kids, she turned all her attention to the men behind her.

"I hear Lawton's planning to make an offer on the Harris place."

"Aw, Guthrie'd never sell."

"No, but that new partner of his might. She wants to take her kids back to Georgia. Hmph. What's so all-fired special about Georgia? I've been there before. Don't never intend to go back."

"Lawton's been wanting that place for years."

"Well, looks like he might get it now—at least half of it— 'less Guthrie does something drastic."

"What's he gonna do? He cain't afford to buy it."

"From what I hear, he don't need to." There was a round of laughter before the speaker went on. "He's already sweet-talked his way into her bed. Now all he's got to do is get a ring on her finger."

"Get married just to get his land back?"

"Why not? Can you think of a sweeter deal? He gets his land *and* a pretty little wife to make his nights long. 'Course, he'd have to take on those kids of hers, but that's worth a hundred and fifty acres."

"Sounds like a smart move to me," one man said, and another agreed. "That Guthrie's a smart boy. He's probably already got it all planned."

A chill stole over Olivia, and she rubbed her hands over her arms to warm them. The men were just gossipy old goats. Just because they said something didn't make it so. They didn't know anything about her relationship with Guthrie...though they did know it was intimate. How had they found that out? She certainly hadn't told anyone, and she couldn't believe that Guthrie had. Maybe they were just guessing...but *He's already sweet-talked his way into her bed* didn't sound like a guess. It sounded pretty damn certain.

It also explained a few other things—like all those sly, calculating smiles she'd been on the receiving end of today. And all those comments about Guthrie, the kids and marriage.

Apparently everyone in town expected him to propose marriage—and not because he loved her, not even because he wanted her, but only because she owned half of his ranch. Only because he wanted something she had.

Well, they were *wrong*. Guthrie didn't have to marry her to get back his land. Hadn't she decided on only her second day here that if she could *possibly* find a way, she would give the land back to him, free and clear, as thanks for his help and support? So there was no reason for him to do *anything* just for the sake of the land. No reason to even think about marrying—

But she'd never told *him* she intended to give him the deed. She'd never told anyone. So he must believe what those men believed—that the land was lost to him unless he did something drastic.

Unless he asked her to marry him.

With another chill, she thought back to that morning in bed, when he'd started to say something important, but Elly had interrupted. *Liv, I love you,* she'd thought.

But maybe it'd been, *Liv, I want to marry you.* Actually meaning, *Liv, I want my land back desperately enough to take you and your kids as part of the bargain.*

Tears welled in her eyes. She'd been through one marriage where she'd been nothing more than part of a bargain, and she'd sworn she would never settle for it again. She wanted passion, devotion, commitment and love.

And Guthrie had them.

Maybe for her. Definitely for his ranch.

The problem was how could she know. And she *really* needed to know.

Fumbling in the deep pockets of her dress for a tissue, she found that and her keys. Suddenly the need to get away was more than she could bear. Clutching the keys tightly, she headed for the midway, where she literally bumped into Shay ending her shift at the goldfish booth.

"Hey, Magnolia, what's—"

Olivia kept her head down. "Do me a favor, Shay," she

said, struggling to sound normal but hearing the tears that clogged her throat. "Find Guthrie and tell him I borrowed his truck. Tell him—" Sniffling, she broke off and started for the parking lot.

"Olivia, wait. What's wrong? Olivia!"

Her voice followed Olivia to the truck, but she didn't. Olivia was grateful, because no sooner had she climbed inside than the tears started falling.

Have you ever had a broken heart? Shay had asked her a few days ago, and she'd answered quickly, confidently. *No.*

It looked as if she might have answered too quickly.

Guthrie was sharing a picnic table with Mary Stephens back in the trees from the pony ride. Though the kids on the other horses changed periodically, Emma and Elly rode past where he could see them every minute or two. He was grateful to Jeff Hendrix for realizing what a thrill this was to them and giving them more than a fair turn—so grateful he might have to look into making a deal for at least one of Jeff's ponies. Maybe Elly was right. Maybe the big guys did need some company.

"I'm still waiting for an answer," Mary said impatiently. "Did you forget my question? Do you need it repeated?"

He hadn't forgotten. He'd been asked the same question— or heard the same suggestion—a dozen times today. Most of them he'd deflected or ignored, but Mary wasn't one to be ignored.

*Are you going to marry that girl?*

"Don't you think I should discuss this with Olivia before everyone in the county knows?"

"She's standing right over there—" She waved a hand in the direction of a broad oak, then shrugged. "Well, she *was* standing right over there. Must've seen somebody she knows."

Guthrie opened his mouth to point out that she didn't know anybody but the two of them and Shay, but that was no longer true. Practically everyone at the festival had taken to her as if she were a long-lost relative. He'd never seen such a warm welcome.

"I don't know where your girl went to, but there's mine," Mary said as Shay separated from the crowd and started toward them. "It was mine and your mama's dearest dream that you two get married and give us grandchildren. When she ran off with Easy, it like to broke my heart. But, you know, I never once saw you look at Shay the way you look at Olivia. I never once saw the two of you together and thought, 'They were made for each other.' But you and Olivia... Lord, first time I ever saw her, I knew."

Shay stalked to a stop in front of them, hands on her hips, eyes blazing. "What did you do, Guthrie Harris?"

Taken aback by her accusing tone, he blinked, then focused on her. "What are you talking about?"

"Olivia just took off out of here in tears. What did you do?"

He stood up, swung his leg over the bench. "I didn't— I haven't— Where was she headed?"

"How should I know? She took your truck and left."

"I haven't even seen her since she went to work in the concessions booth," he said defensively.

"He hasn't, Shay," Mary chimed in. "She was standing over there against that tree until just a few minutes ago, and she seemed fine then. She was watching the kids and smiling."

All three gazes swung to the tree—and the park bench that extended across the back on either side. Guthrie started in that direction. Shay and Mary followed.

There were four men seated on the bench, two more on sandstone boulders a short distance away. Guthrie knew them all—friends of his father's, friends of his. He acknowledged their greetings with a nod, then, with much more respect than he felt like showing, he asked, "You fellas wouldn't happen to have been talking about me and my new partner in the last few minutes, would you?"

Varying degrees of embarrassment marked every face.

"Well," Jed Smith said, then cleared his throat. "I believe you might have come up in the conversation. But, hell, Guthrie, ever'body in the county comes up in our conversations."

"What did you say?"

"Now, son, you wouldn't want us repeating gossip, would you?" That, with a wheezing laugh, came from Bill Taylor, who was ninety if he was a day.

"Olivia was standing on the other side of the tree while you were talking. She's already heard what you had to say—"

"And went off crying because of it," Mary said scornfully.

"Now *I* need to know," Guthrie finished, "so I can try to undo what you've done."

The men exchanged looks, then left it to Velt Taylor, Bill's son, to repeat the conversation. Knowing exactly how Olivia would react to the comments, Guthrie felt sick inside. As if he didn't have enough problems, competing with the whole damn state of Georgia for her affection, now he had to deal with her insecurities, too.

"We're real sorry, Guthrie," Max Owens said. "We didn't mean no harm."

But Guthrie wasn't listening. He looked at Shay, who immediately began digging in her purse for her keys. "I'm parked near the entrance," she said when she handed them over. "We'll get the twins when the ride's over."

As he walked away, Guthrie heard Mary chastising the men for being nothing but a bunch of old hens. Not even that image could lighten his mood.

He drove straight out to the ranch—where else could Olivia go?—and found his truck in its usual space. He parked behind it, saw that the house appeared undisturbed and started across the yard to the cabin.

The front door was open, the screen door unhooked. He didn't knock or call out, but simply stepped inside. From the corner of his eye he caught a flash of bright colors—Olivia's sundress—before it disappeared farther into the bedroom, then heard the bathroom door close. Cutting through the bedroom, he stopped in front of the bathroom, hesitated, then knocked once. "Liv?"

There was a long silence, then… "What?"

"Can we talk?"

Another long silence, broken suddenly by the sound of running water. "I'm washing my face."

"I'll wait." He stood there a long time and heard nothing but the steady, uninterrupted stream of water flowing from the faucet down the drain. When finally he heard a splash or two, he went back into the bedroom, wandered past the dresser, sat on the bed, then went to stand at the window.

By the time she shut off the water, she'd run enough to fill that big claw-foot tub. Another five minutes passed before she opened the door, and yet another minute before she came into the bedroom.

He turned to look at her and his muscles tightened. His throat went dry, and he thought that he'd never faced anything more important in his life. If he couldn't convince her that he loved her for herself and no other reason, if he couldn't persuade her to forget what she'd heard at the park and to believe only what he told her, then he didn't have a future to look forward to, and neither did she.

She stood on the opposite side of the bed, gaze on the quilt, hands demurely clasped. Her face was scrubbed clean, but her lashes were dewy—undried water or leftover tears? She'd rebraided her hair, subduing the few strands that always worked free. She looked incredibly beautiful…and unsure.

He swallowed hard. "Mary calls those men 'old hens.' They don't deny it. They've got too much time on their hands and they use it to talk."

She offered no response.

"Jeez, Liv, what can I say except I live in a town where nothing interests folks more than other folks' business. People love to gossip and speculate, and today, after what Elly said, they wanted to gossip and speculate about us."

Finally she looked at him. "What did Elly say?"

He flushed and shifted uncomfortably. "She didn't mean

anything by it. She was just talking—you know how she is—
and it just sort of slipped out that I—I stay over here…at
night…"

She raised one brow. "My five-year-old daughter announced to strangers that we're sleeping together?"

"Not exactly. Not to strangers. Just one stranger. Well,
actually, she'd met him. Pete. From the feed store. Who apparently told everyone he ran into." He felt as if he were
digging a hole and slipping ever deeper and so he clamped
his mouth shut.

"Well," she said softly. "That's a relief."

"It is?"

"Well, I knew *I* didn't tell, and I thought you were too
much the gentleman to go bragging about it."

"You know I would never do that," he said, then he
looked her over, from her neatly braided hair all the way
down to where the mattress cut her off at knee level, then
back up, and he gently smiled. "Though I might be tempted.
Everyone pretty much agreed that I'm damn lucky to have
you. You're worth bragging about."

Her faint smile came and went. "Am I worth a hundred
and fifty acres of good pasture?"

The ache in his chest tightened. "Liv—"

"Please. I want to know. Am I worth a hundred and fifty
acres of Harris land?"

"How can I put a price on what you're worth? You're
irreplaceable."

Her eyes grew damp, and her lip quavered just a bit before
she got herself under control. "I'll trade you the land."

For a long moment he stared at her as panic ripped through
him. His voice was unsteady, damn near angry, when he answered, "I'm not giving you the money to get back home."

"I don't need money to get home." She met his gaze and
held it. "Those 'old hen' friends of yours said you were a
smart boy. Listen to the terms of my offer before you turn
them down. I'll trade you—not sell, *trade*—the deed to my
half of your ranch for your signature."

"On what?" he asked suspiciously.

Her gaze drifted away, came back, then drifted again, and her hands, so primly folded a moment ago, worked nervously until she took a deep, deep breath. "A marriage license. Adoption papers."

Stunned, he stared at her. He'd come here expecting to plead, to beg, and instead she was offering him everything he wanted and then some. "I don't understand," he murmured.

"Atlanta's not my home. It's just a place I used to live. And the girls *do* need a father, and this *is* a pretty sweet deal, and you *are* a smart boy, and I *am* irreplaceable, and so are you."

"Now I'm really confused."

She moved then, circling the bed, drawing her hand lightly over the iron footboard, then stopping between him and the bed. "Can you understand this?" she asked quietly as she began unbuttoning her dress. "I love you, Guthrie. I love you enough to know that you would never marry anyone just to get a piece of property. I love you enough to know that you're a better man than that. I love you enough to trust you." She looked at him and smiled the sweetest, gentlest, most incredible smile he'd ever seen. "I love you enough to marry you even if the land is all you want."

"Because you know it's not."

She nodded once and slipped the dress off her shoulders. It fell in a brightly colored heap on the floor. "Because I know it's not," she agreed.

His gaze slid slowly from her face down her body—pale, naked but for a bit of lace and ribbons, beautiful and enticing as hell—and his own body responded. He raised one trembling hand to her cheek. "I love you, Liv."

"That's what you were going to say this morning."

"That, and I want to marry you. Raise babies with you. Grow old with you."

With movements so utterly graceful and womanly, she removed the last of her clothing, then started on his. When he tried to help, she brushed his hands away, then continued her sweet, tormenting efforts. By the time she finished, he was unbearably aroused.

She drew him to the bed. When he would have stopped to open the nightstand drawer, once again she brushed his hands away and used them instead to pull him down on the mattress with her. "I already have plenty of reasons for staying. Why don't we work on one more?"

"Getting greedy, Liv?" he teased, and she gave him a smile of tremendous satisfaction.

"You bet. I want it all, Guthrie. Passion, commitment, devotion, love, babies, a lifetime, you."

"Just one thing." He braced himself above her, intimately touching but not yet joined with her. "The land. You keep the land. Put it in the girls' names. Do whatever you want with it. Just don't ever let it come between us."

"Come between us? Darlin', it brought us together." With a husky laugh, she wrapped her arms around him, wrapped her legs around him and tugged his head down to whisper in his ear a wicked invitation he'd accepted once before. "Come inside, cowboy. I want to give you pleasure."

He filled her slowly, completely, just him, her and nothing else, then cupped her face in his palms. "You *are* my pleasure." Then, just before he kissed her... "Welcome home, Liv."

# *Epilogue*

Traditionally July and August were the hot summer months in Oklahoma—though Olivia would have sworn that June was pretty darn hot itself—and the first July Saturday suggested tradition would hold this year. Even at five o'clock, the whole outdoors was like one big oven, roasting everything in sight. It was a tribute to Guthrie and the townspeople's respect for him that so many of them were gathered in the wildflower meadow next door, braving the sun and the heat for a ceremony that could have been held in any air-conditioned church in town.

She stood in front of the dresser mirror and studied her image. There would be nothing fancy about the Harris-Miles nuptials. The bride's hair was done up in a simple twist to keep it off her neck, and her dress was ivory—the dressiest in her closetful of sundresses. It was sleeveless, fitted snugly from shoulder to thigh and closed with the long row of buttons that Guthrie appreciated so much. Her ivory flats kept her outfit monochromatic, but the flowers Mary had picked from her garden for a bouquet provided all the color any wedding needed. Even now Shay was weaving the stem of a delicate lily through Olivia's hair so the blossom was anchored directly behind her ear. It made her look different. Exotic. Happy.

Which was only fair, because she *was* happy.

"What's Guthrie wearing?" Shay asked as she finished with the lily, then stepped back to admire it. "No, wait, let me guess. Faded jeans, a white dress shirt with the sleeves rolled back and his best Stetson."

"Sounds like you've been through the what-will-the-groom-wear discussion with him before." When the other woman looked startled that Olivia had brought up their wedding-that-wasn't, she shrugged. "Hey, he's all mine now. I don't mind acknowledging that he was almost yours first."

Shay mimicked her shrug. "We had that fight—er, discussion—a time or three. I wanted him to wear a tux. He finally agreed to a suit. I wanted something classic. He wanted Western-cut."

"I want him any way I can get him." Olivia sighed dreamily. "Besides, he looks *so* good in jeans and a white shirt." And even better out of them.

Little feet clattered down the stairs, followed by the heavier tread of Mary's. "Mama, Mama, look at us!" Emma cried, dragging Elly into the room. They stood side by side in matching chambray shifts and floppy, sunflower-decked hats, Emma delighted, Elly looking as if she'd rather be strung up naked at sunrise. "We look just alike!"

"Except someone's face is all scrunched up. What's wrong, El? Do you hate it that much?" Olivia asked.

"I don't mind the dress," her older daughter said with a frown. "It's a weddin'. I got to wear a dress. Okay. But the hat...! *Mama.*"

Olivia pretended to study her for a moment, then solemnly said, "But you need a hat because it's still so hot. Do you think if you looked around, you might find another hat you wouldn't hate wearing so much?"

Elly scuffed her denim tennis shoe on the rug. "I think so."

"Well, why don't you go find it and let me see how it looks?"

Everyone watched her shoot out of the room, then Emma sighed. "Mama, you know she's gonna get that cowboy hat. It's red and white. It doesn't *go*."

"The hat's red and white, and your dresses are blue. With tomorrow being the Fourth of July, it couldn't *go* any better."

"Don't worry, Em," Shay said. "Elly wearing her cowboy hat doesn't make you any less pretty."

Emma flashed her a smile.

"Besides," Shay added, "your mama's getting married in a field full of weeds with cows chewing their cud on the other side of the fence, and afterward she's having barbecue, wedding cake, line dancing and fireworks. It's not exactly a traditional wedding, is it, Olivia?"

"It hasn't been exactly a traditional courtship, either. Why get fussy now?"

Outside the door, Elly jumped the last four steps and landed with a loud thud. In addition to discarding the sun hat for the cowboy hat, she'd traded her denim sneakers for unlaced Doc Martens.

"Oh, Elly," Emma said with a put-upon sigh while Shay and Mary worked at hiding their grins.

"How do I look, Mama?"

"I think you look fine."

Elly preened in front of her sister. "I think *you* look fine, too. Can we go see if they're ready?"

"Sure, go ahead."

"I'll go with them," Mary said with a wink. "I'll keep them clean."

Once they were gone, Shay moved to stand beside Olivia,

checking her own appearance in the mirror. Her red dress was as bright as Olivia's was subdued, as short as Olivia's was long, as revealing as Olivia's was— Well, hers was revealing, too, Olivia admitted. The fine ivory fabric fitted so closely that there wasn't room for more than a breath between it and her skin.

"You know, Magnolia, when you ran off from the festival like that," Shay said, meeting her gaze in the mirror, "I thought you were going to pull some fragile-Southern-flower stunt—you know, lots of wailing and pulling of hair and making Guthrie suffer. I thought, when Mom and I brought the kids home, we'd find you over here sobbing and him over there miserable as hell. But that wasn't the case. You behaved in such an adult manner. I was impressed."

"I seduced him."

Shay stared at her. "After all those tears? All his worry? You *seduced* him?"

"It seemed a good way to get my point across."

"Now I'm really impressed. You both looked so relaxed and calm when we got here, as if nothing had happened."

"Relaxed and calm," Olivia repeated with a grin. "We just barely got our clothes on before you got to the door."

"Miss Shay!" Emma called from outside. "Miss Mary says it's time!"

Shay turned to face her. "Are you ready?"

Her throat tight, Olivia nodded.

"You know, I envy you," Shay murmured, her voice husky, her eyes damp. "You're getting a good man who loves you dearly."

"I know. I love him, too."

"Then get out there and claim him, Magnolia."

They left the cabin and circled to the gate around back, then joined their neighbors in the field. Leaving Shay with Mary at the back of the crowd, Olivia followed the kids down the makeshift aisle. Emma walked solemnly, scattering flower petals as she went, while Elly strode confidently, wearing a big grin, bringing her boots down with a loud clump on every rock in the path. When they reached Guthrie, Elly sidled up close to him, grinned at the pastor and loudly announced, "He's gonna be our daddy."

Guthrie crouched to give Emma a kiss on the cheek, then Elly. "I like your hat, El," he murmured.

She tilted her head to look at his Stetson. "Maybe we can get you one like it."

Then he straightened and turned to Olivia and her throat grew tight. He was looking at her in a way no one else had ever looked at her—as if she were the true, great love of his life. As if she were irreplaceable.

As if she *mattered*.

Though it wasn't part of the ceremony, he drew her into his arms and kissed her—a sweet, hungry, needy kiss that promised everything she'd ever wanted. He took her breath away, which was only fair, she thought dazedly, because he'd already stolen her heart and become her life.

The pastor cleared his throat and, with an audible sigh of regret, Guthrie released her. "Jumping the gun a little bit there, aren't you, son?" the man asked with a chuckle. "If we may begin now…"

They were the most important vows she would ever take, yet the words and the promises drifted past Olivia. All she could think was how incredibly lucky she was. How incredibly happy she was. How deeply she loved this man, and how sweetly he loved her back. Before she knew it, the ceremony was over, Guthrie had given her another of those dazzling kisses, and they were on their way down the wildflower aisle to the yard, where tables for food and a floor for dancing had been set up.

They circled the cabin and Guthrie came to an abrupt stop. A few yards away underneath the spreading branches of a maple tree, a table had been set up for wedding gifts. A man stood in front of it, something in hand, looking undecided as to whether he should leave it there and go. As if he felt their presence, he stiffened, then slowly turned to face them.

It was Ethan James.

Guthrie stiffened, too. Olivia felt the tension radiating from him, felt it particularly where his fingers clenched around hers. She pulled free, flexed her fingers, then closed the distance between them. "Mr. James." As soon as she said it, she smiled. "Now that we're in-laws, I guess I can call you Ethan."

"Mrs. M—" He looked from her to Guthrie, who hadn't moved, to her bouquet and the shiny gold ring on her left hand, and swallowed convulsively.

"Olivia," she said gently. "I wish we'd known you were coming."

"I—I didn't think I should call." He addressed the next words to his brother. "I—I'm not staying. I just wanted to bring..." It was envelopes he clutched. He handed one to Olivia, then offered the other to Guthrie. When he didn't take it, Ethan gave it to her, too. "I went to Atlanta to return this to your hus—to—to David. They told me he had died and you had come here. It's not all there, but it's all that's left. I—I'm real sorry."

He moved to a spot a few feet in front of Guthrie—just out of arm's reach, she noticed. "Guthrie, I'm sorry. I don't know—I needed money, and it seemed like easy cash at the time. I just didn't think..."

Guthrie opened his mouth, then closed it again when she gave him a warning look. After a moment, he shrugged to ease the tension in his shoulders, then offered his hand. Ethan warily accepted it. "You can at least stay for supper, meet your nieces and have a dance with your sister-in-law. You can bunk down in the cabin, if you want, but the house is off limits tonight." He smiled at her over Ethan's shoulder. "My bride and I will be staying there."

"Thanks," Ethan murmured as the guests began drifting in from the wildflower meadow. Mary was the first to see him, and she swept him away to introduce him to the girls.

Olivia smiled at her husband as he approached her. "You're a good man, Guthrie Harris."

"Because I didn't kill him?" Shaking his head, he slid his arms around her and backed her against, then around the tree trunk. "All the grief Ethan has caused in his life—and there's been plenty, believe me—can't begin to balance the joy he gave me when he brought me you." He kissed her forehead, her cheek, her jaw, then nuzzled his way down her neck. Somewhere around the hollow at the base of her throat, he remembered that they weren't alone, remembered the envelope she was clenching with nerveless fingers. "Want to open them?" he asked.

"You first."

He slid his index finger under the flap, then took out a single sheet of paper. It was the deed to Ethan's half of the ranch, signed over to Guthrie, properly notarized, all legal this time—except that he didn't own the land anymore. Still, it was a nice gesture, one that obviously touched Guthrie. "Your turn," he murmured.

She ripped the end off the envelope and found two sheets inside. The first contained a brief note—*I'm sorry.* The second was a cashier's check for enough money to make her blink. It wasn't all of what Ethan had taken from David, as he'd acknowledged, but it was a lot.

Guthrie looked at the check, then nuzzled her neck again. "A woman of property *and* cash. I'm a lucky man."

Olivia returned the check to the envelope, folded it in fourths and took her time sliding it into his hip pocket. Then she wrapped her arms around his neck and gave him her best, happiest smile. "You would love me even if I were broke."

"You sound pretty sure of yourself."

"I *am*, and I'm sure of you."

He kissed her, nibbling her lip before sliding his tongue inside to taste her, stroke her, make her tremble. When he was hard, when she was weak, he lifted his head. His brown eyes were dark with desire, with need, with his vow. "I love you, Liv. I always will."

She'd gone through their wedding ceremony too purely happy to hear the vows, but it didn't matter. *I love you, Liv. I always will.* That was the only promise she would ever need.

\* \* \* \* \*

*Look for Easy's story, coming in November*
*from Marilyn Pappano*
*and Silhouette Intimate Moments.*

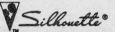

If you enjoyed what you just read,
then we've got an offer you can't resist!

# Take 2 bestselling
# love stories FREE!

# Plus get a FREE surprise gift!

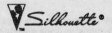

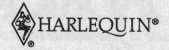

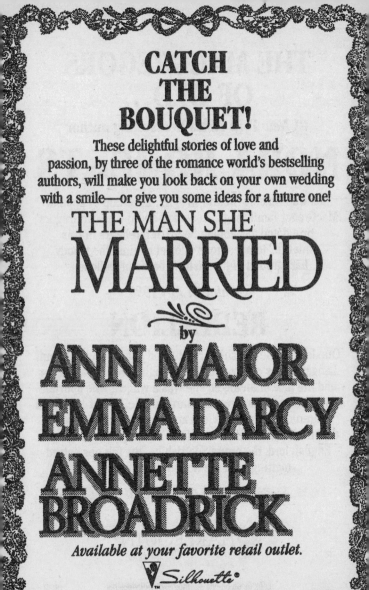

# COMING NEXT MONTH